Dark clouds masked the hot July sun..

as a whining rattle descended upon Vanessa Gallagher. Picking wild violets on her walk home from work, she looked up to see a rusted white car break over the horizon.

On the wrong side of the rural Ohio road, the car wove toward her at breakneck speed. The driver's scraggly white beard tilted forward as his head leaned back, swilling a beer.

Vanessa dove for the ditch. Gravel sprayed her from the edge of the road as her father's car whizzed past. The beer can whipped from his window and bounced across the pavement.

Fear rose in her chest as clouds crashed above her. Clyde Gallagher hit the bars but saved getting drunk for fights with her mother. Ominous dread clutched Vanessa. She leapt from the ditch and broke into a run.

A piercing clap of thunder startled her. She tripped and fell to her knees on the rough asphalt. Jumping to her feet, she dashed toward home, ignoring the trickle of blood pooling in her shoes.

With an approaching rumble, a big blue beast of a pickup roared toward her. Her heart skipped a beat when she recognized the handsome driver.

He nodded.

She kept running until the truck slowed to a stop. Out of breath, she paused beside the enormous tires. Waist-high, raised white letters read Mud Luggers.

Chad James leaned his head out the window. Country music blared from inside, singing *Who's Your Daddy?*

"Need a ride?" Chad asked.

Her stomach flipped and her heart thudded.

"Yes!" she blurted, in a hurry to see her mama.

Yet she cringed at this gorgeous hunk driving up to that shack with the peeling paint and rotting steps. Everyone in Crystal Falls knew where she lived, but he didn't need the close-up view.

Violets for Vanessa

The Crystal Falls Series, Book III

By Dianne Miley

Violets for Vanessa
The Crystal Falls Series, Book III

COPYRIGHT © 2009, 2013, 2014 by Dianne Miley
ISBN 13 – 9780990675327
ISBN 10 – 0990675327

Contact Information: Dianne@diannemiley.com

Visit us at www.diannemiley.com

Cover Photography & Design by Melissa Miley
www.melissamileyphotography.com

Publishing History
The Wild Rose Press
First White Rose Edition, 2009
Second Edition Kindle, 2013
Eden Press LLC
Second Edition Print, 2014

Published in the United States of America

Dedication

This story is dedicated to my children.

My son Nick inspired Chad with his heart of gold, rebellious sense of humor, willingness to help others, and love for big trucks and work boots. When someone's in trouble, Nick always runs to the rescue.

My daughter Melissa inspired Vanessa with her generous heart, strong-willed independence, creative talent, loving ways, and beautiful spirit. When faced with difficulty, Melissa rises to the challenge with determination and strength.

Much like this story's hero, my husband Chip is always there when I need him, and he always makes me laugh.

My mom, Anne Haynes, inspired Darla with her perseverance in the face of difficult circumstances, her breaking the cycle of a dysfunctional family, and her blossoming late in life.

Special thanks to my critique partner, Jennie Atkins. You've been very helpful and so much fun to get to know.

A huge thank you goes to Mick Maloney of the Eastlake, Ohio police department and Eagle Security. Your answers to my barrage of procedural questions has been infinitely helpful. Thank you! Any inaccuracies regarding police procedures are undoubtedly the result of unasked questions I didn't know I needed to ask.

Thanks most of all to our Lord Jesus for his strength and the many blessings He's given me. I couldn't write these heart-wrenching stories without His comfort and peace.

I pray every reader is encouraged that God loves each one of us, no matter who we are or what we've done. Our heavenly Father is always forgiving and merciful, and wants us to turn to Him.

Dear Reader,

Thank you for allowing me to share this story with you. I appreciate your interest in my writing and hope that you've found a message that speaks to your heart. This journey of life isn't easy, but every challenge is meant for our good. When we turn to Christ, we see that every trial is a lesson and God never wastes our hurt. Like tempered steel or a baked cake, each fire we endure makes us stronger and enhances our sweetness.

Maybe you've heard the saying, "A woman is like a tea bag, you never know how strong she is until she's in hot water." That goes for men too! Vanessa loves tea, and she certainly finds herself in hot water – and growing stronger as the heat inches up. Of course she doesn't realize that until she's done steeping. We can't appreciate the sweetness of the tea until the water stops boiling and we've had a chance to brew.

As you endure your own trials in life, I hope you find comfort in our Lord Jesus Christ. My prayer is that every reader accepts Jesus as Savior and lives forever with Him in heaven.

If you have questions or would like to discuss salvation, please feel free to email me at dianne@diannemiley.com. I would be honored to guide you on this journey.

God Bless,
Dianne Miley

"The Lord is my strength and my shield; my heart trusts in Him and I am helped." Psalm 28:7a

Chapter 1 – Mud Luggers

Dark clouds masked the hot July sun as a whining rattle descended upon Vanessa Gallagher. Picking wild violets on her walk home from work, she looked up to see a rusted white car break over the horizon.

On the wrong side of the rural Ohio road, the car wove toward her at breakneck speed. The driver's scraggly white beard tilted forward as his head leaned back, swilling a beer.

Vanessa dove for the ditch. Gravel sprayed her from the edge of the road as her father's car whizzed past. The beer can whipped from his window and bounced across the pavement.

Fear rose in her chest as clouds crashed above her. Clyde Gallagher hit the bars but saved getting drunk for fights with her mother. Ominous dread clutched Vanessa. She leapt from the ditch and broke into a run.

A piercing clap of thunder startled her. She tripped and fell to her knees on the rough asphalt. Jumping to her feet, she dashed toward home, ignoring the trickle of blood pooling in her shoes.

With an approaching rumble, a big blue beast of a pickup roared toward her. Her heart skipped a beat when she recognized the handsome driver.

He nodded.

She kept running until the truck slowed to a stop. Out of breath, she paused beside the enormous tires. Waist-high, raised white letters read Mud Luggers.

Chad James leaned his head out the window. Country music blared from inside, singing *Who's Your Daddy?*

"Need a ride?" Chad asked.

Her stomach flipped and her heart thudded.

"Yes!" she blurted, in a hurry to see her mama.

Yet she cringed at this gorgeous hunk driving up to that shack with the peeling paint and rotting steps. Everyone in Crystal Falls knew where she lived, but he didn't need the close-up view.

Chad jumped from his truck and noticed the bleeding knees beneath her black skirt.

"Did you fall?" His voice held genuine concern as he looked into her eyes. "Are you all right?"

"Yes, but I'm fine. I'm in a hurry to get home." Heat flushed her neck and face, hot to her natural platinum hairline. She had to be as red as a raspberry. There was no hiding a blush like this with skin as Scottish pale as hers. Self-conscious under his scrutiny, she wore no makeup and her plain long hair hadn't been professionally cut in her twenty-five year lifetime. How she wished she were prettier, more outgoing, good enough for a man like Chad James.

"Trying to beat the rain?" Chad raised a seductive eyebrow.

Like an omen, the truck reverberated into low idle and a flash of lightning lit the sky, followed by a thunderous boom. Rain poured from the heavens, drenching them in an instant.

"Too late," she yelled over the din. At least the shower cooled her heated face.

"Come on." Laughing, he ushered her to the passenger side of his truck.

He opened the door, a courtesy that made her stare up at him in surprise.

"Hop in!"

Conflicted between her distrust of men, her attraction to Chad James, and her need to get home quickly, she scrambled to climb in the truck. Her foot slipped on the wet step. She careened but Chad caught her by the waist and hefted her up.

Unnerved by his touch, she ducked just in time to miss banging her head. He shut the door and ran to the driver's side.

In one smooth motion, he was behind the wheel. Rain dripped from the bill of his black ball cap. A lock of dark hair slipped onto his forehead as he jammed the shifter into gear. The truck growled awake and lurched forward. He turned the truck around.

"I hate to see a pretty girl all alone on the road." He winked at her before shifting into second.

Pretty? And was that a wink? Vanessa's heart floated to the sky. She'd had a crush on Chad James forever. Actually, since the day she started working in her dad's bait shop.

Chad had been her first customer. The wiggling worms kept wrangling out of the stinkin' foam cup. Her father humiliated her, as usual, but Chad showed her how to scoop them up.

Unafraid to touch her, Chad gently guided her hands. Then he looked her straight in the eye, right into her soul, without a speck of pity. She had been eight years old and she'd never forget it.

Very few people looked her in the eye, none without pity.

In no time, her family's wooden cabin came into sight looking like a step back to the forties. A sign the length of the sagging roofline read BAIT in weathered red paint.

Chad pulled into the weedy gravel parking lot, past the makeshift clothesline filled with dripping clothes. She cringed at the leaning outhouse, complete with a crescent moon in the door and wasps' nests in the eaves – a remnant of her childhood.

The embarrassing blush returned. Anxious to check on her mother, she offered a nervous, "Thank you for the ride." She reached for the door handle while the truck was still rolling.

"Anytime – Big Blue at your service." Chad caught her eye with a heart-stopping grin. Then his jaw dropped as he looked past her.

Her head spun to see her mother slumped in the doorway. Blood trailed from her nose and one eye swelled shut.

The big truck skidded to a stop. Vanessa bailed out in the rain and rushed to her mother's side.

"Get me...inside," Darla Gallagher choked. Her graying blonde hair stuck out in wet clumps and her rubbery limbs struggled to gain footing.

Vanessa tried to prop her up but Darla lifted from her grasp. Tall, strapping Chad James cradled her mother in his muscular arms and carried her into the house. Back straight and strong, he gently laid her on the sofa. He inspected her arms and legs. "Is anything broken?"

"No, no, I'm fine." Darla covered her face with one hand. "I tripped and fell running in from the rain."

Vanessa recognized the lie and acutely felt her mother's shame. Chad turned to her, brows furrowed and eyes full of compassion.

"Would you like a ride to the hospital?"

"No hospital," Darla growled.

"No, but thank you." Heat rose to Vanessa's cheeks. She hurried to the kitchen and grabbed a clean towel. "I'll keep an eye on her, but I'm sure she'll be all right."

"Okay." Empathy poured from Chad's voice. "How can I help?"

"You've done enough." She smiled uneasily. "I'll take care of her from here."

"If you need anything, call me." His knowing eyes were unconvinced. He dug a wallet from his back pocket and handed her a business card.

Chadwick Builders – Custom Homes Built to Your Specifications. His name and address were printed at the bottom with his office number, cell phone, and a fax line.

His warm hand squeezed her shoulder and he caught her eyes.

"Anything, anytime – really."

Dumbfounded, she tucked the card in her pocket and nodded dismissively. At the sink, she turned on the faucet to wet the towel.

Seeming hesitant to leave, Chad looked at the muddy footprints on the cracked linoleum floor. His shoulders slumped. "Sorry about that."

"No problem." Ashamed to her core, she wanted him to leave, but he pulled out a handkerchief and wiped bits of mud on his way out the door.

Awed by his considerate kindness, Vanessa watched through the window as she wrung out the towel.

Long legs clad in jeans disappeared around the chrome bumper. Black work boots trudged past the front tires. The big blue truck dipped slightly as he climbed in. He looked over with a tentative half-smile.

Heart pounding with longing, uncertainty, and fear, she hurried away to tend her mother. How long before her father returned?

"You can't let him keep doing this to you, Mama. He's getting worse." She dabbed drying blood from her mother's face. Hand-shaped bruises marred Darla's arms. Vanessa lifted her mother's shorts over a purple mass on one thigh. It spread clear to her hip. Biting back angry tears, she checked her torso. Relief washed over Vanessa when she found no bruises that might suggest internal injury. "We're getting out of here. Soon. I almost have enough money saved."

Darla's moans joined the comforting rumble of Chad's truck, punctuated with eerie growls of thunder in the distance.

Big, black *Mud Luggers* rolled past the darkened living room window. Airbrushed white letters screamed across the tailgate: *Rebel*.

Vanessa reached in her pocket to reverently touch the embossed lettering on his card. Fragile hope tugged her heart. Would he really come back if she called?

Did she really want him to?

Long ago, she vowed never to be controlled by a man.

Unlike her mother, she'd make her own decisions and take care of herself. First, she'd get away from Clyde Gallagher as soon as she could. Once she had an apartment, her ticket to real freedom would be buying a car. No man could stop her then.

Love was a nice notion, but men stole your independence – not to mention your dignity and self-worth.

Love or independence – she couldn't have both.

Worried for Vanessa and her mother, Chad couldn't stop the images of Darla slumped in that doorway, nor the suspicion that she hadn't fallen. He wouldn't betray that doubt, but hoped Vanessa would call if she needed help – either him or the police.

He turned his massive truck onto Rose Hill Drive. Just past his parents' home, he pulled into the driveway of his new colonial.

He'd always had a soft spot for Vanessa, but had seen her as a little kid. Five years younger was huge back then. Not until his sister's wedding last month had he seen her as an intriguing woman. The picture of elegance, she looked beautiful with an enchanting air of grace. When he seated her on Rachel's side of the church, Vanessa looked up at him as if he were some Greek god in a tux.

Captivated by her throughout the reception, nothing about her reflected the family that raised her. Refined and gentle, she exhibited fine manners and spoke kindly to children and adults alike. She worked in a quaint little tea room in town. His mother praised her legendary cuisine at The Porcelain Teapot. Her cooking added one more attribute to her kind-hearted personality, hardworking determination, loyalty to her mother and numerous other virtues besides understated beauty and an obvious attraction to him.

That admiration was back full force today, despite his dirty work clothes and smell of sweat and sawdust. Even with her bloody knees and red-faced blush, chemistry smoldered between them.

All weekend he hoped to hear from her, but didn't. He longed to help her, but considering her circumstances, maybe a relationship wasn't meant to be. He prayed for guidance, but felt no leading one way or the other.

Swamped with work on the new construction site, he spent the next week trying to forget her. He strove to avoid an awkward situation by passing her on the road. Unfortunately, Lake Road was the shortest way home from his work site. He wasn't about to drive twenty-five miles out of his way in that gas-guzzling truck. So he worked late, waiting until she'd surely arrived home before heading by her house.

Friday night when he passed the bait shop, Vanessa was out hanging clothes on the line in cutoffs and bare feet. She looked up when he passed and their eyes met.

His heart stopped. They didn't wave, just stared at one another, craning their necks as if neither could look away. It was all he could do to keep the truck from stopping.

With natural good looks, Vanessa lived simply and made the most of what she had. She never wore makeup or cut her hair. She walked to and from work, went barefoot, and picked wild flowers. He was certainly no tree hugger, but something about that earthiness spoke to him.

Later when he sat down to dinner on his patio, he couldn't get her out of his mind. What was with this obsession? His yearning to settle down grew stronger every day. Yet he certainly wasn't prepared to marry her.

He'd known her since they were kids. She knew his family and his history, and he knew hers.

That's what scared him.

He went inside and turned on the television. But he couldn't get her out of his mind all evening.

Giving up, he decided to go fishing that weekend.

He would need some bait.

Bright and early Saturday morning, Chad walked into the bait shop on Lake Road. Clyde Gallagher slouched on a stool, guzzling a beer while his son Junior manned the counter. Two coon dogs lay across the scarred wooden floor.

"Mornin'" Chad greeted the men with a sense of trepidation, scanning the small place for Vanessa.

"Mornin'," Junior replied.

"A dozen night crawlers." Chad pulled out his wallet.

Junior scooped twelve worms into a foam cup faster than his sister ever could.

The house's screen door banged. Chad looked out the window to see Vanessa walking toward the road in her cute little black skirt and button-down white blouse.

"Hoity-toity traitor works for Julia *Calvin*." Clyde scowled. The Gallagher/Calvin feud was alive and well. He whipped his empty beer can at the trash barrel.

Chad's heart wrenched, imagining that anger directed at Vanessa and her mom. Fists clenched at his sides, he wanted to throttle the man. He paid for his bait and stomped out. He needed to see Vanessa and wasn't about to waltz into the tea room and buy scones.

Giddy anticipation mixed with fear and dread when Vanessa saw Chad's truck parked beside the bait shop. She'd heard the familiar rumble, but assumed he was driving by. Did he stop to see her, or just to buy bait?

He wouldn't dare confront her father about Mama's black eye. Would he? His expression that night told her he wasn't convinced Darla had fallen. His insistence on her calling him for help confirmed his suspicions.

She couldn't drag him into her family tragedy. He knew too much already. Yet her heart thrilled at the thought of seeing him again – almost enough to step into the bait shop.

But she had to get to work. She hurried toward the road but knew she'd never outrun that truck.

"Vanessa!" His voice called out behind her.

Stopped in her tracks beside the blue behemoth, she stiffened with frightened joy. Should she smile and chat, or wave goodbye and say she had to go to work?

At the pounding footsteps behind her, excitement bubbled up. She spun around, unable to keep the smile from her face.

"H...Hello," she finally managed.

"Mornin' sunshine," he drawled. He stopped just inches from her. "You look pretty this mornin'."

Heat surfaced at her throat. She willed the blush to stop there, fearing miserable failure. She swallowed hard. His slow smile made her heart thump wildly.

"Thank you." Eye-level with his chest, she avoided his insightful eyes. She dug the toe of her shoe into the dirt. "I'm dressed for the tea room." She motioned up the road, surprised at how sorry she was to say the words. "I have to go to work." She loved her job, and was ordinarily eager to get away from here.

Powerful chest muscles flexed beneath the race car photo on his soft cotton T-shirt. He leaned one elbow on the deep blue fender.

"I could give you a ride." The low, sexiness of Chad's voice startled her. She'd known him practically all her life, but never dreamed she had a chance with him.

She stared at his chest too long. Her gaze shot up to warm eyes sparkling with a smile. One look into those deep blue depths and she was lost forever. She'd never believed in love at first sight, but this wasn't the first time she'd met Chad James. Sudden premonition overwhelmed her. Could he be the one?

He'd never be interested in her.

His smile curved up on one side, showing a flash of straight teeth.

He couldn't really be *flirting* with *her*. She had to be misreading him. She stared dumbfounded at the tricked out truck, in shock that the most eligible bachelor in Crystal Falls was even talking to her – and offering her a ride!

Jumbled emotions overwhelmed her. She focused on the truck's front license plate. It read '1972' and the all-American truck looked about that old. The shiny chrome bumper glinted in the summer sun. Waves of heat rose from the hood into the dewy morning air. Chad's elbow still rested on the fender, as he waited for an answer.

Her gaze shot up to his ruggedly handsome face. The smile she found there set her heart to pounding. She glanced toward the bait shop. Her father leaned against the doorframe with a menacing look of warning.

"I don't think my father would approve." He wouldn't stop

her, not in front of Chad, but she'd pay the price later.

Chad's eyes widened with surprise, then hooded.

"Do you need his permission?" His voice remained polite, but anger stirred beneath the surface.

Mutiny rose within her.

"Actually, no." She tossed Clyde a rebellious glare.

Chapter 2 – Chocolate Blouse

Vanessa walked toward the passenger door of Chad's truck, but he was a step ahead of her.

With a creak of old hinges, Chad opened the door. "I'll help you up. It's a stretch." He pointed below the door to a flattened chrome pipe. "Put your foot here and I'll lift you up."

He sounded like he'd done this before. Nervous at her inexperience with men, she wondered how many girls had been in this truck with him.

She put her left foot on the step.

"On three," he said, grasping her waist.

At his touch, warmth filled her center. Butterflies fluttered in her belly. Usually uncomfortable with physical touch – especially with men, and in front of her father – she was shocked at the yearning to lean back against him. His warm hands were pure heaven, and she wanted him to wrap his arms around her and cradle her forever.

"...Three." He lifted her off the ground and boosted her into the truck. Her hair grazed the door jamb as she nearly cracked her head.

Plopped into the seat, she wondered what happened to one and two. Was she so enamored that she totally zoned out? Whoa. This was downright scary.

Saturday afternoon Vanessa was never so glad to leave work. Everything had gone wrong and her ruined work shirt proved it. She had no idea how she'd ever get the stains out, and it was the only proper white blouse she owned.

"Good night, Miss Julia," she called, slipping out the back

before something else went wrong.

The two-mile walk was balm to her soul. She needed this time of quiet and solitude between a busy day and the stress at home. Maybe she didn't need a car after all.

Until winter.

She passed Mitchell's Garage and the car dealer. Then she turned off Market Street onto Lake Road. She enjoyed the sudden change from town to the country. Woods lined both sides of the road with only an occasional house along the way.

Two miles from town, the houses grew farther apart and traffic slowed to nothing. She heard birds in the trees, frogs down by the creek, and bugs stirring for their evening meal. She most appreciated this quiet ending of her trip – before her father's bellowing and her mother's crying assaulted her sanity. She closed her eyes, knowing the way by heart, basking in the glowing orange sun above the treetops.

Distant rumbling sounded somewhat familiar. She scanned the horizon but saw nothing past the knoll up ahead. The rumbling grew louder, closer. She'd heard that sound before.

A blue truck rose over a far hill.

Chad James.

Her pulse quickened and her mind reeled with the memory of his face smiling down at her.

I hate to see a pretty girl all alone on the road.

No one called the bait shop girl 'pretty.' No one dared come near Clyde Gallagher's daughters. He had scared away her sister Layla's boyfriends, and she rebelled fiercely. Layla had left home and become a stripper, making sure to get the male attention she craved from anyone but her father.

Vanessa shuddered. She hated going home.

She jingled the change in her pocket, touched the wad of tips. Soon she'd be out of there. And she'd take her mama with her.

Meanwhile, the blue truck approached. The rumble lowered in pitch, and the truck slowed to a crawl. Music blared until Chad bent to turn it down.

He was stopping again, and she looked a fright. There was no hiding the mess that covered her blouse.

As his face came into view, she caught his wide grin and smiling eyes.

Maybe if she crossed her arms in front of her…

The big black tires ground to a stop.

Vanessa's heart pounded as she looked up at the truck.

"Fancy meetin' you here." Chad stuck his head out the window and moved the gearshift into neutral.

"What are you doing out this way again?"

"I did a little fishing this morning. Then I checked out the job site."

"What job site?" Her head jerked back with surprise.

"I'm building a few houses on the other side of the lake. Nice property out this way," he commented. He looked around at the nature surrounding them.

"I hope it stays this way." She hated to see the area ruined with housing developments.

"Don't worry. I won't destroy the natural setting. Just a house here and there, tucked in the woods."

"Oh. Good." She squirmed in the grimy shirt, uncomfortable trying to hide it.

"What happened?" He grinned, staring at the front of her.

"Uh – " Her face burned red and she wished to high heaven she could get a tan. "I had a run-in with a chocolate torte."

He laughed out loud. "That's a good one. I have run-ins with subcontractors, homeowners, even the occasional Rottweiler, but I never heard of a run-in with a chocolate torte."

"Occupational hazard, I suppose." Her heart lightened and she felt unbelievably comfortable with Chad James. "Bad day at the tea room."

"Why don't you climb in and tell me all about it?" He opened the door and jumped out. "Let me help you up."

He made it so hard to say no.

"But your truck is so nice. I don't want to mess it up."

"Have you seen me? I've been fishing all day and I'm covered with mud. It's a truck – it's made to get dirty."

She looked over the gleaming blue paint, and then down at her chocolate-stained blouse.

"Come on, humor me." He reached for her hand. "I can't drive by and not give you a ride. It's ungentlemanly. You know, chivalry and all that."

"I heard chivalry was dead," she said deadpan.

"Not quite."

She gave him her hand.

Warm and calloused, his hand felt comforting. More than that, she felt safe and protected in a way she never had with anyone. Towering above her, he led her to the passenger door. Then he turned to face her.

Her eyes came up to that broad chest. Not a good thing. She looked into his vivid blue eyes as they deepened to almost violet. She'd never seen such gorgeous eyes.

She couldn't breathe.

His smile faded. His face was all seriousness and longing.

Did he long for…her?

"R…ready?" His Adam's apple bobbed as he swallowed hard.

All she could do was nod.

This time she knew the routine. His touch was even more enjoyable without her father looking on.

She usually repelled from touching strangers – and fiercely distrusted men. Maybe that was why she felt so comfortable at the tea room – men rarely darkened the door. Her mother had trouble with affection, but she had always been kind. Vanessa felt at ease with women.

Yet something about Chad drew her. She longed for genuine, caring male affection.

"All in?" he asked.

"Yeah." Her voice came out a squeak.

He slammed the heavy door and winked at her through the window.

She was up there. Chad crossed in front of the hood. Of all six foot, four inches of him, all she saw was his head.

The truck was old with no frills. The flat metal dash had a push button on the glove compartment. The vinyl floor mats and bench seat were worn but clean.

Chad's door opened and he vaulted behind the wheel. With a grin, he asked, "So do you want to sit here and tell me what happened to your shirt, or should we drive?"

"Let's drive." She looked out at the open road, sad she was only a mile from home.

He clunked the gearshift into first and with a squawk of tires, the truck growled to life. Usually too shy to touch someone else's things, she couldn't help but crank down the window to feel the wind blow through her hair. Riding high in this cool truck felt as awesome as she'd imagined.

"So tell me about the chocolate torte," Chad prompted.

Amazed at how comfortable she felt with him, she laughed out loud. "I was rushing to serve the Red Hat ladies. Their group is about twenty people."

"Wait a minute – the red hat ladies?"

She chuckled. "It's a social club. Mostly older women, they go on outings and visit tea rooms, stuff like that."

"Oh." He sounded befuddled. "I suppose they wear red hats?"

"You got it," she said with a laugh. "It was someone's birthday so they ordered the whole torte. I was carrying it out when Julia hurried into the kitchen. We ran smack into each other." She looked down at her shirt. "Needless to say, the torte lost and so did I."

Chad laughed heartily. "So did they get their birthday cake?"

"Luckily we had another one," she said with relief. "But we were out of chocolate torte for the rest of the day, and some of the patrons were not pleased. Those ladies need their chocolate."

"I know a few like that," he said with a smile.

"Oh, I assure you, it was no one in your family. The James ladies have the utmost manners. Especially compared to Myrtle Winthrop and her cronies."

He scowled. "Myrtle's started more than one lying rumor to hurt my family and many others in this town."

"I know. She showed up with her gossiping friends right at noon – our busiest time – without a reservation. They were upset they had to wait. Sat pointing fingers and bickering."

"Maybe Miss Julia should hire more help."

"It's not that. We just don't have the room. Everyone knows we're small and they need a reservation. Another tea room might have turned them away, or told them to come back later. But Julia never turns anyone away."

Chad grew quiet as they neared her house. Vanessa cringed at its condition, but she knew he'd seen it all before. He knew where she lived. He knew her father.

And he seemed to like her anyway.

He pulled into her driveway and parked. Thank goodness, her father's car was gone.

"Vanessa, I was wondering if you'd like to go out with me tonight?"

She stared at him, speechless. "Um, I don't know," she finally managed. How she wanted to be with him, but her father would never permit it. Yet Chad's earnest face and seductive voice tempted her to rebel.

"Please?" he begged. "I'll be nice."

She couldn't help but smile at him. Let Clyde have a fit, she was having too much fun to care. Besides, it was Saturday night. Clyde would be hanging out at the pool hall with his buddies until late.

"Uh, well, I'd have to change." She pointed out her chocolate blouse.

"Uh, well, me too!" He pointed out his muddy jeans.

She laughed. "Okay. But what should I wear?"

"Any old thing. Doesn't matter. I'm all about casual, in case you hadn't noticed."

"Good. I don't have many nice clothes. In fact, this is my only good work shirt. How sad is that?" She forced a laugh.

"Wow. Do you think you can get it clean?"

"Probably not."

"We could stop and get you a new one, if you'd like."

This man was beyond kind. He knew she didn't have a car, and Myrtle's Buttons and Bows was closed until Monday morning. By that time, she needed to be at work – and dressed. Not that she could afford the old coot's prices anyway.

She couldn't believe her good fortune. A real date, and this generous offer to boot. She'd gone this far, and it felt great.

"That would be wonderful! Anything beats riding in that rattletrap car of my father's. And I simply cannot abide shopping with that man."

Chad cracked a grin. "No offense, but I can imagine."

She laughed out loud.

An hour later, Vanessa climbed into Chad's truck with his gracious help. She felt giddy as a teenager.

She'd never had a date. In high school, none of the boys wanted anything to do with the girl from the wrong side of the creek. And everyone knew how her father scared off Layla's dates by brandishing his shotgun and yelling threats.

The only guys who gave Vanessa the time of day just wanted a free show at her sister's strip club. But those days were gone –

along with her sister.

Layla had been dead almost two years now, but Vanessa lost her long before that. She and her older sister never had much in common, but Layla had detached completely when their father began crawling into her bed at night.

Vanessa stared out the side window to hide the tears welling in her eyes. She forced the images from her mind. This was no time to grieve for her sister, nor her own lost childhood. After Layla ran away from home, their father's attention had turned to young Vanessa.

She ground her teeth with loathing.

Blinking back tears, she steeled herself from emotion. With her mother's help, she'd stood up to him. She hadn't lost Layla in vain, and she wouldn't allow her father to ruin the rest of her life.

Sitting up straight, she glanced at Chad. He looked over with a flirtatious grin, thankfully oblivious to her disturbing thoughts. A smile bubbled up from within her. This was her first date and she would enjoy it. She flipped back her hair in a flirty gesture of her own.

Chad James was a dream come true.

Working at the bait shop, any decent guy who came in dealt with Clyde first hand. She didn't meet many men at The Porcelain Teapot. The food delivery guy was in his fifties and the package delivery man wore a wedding band. Not that she was looking for a man – she reminded herself of her vow of independence.

Yet she needed a small spot of happiness to break the drudgery of a harrowing home life. She tugged at her faded denim skirt and straightened her yellow tank top so her dingy bra straps weren't showing. Her long hair blew around the cab of the truck as country music played on the radio. The gorgeous man beside her wore jeans and a plain white t-shirt.

"Do you mind if we eat first?" he asked as he drove toward the mall in Springfield. "I'm starving."

"Sure. I'm hungry too."

"Take your pick," he pointed to several sit-down restaurants on either side of the busy city street.

So many choices! Then she spotted her favorite fast food.

"This one!" she hollered before he reached the turnoff.

"All right, a girl after my own heart." Chad hit his blinker.

Starving, she ordered a double cheeseburger, fries and a Coke.

Saying 'Number Two' didn't sound quite so bad. When Chad ordered a triple, she felt relieved that he didn't make her look like a pig.

The food was tastier than ever, especially with Chad's beaming smile across from her. She rarely came to Springfield, even less frequently did she eat at a restaurant.

After enjoying the meal, they wandered aimlessly through the mall.

"What store did you buy your other shirt from?" Chad asked.

"I think the name started with a C. It was a little discount shop with mannequins in the window."

"This one?" Chad pointed out a little store with mannequins.

"No, that's not it." She glanced up and down the row of stores. "They all have mannequins!" She laughed at herself.

"We'll just keep looking 'til we find it." Chad cheerfully looped his arm in hers. Which side of the mall was it on?"

Virtually lost, she looked up at him with puppy dog eyes and shrugged.

He chuckled. "When's the last time you came to the mall?"

"To buy that shirt, when I first started at the tea room about two years ago."

"You really are a girl after my own heart." He wrapped his arm around her. "That store might not even be here anymore."

"Oh. I didn't think of that."

"Regardless, they won't have the same shirt in inventory after two years." His words lacked any hint of condescension. He made her feel like a valued apprentice rather than an ignorant hick.

She reveled in the pressure of his arm around her waist, the warmth emanating from his body so close to hers.

"Let's try this store." He pulled her into a cute little boutique.

They headed for a rack of white shirts. Without any trouble, she found an adorable blouse in her size, at a bargain price too.

"I like this one." She beamed at him.

"Why don't you get two or three?" He winked. "Just in case."

She made mental calculations of the tips Mama told her to keep. "I only have enough money for one." She felt a blush rising.

A young clerk looked over with disdain. Chad kissed Vanessa's forehead. "Don't worry, sweetheart," he said as if they were an item. "I'll get it."

She was so surprised the flush drained away. Before she could find words to protest, Chad had three blouses in his hand and proceeded to the check out. After paying for the entire purchase, he carried the bag as they continued through the mall.

Feeling awkward, she didn't know what to say or how to respond. No one, save her mother, had ever bought her anything. Other than Christmas or her birthday – which were slim pickins compared to what others received – she could count on one hand the purchases made for her.

"Thank you," she finally whispered. She meant it from the depth of her heart, yet the words sounded unsubstantial, not nearly enough.

"You're very welcome." Chad looked into her eyes. "Consider it a gift. I didn't bring you flowers or anything tonight, and I should have. Dinner at a steakhouse would have cost more than this." He held up the bag. "You're a beautiful, vibrant woman and I appreciate your company."

This time, her blush rose with a vengeance.

He grinned. "No need for that blush." He stroked her cheek with his thumb.

The comfort of his touch relaxed her, letting embarrassment fall away.

"Next time, no cheap date, okay?" His face was sincere.

"Next time?" The question slipped out of its own volition.

"Yes. Next time." His arm wrapped tightly around her.

Feeling cherished, she leaned into him, thoroughly enjoying his comforting affection and kindness.

In the mall parking lot, they had no problem spotting the big blue truck that towered over every car, van, and SUV around it. She continued walking on air, not remembering where they exited or even going out the door.

Head in the clouds, she put one foot in front of the other and followed wherever he led her.

When his hands gripped her narrow waist to lift her into the truck, she let herself fall back against him and cuddle into his chest. Right there in the parking lot, he held her. Nuzzling his face in her hair, he didn't say a word.

After a few moments, he turned her to face him. Looking down at her with those indigo eyes, he pulled her closer. Panic rose in her as he leaned close for a kiss.

Chapter 3 – Dinner and a Movie

"Excuse me!" A little boy stood watching them, hands on his hips. Annoyed, he pointed to the car door behind Vanessa. "I can't get in my car," he said with disgust.

Embarrassed, Vanessa moved aside to let the boy pass. She stared at the asphalt.Her amorous feelings evaporated in a cloud of humiliation.

"Sorry about that." Chad mussed the boy's hair, seeming comfortable around kids and not the least bit self-conscious.

A young woman pushing a stroller came quickly behind the boy. She shuffled her son into the car and lifted a baby from the stroller.

Chad nonchalantly opened his truck door and boosted Vanessa inside. His grip around her waist warmed her. Hugs were so much more comforting than kisses. Enticing as his lips were, the thought of kissing created terror in her heart. But how she enjoyed his warm hands.

He climbed behind the wheel and shook his head.

"Kids," he said with humor.

She laughed despite herself. There was no being bashful with this guy.

While the woman folded her stroller, he pulled out and drove toward the cinema.

"Want to see a movie?" he asked.

She had never been to a movie. The idea thrilled her – sitting close to Chad in the dark with his arm around her.

"I'd love to," she breathed.

They chose a cute PG comedy – not too heavy for a first date. Chad insisted on popcorn although she wasn't the least bit hungry. They agreed to share a small box.

"You can't see a movie without popcorn," he said with a wink.

"Tradition, eh?"

"Nah, I just like popcorn. I'm not very traditional."

"Hmm. Is that good or bad?" She raised an eyebrow.

"I think it's good." He seemed very sure of himself.

The theatre filled quickly with people of all ages. For nine in the evening, she was surprised how many kids crammed in.

Shortly after the movie started, people filed into the darkened row behind them, bumping her head and tugging her hair. She casually gathered her hair over her shoulder and leaned closer to Chad. A thrill ran through her when he draped his arm over her protectively. Her head fell onto his shoulder.

She'd longed for this comfort and couldn't believe she'd found it with Chad James, the man of her dreams.

"I can't see!" Some kid behind them whined.

She turned to see the same boy from the parking lot directly behind her.

"You again!" The boy scowled, giving her seat a swift kick.

His mother ignored him, tending her fussy baby.

Chad took her hand and pulled her toward seats near the wall. He positioned his tall frame in the corner and laid his arm over the back of her seat. She leaned into his warm comfort and he wrapped his arm around her shoulders.

"That's better," he whispered in her ear.

His hot breath sent tingles down her spine. Butterflies danced in her belly. Then he gently brushed a strand of hair from her face. His hot, moist lips touched her cheek in a gentle kiss. She reeled from his sensitive touch and her pulse pounded in her ears. Her head fell back against his shoulder and he leaned close, surrounding her with the heat of his chest.

Settled in comfortably, he turned to face the screen. She tried to watch the movie, but Chad's long, denim-clad legs distracted her. The bucket of popcorn was tucked between them. His hand absently reached in for a few kernels.

Her gaze fixed on his long fingers, then his mouth. Unexpectedly, he brought the popcorn to *her* lips. She turned to face him. He gave her a beguiling grin and tugged her bottom lip with warm, slightly rough fingertips. When she opened her mouth, he popped the kernels onto her tongue.

The hot, salty taste mingled with smells of buttery popcorn

and Chad's spicy cologne. Taking it all in, she chewed. A moment later, he held up a drink, tilting the straw toward her lips. She took a sip and swallowed, her senses alert with the cool sweet taste, the warm smells, and best of all, the feel of hot Chad James against her.

If this was a dream, she refused to wake up. As the credits rolled, she wondered what the movie had been about.

Chad escorted her past the rude little boy. Still kicking the seat, he stuck out his tongue. Chad caught her eye, grinning non-stop as he squeezed her hand.

"Kids," he whispered.

Grateful for the warm night air, Vanessa hopped into the truck and rolled down her window as they drove into Crystal Falls.

"Do you ever go to the falls at night?"

Intrigued, she watched his profile. "No, I never have."

"They're beautiful in the moonlight. With croaking bullfrogs and chirping crickets, it's a whole new world."

"How wonderful."

"Downright romantic." He raised an eyebrow. Parked on the square, he led her by the hand onto the old stone footbridge.

Like an enchanted wonderland, the falls rushed below them. Moonlight and distant streetlights lent a faint glow on thick foliage. Night sounds rose from the trees and creek. The scene reminded her of the Thomas Kinkade artwork decorating the tea room.

"You're right – it is a whole new world at night."

He wrapped his arms around her and pulled her close. "Alone at last."

She reveled in his warm embrace. His eyes locked with hers and he leaned down to kiss her.

Almost lost in the moment, she was assaulted by the image of her father's face, mean and angry. His greedy mouth pressed down on hers, tasting of sour breath, moonshine, and chewing tobacco.

She jerked back.

"Vanessa, what's wrong?" Chad's voice filled with hurt.

"I…I'm sorry, Chad. I can't."

"I thought you wanted to. In the parking lot…"

"I do want to, but I can't." She grasped for an explanation that wouldn't betray her secret. "I'm scared. I haven't been with anyone before." Only half was a lie.

"I'll be gentle," he promised, touching her cheek.

"No." She shook her head, turning away. The memory

wouldn't leave her mind.

He stroked her shoulder, comforting her.

"Just hold me." She leaned into him.

He wrapped his arms tightly around her, kissing the top of her head. "It's okay." He rubbed her back, soothing her. She wanted him to never let go.

But the nightmarish vision would not go away.

The clock on the town hall chimed midnight.

Vanessa leapt away from him. "I have to get home." Wild-eyed with panic, she bolted for the truck.

"Whoa!" Chad grabbed her arm, stopping her in her tracks. "Vanessa, what's wrong?"

Struggling to get free, she refused to look at him. She covered her face with one hand.

Shame and humiliation stung her like never before. This gorgeous man had no idea how dirty and defiled she was. Why had she even come? Why had she let herself be fooled into thinking something pure, something good, could ever happen for her?

Tears streamed down her face.

"Please." Sounding crushed, Chad begged. "Please tell me what's wrong."

He wouldn't let go, forcing her to make him understand.

"My father." She couldn't look at him, but he loosened his grip. "He'll have a fit if I'm not home. He's always back around midnight. We have to go, Chad. Now!" Yanking free, she would not let him stop her as she turned to run.

Chad rushed to catch up and grasped her trembling hand, meeting her pace. Understanding dawned as he saw the terror in her eyes. Remembering her mother's bruises, he clenched his teeth. Rage mounted inside him. His long, sturdy legs struggled to keep up with her.

White as a bleached shirt, Vanessa dashed like a fawn running to its mother. Her fragile, delicate condition made his heart ache. Swallowing the anger that could escalate her fear, he realized he had to be gentle with this wounded soul.

He would suppress his own needs until she was ready to accept intimacy. He vowed to let Vanessa make the first move and follow her lead.

Without music or words, only the rumble of the old truck punctuated the ride home. As they neared Vanessa's house on Lake Road, it was ablaze with light. The white rattletrap sat in the driveway.

It was gonna be bad.

Her father was home and there would be hell to pay.

"Thank you, and good night." She felt guilty about her poor manners, but she grabbed the door handle for a quick exit before Chad could interfere. Right now, she had to get inside that house before her father came out.

As the truck rolled to a stop, she flung open the heavy door.

"Whoa!" Chad grabbed her arm.

"Let me go," she cried desperately, wrenching her arm and watching the house. "He'll pitch a fit. Please, Chad, let me go!"

Chad calmly gripped her arm as he batted the gearshift into neutral. He turned his body to face her and held both her arms.

"If your father is angry, then it's my fault. I'm not letting you handle this alone, so forget it." Pulling her toward him, he opened his door, climbed from behind the steering wheel and helped her out the driver's side.

Grateful for his support, at the same time she felt annoyed. No one had ever insisted on helping her this way before. Yet she didn't ask for his help and didn't want it. She told him she could handle this herself.

But could she? And did she really want to?

He led her across the weedy dirt parking lot.

"I'll walk you to the door and compliment your father on his beautiful daughter. We'll see how it goes from there."

"I can tell you how it's going to – " She stopped mid-sentence. "Oh no!"

Her father appeared at the door with a can of beer in one hand. He tossed a menacing scowl at the truck.

"Please, Clyde, come in the house," her mother begged, cowering behind him.

Unblinking, Vanessa leaned toward Chad. He pulled her to his side and slightly behind him, wrapping a protective arm around her.

"Good evening, Mr. Gallagher," he called cheerfully. Familiar with her parents, he'd bought worms at the bait shop since he was a kid. "Evening, Mrs. Gallagher." He peeked inside at Vanessa's mother.

"What are you doing with my girl?" the man roared.

"You have a beautiful daughter. We just went out for dinner and a movie," he said non-chalantly.

"It's after midnight," Clyde growled.

"She didn't turn into a pumpkin or anything." Chad smiled down at her.

Vanessa cringed and her mother's eyes widened. They both knew jokes only made Clyde madder.

"Think you're some kinda comedian?" Eyes narrowed, he pointed the beer can at Chad. Then he threw back his head and guzzled. With the motion, he lost his balance. He caught himself on the door frame, sloshing beer. "Ain't nothing funny about this sitchi-a-tion," he slurred.

"No, I suppose not," Chad agreed as they drew closer.

"C'mon, Dad, I'm twenty-five years old." Vanessa poured on as much charm as she could muster.

Her mother's hand twitched, as if ready to yank him inside.

"You're still *my* little girl." Clyde hurled the beer can into the yard, clenching his fists at his sides.

"No, I'm not." She felt empowered with Chad beside her. "I'm an adult and I can go out when I want to," she said gently.

"Not if I say you can't." Clyde skewed his face. "As long as you live under my roof, you follow my rules," he barked.

"Dad, you look tired. I'm sure you worked hard today." Vanessa changed the subject, betting he wouldn't notice. "Why don't you get some rest?"

Her father raised an eyebrow with a look that only she would interpret. Behind scraggly white whiskers, his lips quivered. He wanted a kiss.

Embarrassed to her core, heat rose to her hairline. Usually careful to be sleeping before her father got home, she hadn't expected this. Glad for the darkness, she never wanted to show her face again.

Why couldn't she disappear and wind up on a deserted island?

Tempted to bolt, she feared a worse scenario if she didn't appease her father. God help her if he chased her down in front of Chad.

"Good night, Dad." Blocking Chad's view with her body as

best she could, she kissed her father's cheek. Like her worst memories, his breath and beard smelled of booze and stale cigars. She stepped away before he took her mouth in front of God and everyone. Namely, Chad.

"Good night, dear." Darla drew Clyde's attention with a sugary voice and planted a big smooch on his lips before he knew what hit him.

"Good night, Mr. Gallagher." Chad politely dismissed him.

Her father glowered and she feared all was lost. But her mother deftly led him down the hall.

Vanessa couldn't even look at Chad, but she felt his presence in the doorway. Why wouldn't he just leave?

Unable to stand still and unable to deal with what just happened, she moved to the window and looked out, wishing she could be that girl she'd been pretending to be.

"Thank you for dinner and the movie. It was really nice."

"My pleasure." His voice was soft and sincere. "Is everything okay?"

She nodded, neither wanting his sympathy nor appreciating his presence in this shack she lived in.

"Will you be all right?" he asked. "Do you want me to stick around until he's asleep?"

Chad was trying to help, but he could never understand.

"No, no – thanks, but we're fine." She scrunched her face as if confused at his assumption, blowing it off. "Thanks again, Chad. Good night." She moved to the door and took the knob in her hand, hoping he'd take the hint. He dallied in the doorway.

"Can I see you tomorrow?"

Her gaze jerked up at him. Was this guy for real? Her father just freaked out on him and he was willing to come back for more? She shook her head hard, squeezing her eyes closed to keep tears from forming.

"I don't dare rile him again," she stammered.

Chad stepped toward her, within inches of her face. His broad chest smelled of manly soap and fresh laundry. Would he safeguard her? The tide of feelings rode high. His hand reached for her cheek and she was powerless to stop him.

"We can meet somewhere else."

Staring at his chest with longing, she couldn't speak.

"My jobsite's just up Lake Road. The roof is on, so you can

wait inside if it rains. Three driveways past Route 4."

She couldn't bring herself to say no.

"Six o'clock tomorrow?"

She nodded.

"See you then." He slipped into the darkness before she could back out.

All at once she understood her sister.

As his truck rumbled away, her mother reappeared.

"Now I understand why Layla ran away and became a stripper," she said.

"Oh honey, please don't say that." Darla wrung her hands.

"She showed Clyde she was free to do as she pleased, to prove he didn't own her."

"I know," Darla said sadly.

"She exploited her body to hurt her father." The realization cut to her heart. Vanessa clenched her fists and growled through gritted teeth. Angrier than she'd ever been, she wanted vengeance too.

"Honey, please don't ruin your life because of him," Darla pleaded.

"I'd never lower myself like that. I definitely wouldn't show my body to any man who walks through the door. But now I understand Layla. And I *will* get away."

"That's right, honey. You stick to your plan," Darla whispered with an eye on the hallway. "Until that day, we need to keep the peace. We can't risk him coming after you again."

Vanessa nodded, that idea refueling her anger.

Then Mama spotted the white bag by the door.

"What's this?"

With a great sigh, Vanessa explained Chad buying her shirts. "I'll pay him back as soon as I can."

She enjoyed the evening with Chad more than she cared to admit. But he didn't need the burden of her baggage. She'd mail Chad the money for the shirts and avoid him for his own good. She would never be good enough for him anyway.

Sunday evening, Chad fired up the truck and headed up Lake Road, announcing his arrival with loud mufflers and thirty-six inch tires.

At the construction site, he scanned the empty stud walls,

peered into the gaping basement, and surveyed the excavated grounds. He sprinted down the driveway and held a hand over his eyes as shelter from the sun.

No one approached down Lake Road. No sign of life appeared at the bait shop on the corner of Route 4, but Clyde's old white car sat in the weedy lot.

After what felt like forever, he pulled his cell phone from his pocket. Quarter after six.

Did Vanessa change her mind, or was she afraid to rile her father? She had feelings for him. He saw it in her eyes, heard it in her breath. He had feelings for her too, and he'd rescue her from that madman if it was the last thing he ever did.

Indignant anger swelled within him. Then fear took over. Had something horrible happened last night – or this morning after Clyde woke up?

If that man hurt Vanessa…

Vanessa rushed out the door with a wicker basket under her arm. It was her safest escape. All night and day she'd debated whether to go. Staying home protected everyone involved. Then she heard Chad coming, watched the blue truck drive past, and saw it waiting for fifteen minutes.

She bustled to the clothesline on the far side of the house and snatched the clothes, still battling her inner fears. Heading back to the house, she spotted him standing in that faraway drive, shielding his eyes from the sun. He waved to her.

She waved back, almost dumping the clean clothes. She set the basket just inside the doorway.

"Going for a walk, Mama. Be home later."

"Okay, Ness. Have fun," her unseen mother replied.

"Bring me some booze!" Her father yelled from somewhere in the dark abyss.

"Yeah, right, on Sunday," she mumbled under her breath. "I'll just pretend I didn't hear that."

Chapter 4 – Coward's Way Out

As she walked across the meadow, Chad came running to meet her. Her heart thrilled at his eagerness to see her. She ran too, stopping breathless where they met on the road.

"Are you all right?" He looked her over with a furrowed brow. "I was worried."

"Yes." Her voice deflated. "Sorry I'm late. My father is home." She seethed through gritted teeth. "Are you sure you want to get mixed up with me?" She narrowed her eyes and nodded toward the house. "With this?"

"Nothing worthwhile comes easily. You're definitely worth the effort."

No man ever found her worth the effort. She blinked hard and looked down. When he licked his lips, she looked sideways. The pout of his mouth drove her mad.

"You have a death wish or something?" she asked.

"I have a wish but it's not for death." He inched closer.

Her eyes widened and her breath caught. He smoothed a blonde strand from her face and ran his hand down the long hair over her shoulder. Scalp tingling, she melted beneath his touch.

"I care about you, Vanessa. I always have."

Stunned, her gaze drifted to his and she couldn't stop it.

"I guess I've just been too busy starting a business to notice that you've grown up. You're a beautiful young woman, inside and out. Five years isn't such a big age difference anymore."

A bashful blush rose to her cheeks. She couldn't hide her transparent feelings. In awe, she looked down at his chest.

"Let's go, Vanessa." He gently took her hand. "Your father will get over it. It's time for him to let you go, and you have to let him go, too."

She searched his gentle, caring eyes for a long moment. She dreaded another confrontation like last night. Yet Chad was right – she needed to break free of her father, and it was time he let her go. Her face burst into a smile.

"I don't think he'll get too drunk tonight. It's Sunday and he's almost out of beer."

Chad held her hand firmly as they strolled down the road, taking in the scenery. They reached his truck and he lifted her into it. He wanted to kiss her, but wouldn't push. She looked so vulnerable and a little sad right then. He dared not scare her off before they left Lake Road.

As he closed the door, she settled in with a bounce on the seat. She rolled down the window and rested her forearm on the old sill, seeming happier already. He climbed behind the wheel.

"Are you building that?" Looking awestruck, she gazed at the house under construction.

"Yeah. Do you like it?"

"Who wouldn't? How do you do all that?"

"One step at a time. Seems daunting at first, but once you break it down into separate steps, it all comes together."

"Wow. I'm impressed."

"Thank you." He couldn't help but grin. "So where to?"

"Would you show me the other houses you've built?" She blinked those innocent doe eyes.

He couldn't believe it – a woman who took an interest in his work.

"Sure." Enthusiasm filled his voice. "But would you like some dinner first?"

"That sounds good!"

"What are you in the mood for?"

"Tacos?" she asked.

"Another cheap date, huh?" he teased.

"Well, the commercials look yummy, and I've never had tacos."

"You haven't?"

"We don't eat out much." She shrugged it off. "You're really spoiling me."

29

The girl was easy to please. Tacos and a tour of Chadwick Homes – it didn't get much easier than that.

After a delightful evening touring Bloomfield County to drive past every house he'd built in the last two years, including his sisters', he pulled into his own driveway.

"My crowning achievement," he exaggerated.

"This is your house, isn't it?"

"Yep." He laughed. "In reality, the mayor's son's house is my crowning achievement to date, and both my sisters have fancier houses than mine."

"They're both so beautiful," she gushed, looking up the road. "Yours is too," she quickly added.

"Mine is simple, like me. I'm finally finished and it has everything a man needs." He paused. "Except a family."

Seeming reflective and unsure, she stared at his house, letting the words sink in without comment.

"Would you like to see inside?"

"I'd love to." She hopped from the truck before he got around to help her.

"You're getting used to the climb, huh?"

"Oh, yeah." She blushed a little, but seemed anxious to see his house. Definitely a good sign.

He proudly escorted her up the recently paved driveway, past freshly mulched landscaping and in the front door.

"Rachel helped me decorate," he admitted as they entered the great room. "I picked the furniture. She added 'art' and plants."

"The furniture's very stylish." Vanessa ran a hand over the back of his leather sectional. "This is beautiful." She gravitated to the soaring stone fireplace.

"You really like it?" he asked.

"Hey, you've seen where I live. This place is gorgeous." She touched a family photo on the mantel with obvious longing.

Of course there was no comparison between her house and his, or her family and his. Feeling like a heel, he explained it away. "Rachel says the rustic stone screams bachelor."

She giggled, a delicate sound. "At least you don't have deer heads on the walls."

"True. But you don't think it's too masculine?"

"Not with Rachel's touches. The artwork and the plants really soften the room. The warm sand-colored walls play off light and dark flecks in the carpeting."

"Dirt-friendly," he said with a grin. "We chose the carpet together."

"You two work well together."

Thrilled with Vanessa's approval, he wondered how well he'd work with *her*. He moved to the kitchen to get her reaction.

"What about my kitchen?" He laid a hand on the counter. White cashmere granite with faint blue streaks accentuated his deep blue walls, off-white cabinetry, and stainless steel appliances. "Some say blue doesn't create an appetite."

"My mother has a collection of old blue and white dishes. I love it and it never affects my appetite."

He couldn't tell by how thin she was, but that was probably due to a lack of groceries, not a lack of appetite. Unlike other girls he dated who were afraid to eat, this girl could polish off an order of tacos with the best of them.

He showed her the informal dining area with his Windsor-style chairs and simple oak table. She approved of the small bedrooms and exclaimed over the master bedroom's private bath. Although nothing fancy, the private bathroom was impressive in comparison to the one bathroom home she was used to.

He opened the closet door just to see her response.

"It's enormous!" She gasped, staring into his four-by-eight walk-in. The closet was nowhere near enormous by his sisters' standards.

They wound back to the great room. He poured her a glass of sweet tea and lit candles on the summertime hearth. He sat close and they talked quietly. Romance stirred the air. She seemed to grow nervous and looked away at the clock.

"I'd better get home." She fidgeted with the hem of her shorts. He yearned to relax those shaking knees. He wanted to comfort and calm her, to hold her and protect her from her father and all her fears.

"I have to go in early tomorrow. Lots of baking to do on Monday mornings."

Disappointed, he understood. The girl so easily pleased wasn't so easy to kiss. The moment was gone so he blew out the candles.

Nearing the old homestead, Vanessa asked Chad to drop her half a mile down the road to avoid Clyde. She regretted staying gone so long. She enjoyed being with Chad so much she completely lost track of time.

"I won't let you walk home alone in the dark. It's not right. I'll take you home and walk you to the door like a proper date."

"But my father," she fretted. "I don't want another scene like last night."

"He went to bed, didn't he?" Chad asked.

"Yes."

"Did he give you a hard time about it today?"

"No, he must have forgotten about it. He was drunk. Plus he had something else on his mind. This morning he found out his friend committed suicide."

"Buddy Rafferton? I heard about that."

"I shouldn't have left. I just needed to get away and didn't consider the consequences. I hope he didn't take it out on Mama." She chewed her thumbnail.

"Vanessa." He gently touched her knee. "I don't want to interfere, but if he hurt your mother, I'm calling the police."

Her eyes widened. She nodded in agreement, but fear ravaged her quaking insides. The last time Darla called the police, it only made Clyde worse. He threatened to kill her, and she knew he'd find her if she tried to run away. She had no money, no driver's license, and nowhere to go. So she laid low and tried to keep the peace.

Vanessa couldn't keep her hands from shaking.

They had one ace in the hole – the incest accusation brought by her high school gym teacher. Too humiliated to take the witness stand, she was relieved her mother insisted on dropping the charges. They couldn't trust the system, and if Clyde beat the rap, he'd torment them even worse. But that threat kept him out of Vanessa's bed since then.

Could she trust the police to protect her? Somehow Chad's strength and confidence buoyed her courage. She felt safer just sitting beside him.

"You need to stand up to him, Vanessa. I want to help you."

She squirmed, but didn't reply. Grateful for his offer to help, he couldn't be there at all times.

As they reached the door, Clyde appeared from the shadows inside. Vanessa's stomach churned and her heart thudded.

"What are you doing here?" Clyde snarled at Chad.

"Walking your daughter to the door, sir."

"Where you been?" Clyde demanded.

"We took a drive, Daddy, that's all." Vanessa pranced nervously.

He narrowed his eyes toward Chad's truck. "In that?"

She nodded, turmoil and fear gripping her insides.

"You said you were going for a walk."

"Well, I did. Then Chad gave me a ride in his truck. He took me out for tacos!" She acted excited to distract him. "You should go sometime. You would love tacos!"

"I ain't eating no tacos and neither are you!" Clyde grabbed her arm and yanked her inside. Stepping out, he slammed the door in her face. She ran to the window.

"Whadda you think you're doing running around with my girl?"

"We went on a date." Chad stood toe to toe with him.

Through the window, Vanessa pointed toward his truck, mouthing, "Go!" Her mother came up behind her with a worried frown, the phone in her hand.

"I'm sorry about your friend, Buddy." Chad wisely changed the subject. Maybe his compassion would soften her dad.

"That coward took the easy way out!" Clyde exploded with rage. "He didn't even stand and fight like a man. He let some fool woman stomp him into the ground and run out on him."

"Poor guy must have been pretty upset when she left." Chad remained calm, with compassionate tact. He didn't realize he was in over his head and sinking fast.

"Stinking coward couldn't hold his liquor. He went and shot his self." Clyde slammed a fist against the doorframe.

That had to hurt, but the man seemed unfazed.

"I'm sorry to hear that, Clyde. He must have really loved her."

"Hogwash!" Clyde narrowed his eyes. "What are you, some kind of pansy?"

"I'm no pansy and you know it." Growing up the florist's son, Chad probably heard enough of that. His eyes flashed, evaporating any semblance of calm compassion. He clenched his fists.

"You stay away from my girl!" Clyde put up his dukes and

drew back.

Chad blocked the punch, smoothly catching Clyde's arm in one hand.

"I don't want to hurt you, Clyde." Chad stood a head taller and easily had fifty pounds on him. Plus he was forty years younger – and sober.

Clyde swung like a demented salsa dancer. Chad caught his arm and her lunatic father sucker-punched him with the other fist. Chad doubled over, but recovered quickly.

"I told you I don't wanna hurt you!" With one quick motion, he grabbed both Clyde's arms and pinned them behind his back.

Vanessa hoped Chad would knock him senseless.

"Keep away from my girl!" The old coot kicked Chad in the shins.

Chad fought to hold him as he tried to dodge the kicks.

Vanessa snapped. She shot out the door and lunged at her father.

"Let me live my own life!"

"You ain't got no life, you worthless wench!" Clyde spat in her face.

"You don't own me!" Incensed with fury beyond control, she beat his chest with all her might.

Chad held her father back as she buffeted him.

"I'm not your little sex slave!"

Chad's face reddened to maroon. With a burst of adrenaline, he hurled Clyde against the house and whirled toward Vanessa.

"Has he laid a hand on you?"

Frozen like an icicle, she gaped in shock, realizing what she'd said.

"Of course he has!" Her brother appeared from nowhere. "Ever since Layla ran off. It's his fault she wound up dead!"

"I ought to – " Chad grabbed Clyde's collar and shook him. The old man came back swinging and Chad blocked every punch. So red he looked like his head would explode, Chad was obviously restraining himself from beating the tar out of the old geezer.

Junior shoved Chad out of the way.

Clyde socked his son in the jaw.

"I've had it with you!" Junior shook it off and showed no restraint. He pounded his father until Clyde cowered against the wall. But Junior didn't let up.

"You're gonna kill him!" Chad tried to pull him off. Clyde saw his opportunity and kicked at his only son, aiming for his groin and barely missing. Junior went ballistic, knocking his father's legs out from under him. The old man landed flat on his back, out cold.

Darla rushed to her son, wringing her hands. "You killed him."

Vanessa heard the relief in her voice. She felt the same relief, mixed with horrendous shame and guilt. An approaching siren spurred tremendous fear for her brother.

"He ain't dead." Junior booted his side and Clyde sputtered and coughed.

"Are you okay?" Chad asked Vanessa. His arm wrapped around her in protection.

She wanted to run and hide, to pretend this didn't happen, to erase her shameful secret from his mind. Yet his warm embrace soothed her like her mother's lap had as a child. She craved that comfort, needed it like a woman in the desert needed water.

The sirens cut. Vanessa watched with trepidation as a police car barreled toward them.

"Who called them?" Clyde struggled to his feet.

"I did." Darla raised her chin. "Right after I called Junior. I'm not putting up with this no more."

Finally! Her relief short-lived, Vanessa sucked in a breath as her father's face twisted with wrath.

"Get in the house, you little wench. You need to learn your place around here." He shoved her mother toward the door.

Darla staggered, and then stood firm.

"Leave her alone!" Junior wedged between his parents, glowering at his father. "You touch my mother or my sister again, and I'll kill you. I swear it, old man!" he shouted. "I'll kill you!"

The police car screeched to a halt, lights flashing.

"Junior." Chad stepped forward, patting his back. "That's enough. I feel the same way, believe me, man. But that's enough."

Chief Hunter climbed from his car with an air of authority. Chest puffed out, he asked, "What happened here, Chad?"

"Evening, sir." Chad returned to Vanessa's side and held her tenderly.

Junior straightened, obviously grappling with his fury. Battered and bruised, Clyde shot the chief a menacing glare.

"Clyde took the first punch," Chad said.

Clyde advanced on him. "Why I oughta – "

Chief Hunter yanked out his billy club. "Against the car, Clyde."

Her father lunged at the officer. The chief whipped him around in no time and had him spread eagle on the squad car. Slapping on the cuffs, he said, "You wait in the car and calm down. I'll get your story later."

He opened the door and shoved her father inside.

Vanessa trembled with an odd combination of dread and relief. Chad held her tight, offering solace beyond anything she'd ever felt.

"Ornery old cuss," the chief muttered. "Let's get your statements, one at a time." Hunter looked from one to the other.

She and Chad were joined at the hip.

Junior stood fuming.

"Darla, we'll start with you."

Chapter 5 – The Next Step

With Darla showered and snoring in her bedroom, Chad took Vanessa a cup of tea. They settled comfortably on the ratty sofa and she leaned close against his side. The girl craved affection; that was certain.

He wrapped an arm over her shoulders and she laid her head on his chest.

"Thank you for sparing us Clyde's wrath tonight." Shame filled her voice even now. "But I'm afraid he'll be even angrier once he gets out of jail."

Chad found it strange she called him Clyde. Yet it distanced herself from a relationship with him. She suffered the ultimate betrayal at the hands of her own father.

Infuriated at her demeaning secret, he understood her reluctance to discuss it. If he brought it up, he felt certain she'd clam up and boot him home. A very private person with a keen sense of modesty, Vanessa seemed to need time and space to open up. Seeing her humiliation, he felt honored that she allowed him to stay with her. He wouldn't embarrass her, but he hoped she'd confide in him when she was ready.

Meanwhile, he stuffed his rage and swallowed the biting remarks on his tongue.

"Why don't you move out?" He worked to keep the anger from his voice.

"Oh, I will. Soon. I've been saving, but I don't have enough money yet. I give all of my tips to Mama. She has so much trouble getting by."

"I'll loan you the money," he offered. "You find a place and I'll see to it that you get the money."

"I couldn't do that." Vanessa sat up and stared at him in disbelief. "Besides, money's not the only problem. I won't go without Mama, and she's afraid to leave him."

"She should be afraid to stay."

"I know. I'm scared for her. She thinks he'll come after her if she leaves." Vanessa looked at her lap and smoothed the blanket he'd settled over her. "But we'd be safer in town than out here all alone."

"I agree. Maybe after tonight she'll change her mind," he offered hopefully. He covered her hand with his, running his thumb over her knuckles.

She nuzzled into him.

"Mama wants to protect me from him, wants me to get out on my own." She took a deep breath and let it out slowly. "She says she doesn't want to be a 'burden' to me." She choked on a sob.

"I know you don't feel that way." Chad stroked her hair. He tenderly held her and let her cry.

After a good cleansing cry on Chad's shoulder, Vanessa gathered her courage. She sat up tall on the sofa and wiped her wet face. But she couldn't look at him.

"I'm sorry for my part in this," Chad said. "If I hadn't come along none of this would have happened." He bit his lip. "I couldn't just drop you off up the road and let you face him alone. But I shouldn't have lost my temper."

"Your temper was perfectly justifiable." Her gaze shot up to meet his. She searched his eyes, unwilling to let him blame himself. "You restrained yourself very well, under the circumstances. It's not your fault."

"I just can't live with putting you in danger like that. Once he gets out of jail, maybe we shouldn't see each other until you get your own place. Not antagonize him."

"I won't live another day under that man's rule. If I hadn't gone with you, it would have been another evening of Clyde speaks, Darla jumps, and Vanessa listens. It's high time we made some changes. I have to take the next step sometime and there's bound to be fallout."

"The next step?"

She'd blurted that out without thinking. He was so easy to talk to, and she really needed someone to confide in. She took a fortifying breath.

"I have a plan." She stared out the window away from him. "The first step was the hardest, but it gave me courage that I could do this."

"The first step?"

She'd set herself up for him to ask. Now she had to admit the harsh reality. She didn't want him to know the horrific truth, but she'd already blabbed. If she wanted a real relationship with Chad, if she ever wanted to kiss him, she had to help him understand.

After a taste of Chad's strength, Vanessa couldn't face this alone anymore. Impossible as it seemed, her face grew even hotter. She stared across the room at her father's gun cabinet.

"What I said about..." Her voice cracked and fury welled within her. "About being a sex slave." Her words took on steely determination. "Not anymore. That was the first step."

Chad seemed to breathe a sigh of relief. He had no idea how relieved *she* had been, or what she went through to get there. But he squeezed her knee in a supportive gesture. He opened his mouth and closed it again.

As difficult as this conversation was, she needed to get it off her chest. She needed his strength and support, and more than anything, his comfort. She rested her hand on his, hoping to let him know it was okay to ask.

"How'd you make him stop?" Chad asked quietly.

She squeezed his hand, holding on for dear life. He already knew the gist of it and hadn't run off. Yet she struggled with divulging the shameful details. "My high school gym teacher saw bruises."

His jaw clenched and anger flashed across his features.

"I tried to hide them, but the marks were pretty obvious. The teacher was compassionate, but she filed a report. I was too humiliated to testify, but I was empowered enough that I threatened to press charges if he ever touched me again."

Chad nodded. "Did you get any counseling?"

"The school required it. I was thoroughly embarrassed but it really helped me not back down – on that issue at least."

"Good." He wrapped his arms around her and held her.

She didn't cry this time, but it felt good to know he cared. She hadn't discussed her problem with kissing, but couldn't deal with any more tonight. Grateful he didn't ask any more questions, she wondered if it was all a bit overwhelming for him too. He quietly held her for a long time.

Ready to think about something else, she asked, "So do you want to hear about my plan?"

He turned to smile into her eyes. "Of course."

"Okay. Well, step two was getting a job outside the bait shop." She smiled wickedly. "I didn't know it at the time, but Miss Julia is Old Bald Calvin's sister. Considering the Gallagher/Calvin feud, that sets in Clyde's craw like no job I could have taken, unless Baldy himself hired me."

Chad smiled. "I guess it would. So what's step three?"

"Moving out and taking Mama with me. I'm saving to rent the apartment above the tea room."

"Please let me help," he said earnestly.

"Thank you." She touched his hand. "But I have to do this on my own. Julia offered to help me with the money too, but I have to do this right. I'm an able-bodied adult, not some charity case. I need to pay my own way like everyone else."

As much as she appreciated his offer, she couldn't depend on a man to get on her feet. Chad might be nothing like her father, but she'd witnessed her mother's dependence and the mess she was in because of it. Vanessa was determined to take care of herself come hell or high water.

He looked like he wanted to argue, but instead pulled her back to his side. Cuddling was so much better than arguing.

"You're a very brave girl."

She looked up with surprise. His face was so close. His lips pouted in that kissable way. She angled her mouth and leaned in. Butterflies danced in her belly and she tingled everywhere.

She searched his eyes nervously as he bent closer. At the last second, the horrid image of her father's face assaulted her.

Repulsion rippled through her and she pulled away.

"I won't hurt you, Vanessa," he whispered. "Do you want to kiss me?"

"No. Yes!" Her cheeks hot as fire, she covered her face with her hands. "I don't know. I just can't." Her voice trailed off.

He gently stroked her hair, smoothing a strand from her

temple. She lowered her hands. She fought the fury coursing through her. Chad could never imagine what Clyde had done to her.

"You're so kind. I'm sorry," she whispered without looking up.

"Don't be embarrassed." He held her hand. "It's just me."

"Just you?" How could he be so clueless? "The handsomest man in town? Most eligible bachelor with a successful business, a custom-built home, and a stable family? What on earth is a son of the founding fathers of Crystal Falls doing with a wretch like me?"

"You're no wretch, Vanessa." He winced. "You're beautiful and smart, talented and amazing and compassionate and kind."

Did he really think that? Her red-faced shame dissolved.

"You're the kind one," she said.

"We don't have to kiss if you don't want to." He wrapped his arms around her and hugged her close. She buried her face in his chest and held him tight.

"It's not that I don't want to," she whispered.

"I know." He stroked her long blonde hair, calming her with his gentle touch.

"Tonight you saw how possessive he is." She trembled violently. "I never wanted anyone to witness that, much less you!"

"But I did, Vanessa." He clenched his jaw. "I'm furious with your father, but I don't think any less of you. If anything, I respect you even more."

She pulled back and looked at him. "Why?" Her eyes bulged in disbelief.

"You've been through so much, yet you remain strong. You went out into the world and you're taking steps to change your situation. You're the strength for your mom, too. You're pulling yourself up by your bootstraps and that's no easy feat."

A small measure of pride filled her chest. "It certainly isn't easy, but I'm determined."

"I see that, and I'm proud of you."

"Thank you," she whispered. His affirmation meant more to her than she could possibly express. She stared into his kind eyes, grateful some miracle had brought him into her life.

"No need to thank me. I admire you, Vanessa. You're simply amazing to me. And if I didn't think it would frighten you, I'd kiss you right now."

She stared at his mouth. "I want you to…" Desire and fear

mingled in her gut. Her lips twitched but she kept her distance.

"But?" He waited patiently. "Tell me how to make it better."

"I don't know how." She shook her head sadly. "Every time we get close to kissing, I have visions of him…" She shivered. "Those scratchy whiskers, his sour breath, the booze and smoke and chew!" She made a face. "Yuck!"

Chad stroked her hair, listening.

"But he never held me." She crossed her arms over herself protectively.

Chad wrapped his arms firmly around her and subdued the fear welling inside her. She clung to him.

Eventually she squirmed. "You shouldn't get tangled up with someone like me, Chad. I'm damaged goods. You deserve better than that." Fear ravaged her. She was falling for him, but she'd never be good enough.

He lifted her face to his.

"Vanessa, *you* deserve better than that." He searched her face. "You're a beautiful woman. His abuse is not your fault. You deserve a better life and I want to help you make that happen."

Her eyes misted. "You're way too kind, Chad James."

He gently touched her mouth. He ran his thumb over her trembling lips. The sensation stirred her and she didn't want it to ever stop. He locked his eyes with hers. Overwhelmed with yearning, her eyelids fluttered.

"Look at me," he begged. "Think about me."

She looked deeply into his indigo eyes. Then her gaze dropped to his gorgeous mouth. She nervously lifted her fingers and cautiously touched his soft, kissable lips. He gently kissed her fingertips. She wanted more. She wanted to feel his lips on hers. He caught her eyes again.

"You're very handsome, Chad." Her fingers trailed up his jaw and she held his cheek. Then she ran her hand down his throat.

Breathing heavily, he sat very still. She explored his face, his neck, and ran her fingers through his hair. A ball of flame began to burn in her belly. Every female desire she'd ever felt battled fiercely with her fear, nearly overpowering her with the onslaught of emotion.

Chad closed his eyes and swallowed hard. His barely controlled passion set her on fire.

"Kiss me, Chad."

Chad's eyes sprang open and met hers. Pale blue, her eyes held all the desire and passion he'd felt in her embrace. He wanted to ravage her with kisses. His fire raged, threatening to engulf him past the point of no return.

Deliberately, gently, he took her face in his hands. With all the restraint left in him, he softly touched his lips to hers. She moaned beneath his caress. That shattered his control.

Chad took her mouth, kissing, nibbling, licking her lips. She responded passionately, meeting his every move and pushing for more. Deeper, harder kisses had him panting with need.

She arched up to him and he held her there. His hands spread across her back, stroking her, pressing her firmly against him. She writhed and moaned, completely letting go.

He had to stop before he lost control – and lost her.

He stilled, holding her tightly. She caught her breath and the kiss ended. He rested his face in her hair and his chin fell to her shoulder. He embraced her tighter, holding onto her with all his might, crushing her bones against his.

"Never let me go," she murmured.

"I won't," he promised.

They lay entwined on her mother's sofa, letting emotion catch up with desire, letting desire fade to comfort in each other's arms.

"I like kissing you," she whispered in his ear.

"Oh, really?" he whispered back.

"I like it when I think about you."

He rubbed her back. "Your kisses set me on fire," he breathed into her ear.

He felt her jaw move against his cheek and he knew she was smiling.

"Do you want to kiss me again?" she teased.

He pulled back to look into her eyes. "Do I dare?" he asked with a wry grin.

"Why not?" She pouted like a little temptress.

With all seriousness, he caught her gaze. "I love kissing you. Too much."

"What do you mean?"

Touching her cheek, he searched her eyes. "I want you, Vanessa. But I can't have you. Not now, and not without a marriage certificate."

She stared at him, dumbfounded.

"I don't believe in sex outside of marriage." He shrugged. "My moral upbringing. So you have no worries about that."

She looked forlorn.

With a gentle touch, he smoothed the disappointment from her face. She clung to him. Long into the night, they held each other tightly.

He was falling hard for Vanessa Gallagher. That marriage certificate might come yet.

Chapter 6 – Julia's Heritage

Vanessa woke in the night with Chad's arms wrapped firmly around her. She nuzzled into his sweet-smelling chest, reveling in the comfort of his body against hers. He stirred, moaning softly as he dozed. His arms tightened around her, warming her body and soul.

Where would a relationship with this man take her? She had so much to consider. His loan offer tempted her, but she couldn't accept it. She'd move out on her own terms. But it sure was nice to feel protected and safe.

And his kisses were heavenly.

With a smile, she drifted back to sleep.

Sizzling crackled Vanessa's consciousness. With a deep, waking breath, the smell of bacon tickled her nose. Mmmmm. Her eyes cracked open. Lying on the couch, she snuggled under a fuzzy plaid blanket that smelled like Chad.

Her sleepy eyes looked around although her body was too tired to move. In the kitchen across from her, it wasn't Mama frying the bacon.

His back to her, Chad James stood at her mother's stove in his wrinkled shirt. Broad shoulders narrowed to a trim waist. Low-riding jeans hugged his little butt and long legs. Stocking feet planted on the cracked linoleum floor.

Taking him in, she stretched.

As if on alert, he turned. A slow smile graced those kissable lips.

"Good morning." He took the skillet off the burner and walked toward her. "Did you sleep well?"

Sitting up, she felt a blush rise up her neck. She cleared her throat, willing it back down.

"Yes," she said with a grin. "I was quite comfortable. And warm." She tugged at the blanket. "Where did this come from?"

"My truck. I woke up about an hour ago and put that over you so you wouldn't get cold."

How did she sleep through that? She imagined his warm hands tucking the blanket around her and wished she'd been awake to enjoy it.

"Then I ran to the store for bacon and eggs. I hope your mama doesn't mind me using her stove." He leaned down to kiss her, but stopped suddenly and looked down the hall. His smile vanished, replaced with concern.

"Mrs. Gallagher," he breathed.

Vanessa turned. Her mother came toward them, clutching a tattered bathrobe around her.

"Mind a man cooking breakfast? I don't think so." Darla grinned.

"I didn't intend to spend the night, Mrs. Gallagher. But I didn't want to leave Vanessa, and... and then we fell asleep." His cheeks pinked.

"He was a perfect gentleman," Vanessa vouched for him.

"What fun is that?" Darla remarked deadpan. "So what's for breakfast?"

"Bacon and eggs, ma'am." Chad scurried to the stove and turned the bacon.

Vanessa cringed at the awkwardness. Chad wasn't used to her mother's dry humor. After his hasty retreat to the kitchen, he fed them breakfast without letting them help or clean up. Poor guy probably felt like he had to redeem himself for sleeping on their lumpy couch. Yet his attention made Vanessa feel pampered and loved.

Then the lecture began.

"You two aren't safe here once Mr. Gallagher gets out of jail," Chad insisted. "You need to find a place before then."

"No." Darla stood, defiant. "Vanessa can leave if she wants, but I'm staying in my home."

"You can't stay here." Vanessa couldn't believe this. She'd been planning her mother's escape for months. How could she stay with that madman? "He's gonna kill you, Mama."

"No, he won't." Darla waved a hand at them. "This is nothing. I've been through a lot worse."

"And you want to relive it?" Vanessa pounded her fist on the table.

"Of course not. But Clyde's in jail." Darla tightened the belt of her robe and faced Chad. "Thank you for breakfast. Stay as long as you like." She headed for the hallway. "I'm taking a shower."

"Wait." Chad gripped her arm, letting out a sigh. "If you won't leave, at least file a restraining order against Clyde. Please."

Darla's shoulders drooped, but her face lit with a shy smile. "You sound just like the chief. But don't go gettin' no fool ideas." She wagged a finger at him. "I'm stayin' in my home."

Chad searched her eyes with resignation.

"Yes, ma'am."

Vanessa was grateful when Junior's truck pulled in behind the bait shop. He stopped in to check on them.

"You're here early." Junior eyed Chad's sleep-rumpled shirt, the same one he had on last night.

"Chad made us breakfast." Vanessa took the focus off Chad's attire.

"Will you be around when your father gets out of jail?" Chad asked.

"Yeah. I'll make sure he doesn't hurt Mama no more." Junior patted a pistol in his pocket. "I nabbed his key to the gun cabinet." He pulled a string from his shirt pocket, dangled the key for a moment and then handed it to Vanessa. "This should be safe with you, Ness. Mama and I have keys too."

Vanessa tucked the key into her purse.

"Okay." Chad started to say something else but apparently decided against it. "I feel a little better knowing you're here to protect them."

His protectiveness, while flattering, worried Vanessa. She didn't dare depend on a man to protect her. Not when the one man who should have protected her from birth had betrayed her trust and hurt her beyond what she could bear.

"If you want to get ready for work, I'll give you a ride." Chad's offer, though generous, made Vanessa squirm. Feeling vulnerable, she feared any dependence on him, panicked he would gain control over her.

"I don't mind walking," she said distantly. Yet the July sun was already hot. How tempting to show up for work without having to towel off sweat in the rest room, reapply deodorant, and change her shirt.

"I don't mind giving you a ride," he insisted with a grin.

"Okay," she conceded against her better judgment. Again faced with a difficult choice, she couldn't bring herself to thwart their blossoming relationship.

Yet she'd fought so hard and so long for independence. She refused to give it up.

Busy for a Monday, The Porcelain Teapot buzzed with customers. Clearing the tables, Vanessa collected several ten-dollar tips and even a twenty from a larger group. She cringed as she scraped plates. So many times she had gone without a decent meal, while these ladies threw away homemade chicken salad with cranberries and pecans, barely touched raspberry scones made fresh that morning, and half-eaten slices of gooey chocolate torte that made her mouth water. Thank heaven the lunch rush finally waned and she could take her meal break.

Julia always ate first while Vanessa waited tables. She rinsed her lunch dishes and then piled a clean plate with generous portions of delectable food. She set it on the kitchen worktable.

"Eat." Julia knew Vanessa wouldn't stop working unless prodded.

Vanessa savored the delicious meal while Julia served the late afternoon crowd. At closing time, her kind boss filled large take home containers with sumptuous morsels and set them in the fridge. Every day Vanessa took home enough food for a delicious supper with her mother. After a long day in the kitchen, the care packages were a godsend.

She carefully hand-washed each delicate teacup and saucer. With the plates, glasses, and silverware loaded into the dishwasher, she scrubbed the steaming teakettles and wiped down the counters. After mopping the kitchen floor, she dusted each antique chair in the dining room, polished the hardwood floor, and shined each glass-topped table. As she put away the cleaning supplies, Miss

Julia touched her shoulder.

"Can I speak with you a moment before you go home?" the elderly woman asked.

"Of course." Vanessa loved chatting with Miss Julia after work. Any delay in returning to that dreaded bait shop was welcomed.

Julia sat two hot cups of tea on the small table in the corner of the kitchen. Heaping plates of finger sandwiches and pastries graced the center of the table. Chocolate ganache glistened on a slice of expensive torte in front of the chair where Julia motioned for her to sit.

"Eat dessert first if you want to," she said with a warm-hearted laugh. "Take home the leftovers for your family."

Hungry again after the hard day's work, Vanessa devoured a tiny sandwich in two bites and grabbed another, eyeing the chocolate torte to savor last.

"I had a phone call from the mayor this afternoon," Julia began as she folded her tiny frame into a chair. Taking her time as the elderly do, she adjusted her demure pink sweater.

Although the tea room was air conditioned, come July the ovens and steaming kettles made the kitchen hot as a tin roof in August. With a wrinkled, shaking hand, Julia stirred honey into her tea. "The mayor received the security deposit and first month's rent on the apartment upstairs."

"He's renting it to someone else?" Vanessa slumped in her chair. "But he promised to let me know if anyone else was interested."

"It's not for someone else. An anonymous donor paid the rent for *you*."

"But I – " She was about to say she couldn't imagine why anyone would do that. But suddenly she knew exactly who would. "He didn't dare!"

"You know who it was?"

"Only one person I can think of." Vanessa tossed her napkin to the table. She explained Chad's offer and his reasons behind it.

"I didn't realize your situation was that bad. So Clyde's gotten worse?" Wrinkles creased Julia's forehead and frown lines furrowed around her mouth.

"He's the same as always," Vanessa retorted. "I won't be dependent on another man."

"Chad wants to protect you," Julia soothed knowingly. "He must truly care for you."

Her response blindsided Vanessa. "You really think so?"

"Why else would he do this?"

Ashamed of her assumptions, Vanessa's anger deflated. "It feels like he's trying to control me."

"I think he's showing you how much he cares," Julia said.

"I can't accept it," Vanessa said with resolve. "I won't be under another man's thumb. When they provide for you, they own you. What's the difference if it's my father or Chad?"

"There's a very big difference, and you know it."

She shook her head. "Either way some man's trying to run my life." Vanessa's anger built again. "I refuse to be manipulated by that macho Chad James."

"I love your spunk." Julia chuckled in that dainty, old lady way of hers.

"I finally stood up to my father and it feels good. I won't be a doormat like my mother."

With a gentle expression, Julia took her hand. "I'm sure Chad's concerned about your mother's welfare as well as yours."

"Rightly so." Worry replaced Vanessa's irritation as realization dawned. "If I refuse his offer, and something happens to Mama, how will I ever forgive myself?" She dropped her head into her hands, agonizing over her mother's refusal to leave. "I don't know what to do."

"Just take it," Julia said. "Get your mama out of there and move into the apartment. I'll return Chad's money and explain the rent's already been paid. Repay me as you can. I can take payments from your check if you like."

"No." Vanessa raised her head. "You already offered to loan me the money. I need to do this myself." She suddenly understood her mother's determination to stay and fight for her home. At long last, Darla needed to make a stand the same way Vanessa did. She didn't want to be coddled by her daughter.

"I know, but we want to help. Don't be angry with Chad. He's a good boy. I can see you two together. What beautiful babies you'd have!" she said with a wink.

"I don't know about that." Although flattered by Julia's compliment, Vanessa couldn't imagine Chad James settling down with the likes of her. He might care about her, but she was nothing more than a charity case. He wasn't about to *marry* her. She toyed with her fork, poking at the chocolate torte as she gathered her defiance. "I'm not sure I want to get married. I need to rely on myself."

"I understand. But you don't want to end up an old spinster like me." Julia got quiet and sniffed.

"What's wrong with your life?" Vanessa asked.

The woman shrugged a bony shoulder beneath her lace collar. "I have no one, Vanessa. You're the closest I've ever had to a daughter, and you mean the world to me. Please let me do this for you."

Vanessa stood and hugged her. Julia's petite body shook with emotion.

"Okay, okay. Don't cry. I'll take the apartment."

"Good!" Julia squeezed her tightly. After Vanessa sat back down, her boss slipped an envelope into her hand. "Now there's something else we need to discuss."

Waiting for Julia to continue, Vanessa was puzzled.

"I'd like to retire soon. And I'd like you to own the tea room," Julia said.

Vanessa's jaw dropped. Blinking, she tried to speak but no words would come out. "But...but – " she said finally. "Julia, I'd love to buy it, but – "

"Shhh. Quiet, child. Let me finish. I have it all figured out. You can make payments based on a percentage of income. That way you won't be strapped during the off-season. It'll provide a little retirement income for me. I have money set aside and don't need much, so not to worry. You won't need to get a loan or scrape up a down payment."

Vanessa stared at her in awe. Her heart threatened to burst with love for this dear woman, with excitement for the opportunity presented.

"You don't have to decide today." She covered Vanessa's hand with her age-spotted one. "Just think about it. If you'd rather not own the tea room, just tell me. I'll figure out something else. Don't be afraid to be honest with me. Owning a business requires dedication and a lot of work. You have to love it. Take your time to think it over and let me know."

As much as she needed to do things for herself, this was an opportunity to purchase the tea room fair and square, secure her employment at the place she loved, and provide Julia with a retirement income as well. The chance of a lifetime, she'd be a fool to pass up this opportunity.

"I don't need to think about it." Antsy, Vanessa bounced on her chair. "I'd be honored to accept your offer. Owning The Porcelain Teapot would be a better future than I ever could have imagined."

Julia's blue eyes glowed behind the cataracts. "Are you sure?"

"Yes!" She squeezed her friend's hand. "Thank you, Julia. I never dreamed I'd get an opportunity like this. I feel so honored. How can I ever thank you?"

"By giving me a heritage," Julia said with a smile. "With no children of my own, you, my dear, are the only chance I have."

Vanessa's heart brimmed with joy. "Thank you so much."

"Now, one more thing." Julia pulled a thicker envelope from a shelf near the table. "This is my will. I'd like you to have a copy for safekeeping. There's a duplicate in the safe, and another copy in my safe deposit box at the bank."

Despite Julia's advanced age, Vanessa had never considered her dying. She couldn't bear to think of it. Her heart thudded against her chest as Julia slid the envelope under her palm and clasped her hand.

"I love you dearly, and I have no one else. When I pass, the tea room is yours, free and clear. You can sell it if you like."

Sudden tears stung Vanessa's eyes as sadness mingled with overwhelming gratitude. She wanted to assure Julia she could never sell it, but the enormity of this miracle rendered her speechless. Her tears burst forth.

Julia's eyes glistened with understanding and joy.

Chapter 7 – Packing

Chad pulled up in front of The Porcelain Teapot. He shut off the rumbling engine as quietly as he could, wanting to surprise Vanessa when she got off work. The mayor said he'd notify Miss Julia right away that the rent was paid. Now way past quitting time, they were probably discussing the move.

After cutting his workday a bit short, Chad had gone home to shower. He couldn't show up soaked in sweat and sawdust, even though he planned to load Vanessa's belongings into the truck and help her and her mother move tonight. No sense having them spend one more minute under Clyde Gallagher's abusive rule.

Cradling his arms behind his head, he waited in the truck as the town closed down for the night. Next door to the tea room, Myrtle Winthrop swept the sidewalk in front of her dress shop, Buttons and Bows. On the corner, his sister Rachel carried galvanized buckets of flowers into Rosebuds for the night. He jumped from the truck to offer assistance.

"Hey Chad, what are you doing here?" Rachel looked up with surprise.

"Waiting for Vanessa." He casually picked up several buckets of flowers. "I'm giving her a ride home."

"Vanessa Gallagher?" She stopped with a puzzled look.

"Yeah." He figured he'd get caught on this mission – Big Blue was a bit conspicuous. He didn't want his family worming their way into his relationships and offering unwanted advice, but Rachel was least likely to do so.

"We've gone out a few times. Despite her crazy father, she's a great girl."

"Oh, I agree. She does a wonderful job at the tea room."

"Hey, don't mention this to anyone, okay?" He carried the buckets inside the flower shop and set them down. "I don't need the family playing matchmaker and the drama that goes with it, if you know what I mean."

Rachel laughed. "I know what you mean! Although you deserve it. Elliot told me about your little conversations on the porch last summer."

"What conversations?"

"Don't play innocent with me, big brother." Arms full of flower-filled buckets, she leaned a shoulder into him with a light-hearted shove.

"Elliot said you were cool about it in front of everyone else, but you prodded relentlessly when he was alone with you."

"Hey, I was right, wasn't I?"

"Yep." She plopped down the buckets just inside the door. "So that justifies me doing the same for you, right?"

"Hey, come on, Rach. You're the one in this family I thought would understand."

"And I do." She grabbed a broom and he followed her back outside. "Don't worry, I won't let on. But if I feel Vanessa's right for you, I won't hesitate to let her know." Mischief sparkled in her eyes.

"Great. Thanks a lot," he grumbled.

She handed him a pink rose and nodded toward the tea room. "Better go catch her. That girl's in a hurry to get somewhere."

Chad grabbed the flower and looked past his truck. Vanessa was practically running across the street.

"See ya, Rach." He waved and ran after his favorite girl.

Carrying several white bundles, Vanessa dipped beneath the willow trees surrounding the swan pond in the park.

"Vanessa!" he called. She kept up her pace, as if she didn't hear him.

He poured on the steam, gaining on her. One of the bundles slipped from her grasp, smashing to the slate pathway. As she tried to save the others, Chad reached her and scooped up the torn package. He tried to salvage the ripped paper bag, but the foam containers fell to the ground and popped open. Tiny sandwiches and pastries teetered toward the edge, but stayed inside.

"At least your food's intact." He closed the lid and Vanessa snatched it, trying to keep the container contained. Her red face looked like she'd been crying. He hoped that didn't have anything to do with his paying her rent, but her avoiding him made that an unlikely coincidence.

"I have some duct tape in the truck." He reached for the torn bag, desperate to make things right.

She yanked it from his reach. "I don't need your help. I know you paid for that apartment." Her voice edged with anger. "I told you not to do that."

Okay, the anonymous donor idea didn't work. He had no idea she'd be this upset. Bewildered, he touched her face. "Vanessa," he said softly. "I'm sorry."

Struggle warred in her pale blue eyes. Fire and ice – passion and anger – fought for control. He stroked her cheek, knowing she couldn't resist his touch.

"Stop it," she said without conviction.

He leaned closer, searching her eyes.

"Don't," she breathed. "Stop."

"Don't stop?" he teased.

She didn't respond, but she didn't pull away either. Her beseeching eyes locked on his.

Okay, he wouldn't. He cupped her jaw. Her face leaned into his hand and her breath quickened. Her gaze never left his.

He touched his lips to hers, ever so gently. His hand cradled her neck, running his fingers up into her hair. Her head fell back and her eyes drifted shut.

He deepened the kiss, wrapping his other arm around her delicate waist.

A soft moan escaped her. He placed both hands on her waist before she changed her mind. Still holding those cumbersome bags, she laid her head on his chest. Surely she heard his heart pounding. Surely she knew, and felt, what she did to him.

As long as she wanted, he would hold her. There in the park, in the middle of town, teenagers drove by in their beat-up hotrods, honking horns and pumping fists in the air when they spotted him. The old timers, namely Myrtle Winthrop and Barber Bob – glared with disapproval and, he suspected, more than a hint of envy. Swans swam across the pond, their babies trailing behind single file like a class of obedient children.

Except for one. Out the corner of his eye, Chad spied the

largest male swan. He'd heard stories of that food-snatching thief. The bird ambled toward them, sniffing the air and eyeing Vanessa's bundles of food.

"Vanessa," Chad whispered. "We'd better go."

She stirred, not letting go of him.

"I'm not kidding." He nudged her to face the approaching swan. "He's after your food."

With a start, she pulled back, gathering the packages in her arms. Chad carefully took the torn one and they moved toward the truck.

Squawking, the swan spread its wings to block their path.

Chad laughed. "Go away, you stupid bird."

It lunged at Vanessa.

"No!" She ran for the truck as the ravenous bird nipped at her heels.

Chad scrounged in the bag and pulled out a morsel. He tossed a little sandwich in front of the swan, deterring it from Vanessa. She reached the truck safely, but he had to toss another sandwich to get past the swan himself. He barely made it to the truck without losing everything from the shredded bag.

He climbed inside with the tattered package on his lap. He pulled a roll of duct tape from his glove box and secured the bag.

Head drooping, Vanessa's shoulders slumped as she pulled the package to her belly. She blinked quickly and faced the window. Her throat bulged as she swallowed hard.

Was she crying? Just great.

"Vanessa." He touched her leg. Affection was the only way he could reach her. Not that he minded. "Please talk to me."

Sorrow pulled down her mouth and eyes. Her brows crinkled and her nostrils flared as if she might burst into sobs.

Vanessa sniffed, staring out the truck window as she wiped a tear. A lump clogged her throat and her eyes stung. She was powerless to keep her emotions in check.

"You saved my butt again. I've tried so hard to be independent. Everyone wants to help me and I'm grateful. But it makes me feel so helpless. Like everyone else has more control over my life than I do."

"I'm sorry, Vanessa. I never meant to make you feel that way.

I wasn't trying to control you. I just wanted to help."

"If you want to help, listen to me," she choked out. Her heart ached with the wound of being wronged. "I made it clear I didn't want your money, but you didn't even consider my feelings. You went behind my back and rented that apartment."

"You're right and I'm sorry." He looked sheepish. "I'm just afraid for you."

"I'm afraid too," she admitted. "But not for my physical well-being. I've grown stronger while my father's grown old and weak." Her stomach roiled, distressed at the confrontation, yet more fearful of ignoring his affront. She gathered her nerve and wiped her tears, determined to make Chad understand how much he'd offended her.

"I'm afraid of winding up powerless and dependent on someone else – just like my mother." Hurt rang through her cracking voice as she stared at the windshield, seeing nothing but the blur of tears. "It's time to stand up for myself and claim my independence. I won't be bailed out and manipulated by another controlling man."

"Whoa, slow down." He grunted at the utmost insult. "Are you comparing me to your father?"

"I'm still trying to get out from under his thumb and I won't let another man run my life."

Feeling victimized and bullied, she swiped at her tears. Then she finally calmed down enough to look at Chad, really look at him.

Shock registered in his face and his expression fell. Her anger dissolved but she'd been down this road before. She wouldn't let his surprised hurt make her back down.

"Don't look at me like that," she rebuked him. "I'm sorry to compare you to my father, but he's the man I know best. Big surprise if I have trust issues with men." She let out a sarcastic little laugh. "He makes me feel like I'm worthless, unable to think for myself or take care of myself. That's his way of holding me down."

She squeezed her eyes shut, tormented by the endless persecution. Taking a cleansing breath, she turned to Chad. She didn't want to hurt him, but she would not allow her feelings to be ignored. Speechless, he searched her eyes with compassion and empathy, bolstering her courage to continue.

"When I found out you paid that rent, I felt the same oppression. As if you think I'm some poor little scamp, incapable of paying my own way."

"I don't think that at all." His whisper filled with nurturing concern. "I just wanted to protect you."

"I'm very grateful for your concern. But if you really care, please listen to me. It really hurts that you completely disregarded my feelings. I can't do this if you don't respect me."

Her tyrant father had jaded Vanessa, abused and violated her, made her distrustful and quite possibly ruined her chance at a solid, loving relationship.

Chad reached out to touch her.

"Please don't. Not now." She closed her eyes, pressing her fingertips to her forehead. "I'm sorry, Chad, but I'm feeling vulnerable right now and I can't think straight when you touch me. We need to talk about this. I need you to understand."

Aching to hold him, she felt a glimmer of hope. She knew he was insulted, yet he listened to her without anger. He wouldn't be so patient if he didn't truly care.

She remembered the passion in his kisses last night, his gentle caresses as he held her until they fell asleep in each other's arms. She had wanted him so badly it hurt. Now she hurt just wanting him to hold her. Yet they needed to settle this first.

"I want to understand, and I do now." Regret lined his features. "I care about you, Vanessa. Very much. I'm sorry I overlooked your feelings with my own agenda." He frowned sheepishly. "If someone did that to me, I'd be livid."

"So you do understand." She crossed her arms over her chest, balancing the package of food that was getting cold. Her mother would start to worry soon.

"You're right to be upset. I shouldn't have jumped the gun by paying your rent. Yet I'm afraid if you stay in that house, with that...that *man*, something horrible might happen to you."

She nodded, staring at the dash.

"I couldn't live with myself if I hadn't done everything I could to protect you," Chad said. "But I should have discussed it with you further instead of taking matters into my own hands."

She stared at him, astounded at the worry in his eyes.

"Yes, you should have." Her voice held firm and strong.

"Can we discuss it now?" he asked with hesitation. His pleading eyes made her want to crawl into his lap for a big hug.

She swallowed hard, steadying the package of food on her lap. "We can talk but my mind's made up."

"You have to get out of there, Vanessa." Desperation filled his low voice.

She nodded in agreement. "I worked it out with Julia. I'm moving in tonight."

"Oh, thank goodness." Chad breathed a huge sigh. "Glad I'm here with the truck."

Her heart swelled with joy and love at the relief in his expression. His genuine concern filled her with anticipation and longing for him. No one but her mother had ever cared that much. Vanessa had always yearned for affection, but her mother had a hard time showing it. Too many years with Clyde, she supposed.

Vanessa couldn't hold back any longer. She placed her package on the dash and leaned across his bench seat to melt against Chad. He wrapped his arms tightly around her, caressing her back, kissing her hair. She craved affection and this man had no problem showing it. Falling recklessly in love, she clung to him for all she was worth.

His passionate kiss lingered in her mind. The attraction frightened her, but she couldn't resist lifting her face to his.

Chad's blue eyes deepened to violet, filled with longing. Locking her gaze on those beautiful eyes, she parted her lips for his kiss. Desire set her on fire with his soft, firm lips pressed against hers. She intensified the kiss, wanting him to engulf every inch of her.

His muscled arms gripped her waist, pulling her to him. Reveling in the feeling, she was suddenly assaulted by memories of her father's bony arms grabbing her, forcing her beneath him.

She shuddered, scathed with relentless shame. Pulling back, she turned her face away.

Chad loosened his grip. Seeking her gaze, he smoothed the hair from her forehead.

"Vanessa? Are you okay?"

Covering her face with her hands, she shook her head in disgrace.

"Bad memories?" His loving voice held more compassion than anyone had ever expressed to her.

She nodded behind her hands, curling into a ball of humiliation. How could he possibly understand? She wanted to fall in a pit and die.

"You have nothing to be ashamed of," Chad tenderly assured

her. He stroked her hair, comforting her beyond measure. At that moment, nothing could have made her feel more cherished. "Let's take it slow," he suggested. "I promise to be more gentle."

All she could do was nod. His understanding won her heart more than words could ever express. But she didn't want him to be more gentle, and she certainly didn't want to take it slow.

She wanted Chad, yet her abusive father kept coming between them. Anger swelled in her gut, filling her with resentment.

She needed her father out of her mind, and out of her life.

At Vanessa's house, she and Chad shared sandwiches and pastries with Mama. Thankfully, Clyde was still in jail, but Junior wasn't around either. They needed his help moving the furniture, especially up the steep stairway at the apartment.

"He's probably out at the cabin by the lake," Darla said.

"Would you like me to find him while you pack?" Chad asked.

Vanessa noticed how he'd worded the question, offering a suggestion rather than commanding. She appreciated the effort, knowing he was used to taking charge.

"That's a good idea. It won't take long." She glanced at her sparse bedroom with its half-empty dresser and old twin bed.

Chad left to find Junior. While Vanessa packed her clothes, Darla set aside an old table, a well-worn chair, and a handful of dishes.

"Why don't you pack your clothes, Mama," Vanessa suggested.

"I'm not going." Her mother jutted her chin stubbornly.

"You have to come! Dad will hurt you again. You can't stay here anymore. Especially once I'm gone." Vanessa panicked. "I can't afford rent and helping you too."

"No, you go stay near the tea room with Julia." Her voice hinted at jealousy.

"I'm not staying with Julia, Mama. I have my own apartment, with plenty of room for you. I want you to come. That was the plan all along."

"Junior will look after me," her mother insisted.

"But Junior..."

"Junior what?" Clyde growled from the doorway.

Vanessa gasped in horror.

"What's going on here?" He narrowed his eyes at the packed boxes.

Chapter 8 – The Devil Himself

Vanessa's gut wrenched.

Clyde stormed into the room.

"How'd you get out of jail?" Darla asked.

"My buddies bailed me out. No thanks to you," he spat.

When he yanked her mother's arm, Vanessa cringed with dread and fear. Darla probably never filed the restraining order.

"Don't get no fool ideas about leaving," he warned.

"I'm not, Clyde." Darla's voice murmured sweet as chocolate silk. "Those are Vanessa's things."

The familiar rumble approached and Vanessa sighed with relief as Chad's tires hit the weedy gravel drive.

"What's he doing here?" Clyde scowled at the screen door.

Grinding to a halt at the back door, Chad leapt from the pickup with Junior right beside him.

"Let her go!" Junior bellowed. Pushing past Chad, he yanked his father away from his mom. "Leave her alone!" Fury simmered in his voice but fear tainted his expression. "For once, just let her be," he pleaded with obvious dread.

"She's my wife," Clyde snarled, blocking her into a corner.

Vanessa's face burned. Her fists clenched as she struggled to restrain her temper, fueled by the resignation in her mother's eyes.

"I don't wanna go," Darla looked to her daughter. "I never planned on leaving. I know you want something better for me, Ness, but this is my home."

Vanessa shot a look at her father. "I'm concerned about my mother's safety," she hissed. "We all are."

"Ain't no place safer than yer own home," Clyde scoffed.

"Now get on out of here, if that's what you're planning. Go on, git!" He shooed Vanessa away as if she were a stray dog begging for a handout.

She closed her eyes against the assault, determined it would be the last. Gritting her teeth, she faced the boxes and hefted as many as she could carry. Her heart turned stone cold at the mere sight of her father sneering in the corner. Stomach churning, she recoiled at the insult, the callous betrayal of her own father.

Headed for the door, she recognized barely contained anger in Chad's face. He looked like he wanted to deck Clyde, then and there. But that would only make things worse. He hoisted one end of her dresser and Junior wordlessly heaved the other end.

As they carried furniture to the truck, Junior's angry red face grew harder with each load.

Vanessa silently slid boxes between the loaded furniture, scampering like a mouse near a waking cat.

Darla cowered in the corner as Clyde scrutinized the process.

"That's mine!" he barked when Chad picked up the scruffy wooden chair that didn't match the others.

"I told her she could have it," Darla insisted. "I can't give her much, not like Julia can, but I can spare an old chair and a few dishes."

With a glare, Clyde grunted. Not one to be outdone by Julia Calvin, he eyed Junior's red face and Chad's muscular build. "Just take it, then."

After loading the last box, Vanessa hugged her mother like she might never see her again. "Be careful, Mama. Please."

"No worries, baby." Darla patted her back in dismissal. "I've been taking care of myself all these years. I'll be fine."

She wasn't fine on Sunday night. Clyde's bullying threats had grown increasingly violent. His arrogant smile sickened her. Vanessa glowered at him, then turned back to her mom.

"I love you, Mama. If you ever need anything, you know where I am. You're always welcome to stay with me." She kissed Darla's cheek and turned to go, tears pooled in her eyes.

"When you comin' back to see yer mama?" Clyde sneered.

"I'll be around, don't you worry." Her expression dared him to try and get away with anything.

"Bring me a six-pack," he demanded.

Tuesday afternoon, Chad couldn't stop thinking of Vanessa. She had her own apartment now, so he could finally stop and see her without a nasty altercation with Clyde. Anxious to finish working, he whizzed through a two-by-four and shut off the buzzing saw. He carried the board to his apprentice, a punk kid in his second summer on the job who still couldn't hold a candle to Brett Mitchell. Carpenter or not, Brett had been more help than he realized when he worked for Chad two summers ago.

Then Brett landed his dream job and married Laura.

Laura and Brett, Rachel and Elliot. Chad's little sisters both married before him and his turn was long overdue.

"Here ya go." He dropped the plank near his helper. "I gotta make a call, be right back."

The lanky kid nodded, sweat dripping down his face. Tongue sticking out in concentration, he measured a board twice before cutting it, just like Chad had taught him. But the kid always had to measure three or four times before two measurements matched.

Chad shook his head. He pulled out his cell and walked away. The phone read 4:40 p.m. The tea room closed at four thirty so Vanessa should be cleaning up and getting ready to go home.

He hit the speed dial number.

"The Porcelain Teapot," Vanessa answered a bit out of breath.

"Hey, it's me," he announced excitedly.

"Hi Chad." She sounded annoyed.

"Is everything all right?"

"Yeah, I'm just exhausted. I was up late unpacking and getting settled in. Before I realized it, it was two a.m."

"You're kidding. You told me there wasn't much left to do. I would have stayed to help."

"I know, but some things I just wanted to do myself," she replied awkwardly.

"Pretty nice having your own place, isn't it?" He couldn't keep the pride from his voice. Vanessa had a more difficult start than most but was well on her way in this world. She'd confided last night that Julia had offered her the tea room as well.

"So what did you need, Chad?" Her voice edged with urgency, as if she were too busy to chat.

"I just wanted to see you tonight. Want to call me later?" She was at work, after all. The last thing he wanted was to jeopardize her job.

"Sorry, Chad. I can't tonight. I have to check on my mom."

"Oh. I understand. I hope she's all right." Pacing the ground, he fought disappointment. He'd so looked forward to hanging out at her apartment and seeing what she'd done with the place. He longed to spend some time alone with her. Yet with Clyde out of jail, he understood the need to check on her mom.

"I'm sorry." She sounded as let down as he felt. "I need to keep Dad on his toes so he doesn't think he can treat her any way he chooses and no one will be the wiser."

"Would you like a ride?"

"That's tempting, but I'd better not antagonize him."

Julia's voice sounded in the background.

"I'm sorry, Chad. I have to go. Can you come over tomorrow around six?"

"You don't have to ask me twice!"

"Good. Gotta run. See ya tomorrow!" Excitement filled her breathless voice and she was gone before he could say goodbye.

At five, Chad sent home the apprentice. He'd wanted to take Vanessa out for a nice dinner to celebrate her new place, but that had to wait until tomorrow. He hoped. He hadn't had a chance to ask.

He refused to stomach another fast food meal. Craving a juicy steak, he headed to the grocery store.

Chad tossed numerous items into his basket: a thick rib eye, a bottle of steak sauce, a ready-made salad, and a twice-baked potato from the deli. He added his favorite cold green tea with honey and ambled to the checkout line.

Who should he find in front of him but that sassy platinum blonde?

"Fancy meeting you here," he joked as he came up behind Vanessa.

She turned in surprise, not looking all that happy. "Fancy meeting *you* here."

The big-haired cashier slid a six-pack of beer across the scanner. Sadness washed over Chad as the woman bagged a frozen pizza and a pack of cigars. He understood all too well that Vanessa was afraid for her mother. Appeasing Clyde with beer and cigars might keep him at bay, yet she was enabling him.

She paid for the purchases with a characteristic blush and waited for him outside the door. Obviously embarrassed and frustrated with her situation, her dejected frown made her look ten years old again.

"Can I give you a ride out to the cabin?" he asked.

"No thanks." She headed outside and he followed. "I'm sorry. You know I'd rather be with you." She offered a faint smile. Her hair shone golden in the sunshine.

"I understand, Vanessa," he said gently. "You want to be strong and independent, and you need to watch out for your mother. But if you ever need me, for whatever reason, I want you to know I am always here for you and for Darla."

Staring at the bags in her hands, the dilemma etched her features. She looked up at Chad, then back down at the groceries.

"I'm still letting him control me." Deep sadness filled her voice.

"I'm sorry you have to deal with this, Vanessa. I wish there was something I could do." He tenderly rubbed her back.

Her eyes fluttered at his touch and heaved an exhausted sigh. Then she squared her shoulders.

"This is the last time," she vowed. "And I'm telling Clyde so."

"Are you sure that's wise?" Worry churned his gut.

Vanessa lifted her chin. "I have to stand up to him. Now is as good a time as any."

"Okay." He nodded. "Are you sure you don't want a lift? Those bags look heavy."

"Nope, I gotta do it my way." She headed off, swinging her arms with determination.

Those bags might not make it all the way to Lake Road.

He wanted to chase after her, to take care of her and protect her. Yet she needed to do this herself. At least by the time she got there, Clyde's beer would be warm.

Encouraged by Chad's understanding, Vanessa rounded the curve on Lake Road, amazed that she'd walked that far so fast. Adrenaline was powerful stuff.

The bait shop came into sight, with the rusty white car in the driveway. Her heart sank as dread swept over her.

She braced herself as she neared the cabin.

Then she heard the screams.

The bags dropped to the road, beer cans clinking and rolling toward the ditch. Vanessa took off running across the yard, toward her mother's terrified voice.

Crashing furniture punctuated her father's bellowing. A splintered chair blocked the doorway. Vanessa thrust it aside and leapt across broken dishes littering the floor.

Cornered in the front room, her mother wasn't whimpering for mercy. She was fighting back! She landed a blow to Clyde's jaw, and he staggered in shock.

Wild with rage, he lashed out, swinging fists and kicking feet.

Vanessa grabbed his collar, pulling him off her mother. His foot struck Vanessa's shin. On her adrenalin high, the pain registered but she didn't give in to it. Hands planted on his chest, she pushed with all her might. He slammed against the wall. Jarred, he slid to his haunches before shaking it off.

"You little..." He rose to come at her.

"Leave her alone!" Darla bolted to block his path, forcing him to hear what she said. "You're not her father any more than you were Layla's!"

Shocked at the revelation, Vanessa was horrified when he hauled off and slugged her mother in the face.

Clyde wasn't her father?

Knocked to the floor, blood gushing from her nose, Darla spat, "Baldy's her father, same as Layla. He's the only man I ever loved. The man I should have married." She scowled spitefully.

Red with rage, Clyde's wrinkled face contorted. His white hair and scraggly beard stood on end. As clearly as if horns and a tail sprouted, Clyde looked like the devil himself. As Satan took control of him, he stood over her like a boiling kettle ready to explode.

Yet her mother didn't stop.

"Junior is your only child and you treated him like dirt from the day he was born."

Clyde let her talk, but as his anger grew, he seemed larger, more ominous. Evil engorged him.

"You've seen how he degraded Junior." Darla looked to her.

Vanessa shushed her, but she continued as if suicidal.

"He put him down and kept him down – either by depriving him, or by bad mouthing him and smacking him around. He's nothing but a low-life scum bag."

"Quiet, Mama, don't provoke him."

"Too late." The bellowing words reverberated inside the cabin. Clyde grabbed his wife's arm and yanked her to her feet. Fist clenched, he punched her again.

Darla collapsed into a ball of pain, her face covered with blood. She glared up at him with hatred.

Vanessa grabbed an empty beer bottle.

"You don't sass me!" he boomed, reaching down to snatch her mother up again.

"Stop right there."

Vanessa whirled around to see Junior in the doorway, face red with rage.

Darla gasped.

"You ain't got the guts to stop me," Clyde sneered. He held a fistful of his wife's shirt.

"This has gone on long enough." Junior's face fell as he looked down at his wounded mother. "Too long."

Shameful regret filled his voice. His gaze locked on Vanessa, poised with that empty bottle. He straightened and stuck out his chest.

"Let...her...go." Each word boomed fiercer than the last.

Clyde held his grip. His hair still stood on end, but his monstrous presence shrank as fear settled in his eyes.

Junior came at him like a rabid coon.

Clyde threw up his hands as a shield, cowering beneath them.

Junior plowed into him. In a flash, he twisted Clyde's arms in a lock behind his back.

"You gonna let your kid treat me this way?" Clyde narrowed his eyes at Darla.

"Get outta here, Clyde," she sneered. "Go to your precious huntin' shack and stay there!"

He snarled. Satan's hold remained, but his power deflated.

Junior hustled his father to the door.

"You made our lives miserable long enough. I'll die before I let you hurt my mother or my sister again." Junior tightened his hold, making the old man flinch. "I should have done this years ago. Now get out and stay out!" He shoved his father out the door.

Clyde staggered around and scowled at his wife.

"He said get out and stay out!" her mother bellowed, eyes flashing. She dramatically wiped her nose and showed him the blood on her hand. "This is the last time you'll see my blood."

Clyde stared in shock. His anger visibly dissolved as he seemed to realize he'd finally gone too far. Junior had grown up strong while Clyde's strength now waned.

Regret lined his features.

"Now, Darla," he said more gently than Vanessa had ever heard him speak.

"That tone's not going to work this time." Her mother's voice was steel.

Junior blocked the doorway, fists clenched and ready.

Beaten down and sniveling, Clyde slunk off. On the other side of Junior's truck, he opened his car door and scrounged around. For what felt like forever, only his feet were visible as he shuffled between the vehicles. Fresh fear rose in Vanessa.

"Watch out, Junior," she whispered. "He might have a gun in there."

Junior barricaded the doorway until Clyde climbed in his car. Without fanfare, he started the engine and took off.

Vanessa rushed over to hug her brother.

"Thank you so much," she cried.

"Good job, son," Darla said with pride.

Junior hung his head. "I don't deserve that. I should have protected you long ago, Mama." He stood tall. "But I'll earn your trust."

Pride welled in Vanessa at the change in her brother. All three of them finally stood up to Clyde.

"Let's get Mama to the hospital," Junior said.

Vanessa grabbed a cool washcloth and Junior helped their mother out to his truck.

Both passenger side tires were slashed.

Chad pushed his plate across the glass-topped table on his patio. Most of the grilled rib eye lay untouched. He had half a mind to toss it in the trash, to get rid of any reminder why he'd lost his appetite.

But his mother's admonition not to waste food rang in his ears even now. Forget starving children in Africa, starving kids in Appalachia had never *seen* a steak, much less tasted one.

Emily James' upbringing in the poverty-torn mountains of Virginia had shaped his childhood as well. Convinced he was a better person because of it, he refused to waste food.

Too bad Vanessa wasn't here to share it. He wouldn't mind waiting on that infuriating cutie who waited on everyone else all day. If he ever got her to his house for dinner, he'd treat her like a queen. He pictured his parents' relationship and the delight they took in spoiling one another.

Would he ever find marital happiness like that? He longed to pamper a good woman – waiting on her hand and foot, indulging her every whim, and providing nice things. He hoped to someday have a relationship like that with Vanessa. He might even get a little royal treatment in return.

He pushed back his patio chair. Some throne!

He carried his plate to the kitchen and began cleaning up after himself. If only she were here, instead of that house of terror. He was tempted to drive by and make sure she was all right, but he had promised that he'd help, not try to control her handling of the situation. He grinned, thinking of Vanessa drawing up like an enraged hen, fighting her own battles.

Up until now, she'd clammed up when something bothered her. The confrontation proved she'd gained self-confidence.

The quiet little imp stood up to her father and she stood up to him. Funny how that made him respect her even more.

He prayed he hadn't blown it. The better he got to know Vanessa Gallagher, the harder he fell for her.

Spraying down the sink, he imagined all his notions of Vanessa swirling down the drain. She would never be a doormat like her mother – thank goodness for that. She'd look pretty on his arm, but she'd never be a trophy wife, either. As much as she enjoyed her job, he suspected she'd want to keep working – especially if she owned the tea room. He hoped she wanted children.

Putting the sprayer back in its place, he jumped when his cell phone rang.

Vanessa!

He trounced on the vibrating phone in his pocket. Clyde Gallagher's name showed on the screen. Without a second thought, he answered with an enthusiastic hello.

"Chad, it's Vanessa," she said breathlessly. "Can you come quick? My mother needs to go to the hospital."

"I'll be right there. Does she need an ambulance?"

"No. She's bleeding but it can wait. We can't afford an ambulance."

"I'll get there as quick as I can. Try to stop the bleeding."

"Thank you, Chad," Vanessa said fretfully.

"Be right there." Chad shot out the door. Vanessa had called *him*. At last, she was learning to trust.

The drive to Lake Road flew by. He remembered nothing along the way until he spotted a six-pack of beer lolling toward the ditch just before her parents' house. He veered to the edge of the road and smashed the entire six-pack with one massive tire. The cans exploded and beer spewed ten feet into the air.

Well worth the slight diversion, it wouldn't hurt that tire a bit. Energized with the small vindication, he pulled into the drive and bounded inside.

Vanessa ushered her bleeding mother toward him, holding a blood-soaked rag on her face. Her brother helped the women get into Chad's pickup. Junior's truck sat with two flat tires. There wasn't room for four of them so Junior kissed his mama and headed into the bait shop.

With no time to ask the million questions that ran through his mind, he feared he knew the answers. Anger had fueled his drive here, but now he needed to stem that emotion and concentrate on getting Darla help.

Good thing the rusty white Chrysler was absent. Beating the tar out of Clyde would delay Darla's treatment. And getting arrested could seriously derail Chad's life. Taking a deep, cleansing breath, he unclenched his fists and wiggled his fingers.

Get this woman to the hospital.

Chapter 9 – Leap of Faith

While the doctors straightened and bandaged Darla's broken nose, Chad had a few minutes to speak with Vanessa. They sat on a stiff sofa in an empty hospital lounge.

"So what happened this time?" he asked.

Vanessa sighed. "They were fighting before I got there. I heard them screaming from up the road."

"That explains the six pack in the middle of the road."

"Oh!" she gasped. "I hope someone doesn't run over it."

"Crushed," Chad informed her. How had she missed the beer foam running down the side of his truck?

She frowned, and then got back to the story.

"Of course, Clyde was mad about his stint in jail, and my moving out. He yelled something about her belonging in that house and she wasn't going anywhere."

Vanessa paused with great sadness.

"In the end, Mama agreed with him. She has no intentions of leaving her home. She kicked *him* out," she explained with wide eyes and a dropped jaw. "Get that!"

"No kidding!" Chad didn't think Darla had it in her. Now he saw where Vanessa got her spunk.

"Of course Junior's arm lock on Clyde helped bolster her courage."

Chad smiled. "Good for him."

She nodded, seeming ashamed it had come to that. "Mama said I made her see that she didn't have to put up with his abuse." Vanessa wiped a tear. "She told him to stay at his precious hunting shack and not to come back."

"Isn't that a good thing?"

She shrugged, sniffling. "A lot was said. Mama and I need to talk. There are issues far deeper than I ever realized."

That riddle didn't surprise him. "I'll pray for you," he offered.

Vanessa got a funny look on her face. "I'm relieved for her. She certainly deserves a better life. But as angry as I am, I have to admit I'm worried about Dad – Clyde. I don't know. I kind of feel sorry for him. Not that he doesn't deserve it, but I don't want anything bad to happen to him."

That man had abused and degraded her. And he'd beaten up her mother – given her two black eyes and a broken nose. Chad wondered how many countless times Clyde had hit her over the years when no one was looking. Not to mention her broken spirit, mental trauma, and emotional suffering.

How could Vanessa feel sorry for him? That man deserved any punishment God brought down on him. Chad hoped he'd rot out there in the woods. He'd been wondering about Vanessa's spirituality and was ashamed that she was more forgiving than he could even imagine being. Some Christian example he was.

"I called Chief Hunter to file a police report," Chad told her. "He's on his way here. He recommends a restraining order."

"Yeah. I'd planned to do that once we got Mama bandaged up." Vanessa frowned. "You didn't have to take care of that. I would have handled it."

He was being overbearing again.

She shook her head. "One minute I tell you I can handle things myself, the next minute I'm calling you in panic."

"I'm honored that you asked me."

She offered a sheepish grin. "Thank you for coming when I needed you."

"You're welcome." He took a deep breath before continuing. "I don't want to scare you, but I'm not sure the restraining order will 'restrain' your father."

"I'm not either." Her brows furrowed.

"I'd like to keep watch over you." He paused. "If that's okay with you and your mom."

"Thank you," she said with relief. "Just don't hurt him, okay?"

"I'll do my best," Chad vowed. "But I won't allow him to hurt either of you. So no promises, okay?"

Vanessa nodded, pulling a tissue from the box on an end table.

She wiped her eyes and blew her nose. Seeing her compassion for her abusive father, Chad quickly realized what a devoted wife she would be. It was a strange feeling to know that in his family, compassion and trust were taken for granted. He'd never had to earn it before. He felt humbled.

He squeezed her knee. She looked up at him with watery eyes of the palest blue. All at once he realized the tables had turned. Her wide-eyed innocence and easy forgiveness could teach him a thing or two.

So how would he approach a discussion of God when the girl had more Christianity in her pinky than he had in his whole heart? How ironic that he expected to share his faith with her, and she'd been an example to *him*.

Friday night, Vanessa swung her bare feet over the tailgate of Chad's truck and looked out over the lake behind the bait shop. She'd finally agreed to talk to him, even if she wouldn't leave her mama any further away than the 200 yards to the lake.

Her brother must have felt the same way. Junior appeared along the far edge of the pond with a stylish, auburn-haired girl in a trendy orange halter. Wearing his characteristic overalls and carrying a fishing pole and tackle box, shy, red-headed Junior chatted away.

"Is that Brandy Kennedy?" Chad asked with surprise.

Jealousy welled in Vanessa as the perky redhead swung her hips in a pair of shorts that flattered her shapely legs. She didn't want Chad noticing a girl like that.

"As in Kennedy for Senate?" she asked warily.

"Yep. Carpetbagger left town after losing the election, but his daughter stuck around. I thought she was dating the mayor's son." Chad shook his head. "Another politician like her father."

"What's a girl like that doing with my brother?"

"Maybe she's tired of politicians. My sister dated Daniels for a while." He scowled. "He doesn't treat women right. Brandy's better off without him."

"How do you know her?" Vanessa didn't like Chad's familiarity with that woman and couldn't hide the suspicion in her voice.

Chad's eyebrows rose and a smile curved up one side of his

mouth. "She works for my brother-in-law, Elliot. If anyone should be jealous of Brandy, that would Rachel." He had a knowing glimmer in his eyes.

"I'm not jealous." Vanessa drew her eyebrows together with a defensive frown but he'd seen right through her.

Chad pulled her close and kissed her cheek. With a empathetic smile, he lapsed back into their conversation.

"So let me get this straight," he furrowed his brow. "Junior is Clyde's only biological child?"

"Yep, red hair and all. Lucky him."

"Wow. Everybody knew about Layla. I mean – she had that little cleft in her chin and dark eyes. She looked just like Baldy."

"And I look like my mother. But she said I have my dad's personality." Even as she said it, relief poured over her. Calvin was no man-of-the-year, but he was a saint compared to Clyde Gallagher. "It's still sinking in, but I'm really glad Clyde's not my father."

"So Clyde abused Layla to hurt Baldy, but when she ran away from home he took it out on you?"

"Uh, huh." Vanessa swallowed, gritting her teeth to keep the grief at bay. She hated crying. It made her feel vulnerable and she needed strength right now.

"And Clyde backed off after the incident with the gym teacher, right?"

"Yeah. Until Layla died." Fury rose in her. As if she hadn't suffered enough, that scumbag took it out on her when her sister died. Worse yet, he was the one who had driven Layla away.

"The rumors about her paternity surfaced again." Vanessa fidgeted with the hem of her shorts, bashfully tugging them over her sun-pinked thighs.

"Clyde went off the deep end, and got really mean. He threatened to kill Mama if she left him, and then take me back..." She brought her knees to her chest protectively. "You know."

A whirlwind of emotion swirled through her gut – terror, shame, indignation, and sorrow. Fury overshadowed them all.

"That's never gonna happen." Chad's face reddened all the way to his scalp beneath the short dark hair. "I won't let that happen. Ever." His fists clenched. "I'd kill him."

"Don't worry, you won't have to resort to violence." She pulled a small bottle of mace from the pocket of her cut-offs. "I carry it all the time. Mama has some too. And his guns are still at the house."

"But are you prepared to pull the trigger?"

"Yeah, I can defend myself." Self-respect felt incredible, empowering. And she couldn't take another minute of despair. With a light tone, she teased, "And don't you ever forget it, Chad James."

"I won't forget it." The blood drained from his face. "I'll be praying for you."

Chad prayed for her? That too-personal sentiment made her feel odd and uncomfortable. Religion had never been a part of her life. She had no idea how to respond, so she ignored it.

"I'm proud of you, and your mother too." A smile played around his eyes. "Don't let anybody push you around, okay?"

"Nope, I won't." She ribbed him good-naturedly. "Not even you."

Carrying a small cooler filled with food from the tea room, Vanessa walked into the bait shop driveway. Clyde's hound dogs pulled against their chains to greet her with tails wagging.

"Hey Smith, you miss old Clyde?" She walked to the tree where the dogs were chained and petted Smith's head while the other dog sniffed the cooler. "Get outta there, Wesson," she said with a laugh. "That's not for you."

Even the dogs seemed happier with Clyde out of the house. Vanessa unhooked their chains to let them run loose. The dogs howled with glee and took off across the yard.

Darla appeared with a broad smile. "Hi honey."

"Hi Mama." Vanessa kissed her mother's cheek. "Hungry?"

"Yes! So what do you have there?"

They moseyed inside and Vanessa opened the cooler.

"Julia can't pay a lot, but the perks are delicious!"

They enjoyed blackberry scones, spinach quiche, salad, and lemon squares, saving some for Junior who was still working.

Vanessa patted her belly. "It's a good thing for that two-mile walk or I'd be getting fat!"

Waving a hand, her mother said, "You're thin as a rail."

"Just like you." Her mother was lean and muscled from years of hard work. "And Dad is skin and bones." Vanessa caught herself as a funny look came across Darla's face.

"Baldy's thin too." Her mother said with a smile. "You keep forgetting, don't you?"

"It's really weird." Bewilderment settled over Vanessa. How strange to find out her father wasn't her father at all. She didn't know how to feel other than relieved – and confused. Some stranger, the town hermit, was actually her father. She knew nothing about him except that Clyde hated the man and they had some age-old feud. All her life she'd been a Gallagher, when her name should be Calvin.

Then it dawned on her. Just like Julia. She was Baldy's sister – Vanessa's mind spun and her mouth fell open.

"Julia is my aunt!"

"Yes, of course." Darla's matter-of-fact words belied the trepidation in her eyes. "That's probably why she was so willing to hire you without experience. And why she's been so generous." She toyed with a gold medallion around her neck.

"She never said a word." Vanessa's mind was reeling. Her mother had worn that necklace every day for as long as she could remember. In the recesses of her mind, she recalled an argument her father started over the medallion. Her mama had claimed it was a gift from a friend. Clyde had insisted that she stop wearing it, but Darla had refused. Had Baldy been that friend?

"The truth is out." Darla didn't sound so happy about it. Her unspoken jealousy of Vanessa's relationship with Julia now made all the sense in the world.

"Don't worry." Vanessa hugged her. "You'll always be my mama and no aunt can ever replace you."

"Don't be silly." Darla waved away her comment, but her face glowed. "Let's go get the wash." She grabbed Vanessa's arm and pulled her outside.

As they took clothes off the line, the dogs started howling, chained to the tree again. Before they realized why, Clyde slunk around the corner and grabbed Darla. She jumped nearly a foot when he nuzzled his grizzly face to hers.

"What are you doing here?" She pushed at his chest to break free.

"Surprise!" He kissed her cheek. "Didn't hear me, did ya?"

"No." With astonishing force, Darla shoved him away. "You're not allowed to be here. I have a restraining order."

"Come on, Darla, forget that nonsense. My car's broke down.

I need something to eat, and I miss ya." He drew close. "You know I'm sorry for what I done," he sweet-talked.

The words and actions were too familiar. Vanessa hurried inside and dialed 911 as she watched from the doorway.

Seeming to gather her courage, Darla wrenched away. "You're not sorry and don't you dare touch me." She stepped quickly toward the door, turning to sneer in his face, "I wish you were dead."

Changing like Dr. Jekyll to Mr. Hyde, he caught up to her at the doorstep and yanked her arm. "You don't talk to me like that, woman."

"I'm done with you. I'm filing for divorce," she spat.

Stunned, his eyes went wide. Then he lowered his brow and grabbed her by the collar, catching her necklace in his grip.

"It's high time I did." She jerked away from him, and the gold medallion fell in the dirt.

Junior bolted from the bait shop. "Get away from her!" He grabbed Clyde and hurled him to the ground.

Just then, a fancy car barreled into the driveway. Junior turned and Clyde scrambled to his feet. Brian Daniels, the mayor's son, burst out of the car.

Smith and Wesson barked and growled, yanking at their chains on two legs, pawing at the air.

"You redneck hillbilly!" Brian screamed at Junior. "What kind of man treats his own father like that? I don't know what Brandy ever saw in you but its over, dude. She's mine and I aim to get her back. So lay off."

"You don't own her." Junior's face turned red. "Brandy can decide who she wants to be with. She's tired of politicians and their *lies*."

"All politicians don't lie."

"Maybe not, but you do."

"I never – " Brian stammered.

"What makes you think your false pretenses would impress her anyway? You don't know Brandy at all."

"I don't have false pretenses. I have clout in this town and you'd better remember that." Brian shoved Junior's chest. "Back off or you'll be sorry."

Vanessa felt someone sneak up on her. With a jerk, her arms twisted behind her back. Shock and fear welled within in her as she struggled to get free.

"I know this one," Clyde snarled in her ear. "I own her and I'm taking her back."

"Let me go!" Intense hatred surged in her gut. She kicked and fought.

Hurry up, Chief Hunter!

Junior shoved Brian away from him, rushing for Clyde. He knocked his father away from Vanessa. Clyde came up swinging and Vanessa ducked.

Darla went ballistic and Vanessa couldn't stop her. She scrounged a rock from the ground and pounced on Clyde.

"You touch Vanessa again, you lay a finger on her and I'll kill you myself!" Darla screeched.

"You people are crazy!" Brian dove behind the wheel of his fancy-pants car and skinned out of there like a bank robber with cops on his tail.

Where were the cops anyway? With barely a glance at the plume of dust in Brian's wake, Vanessa ran from her father.

She should have called Chad. The faint sound of hammering came from the other side of the lake. He could have been here by now, but she didn't want to burden him with her problems.

Finally, sirens sounded in the distance.

Clyde yanked Junior's feet out from under him. They fell into a kicking, flailing pile. With a high-pitched scream, Darla lunged into the fray.

"No!" Vanessa jumped in and dragged her mother out before she got injured again.

Police cars peeled into the driveway as Darla bashed Clyde in the head. Chief Hunter rushed from his car.

"Break it up!" He yanked Darla off of Clyde and pulled the men apart.

Taller and stronger, Junior shook it off and stood steadfast. He crossed his arms with disgust. Clyde shrunk against the house, wailing as a bleeding lump rose on his head.

With no sympathy for the man who terrorized her mother, revulsion and loathing swelled in Vanessa. She wished he were dead, too.

"What are you doing back here, Clyde?" Hunter slapped the cuffs on him. "Didn't get enough of my penthouse suite the last time?"

Shoulders slumped with defeat, Clyde groaned. He shot a pleading look at Darla.

"Don't *ever* come back." Feet planted in a firm stance, she pursed her lips. Her brow drew low with determined resolve.

Vanessa knew those were the toughest words she'd ever said. The dogs now whimpered and whined.

Genuine remorse radiated from Clyde's tear-filled eyes and quaking lips.

Beneath the low August sun, Chad pounded a nail into a two-by-four. A distant siren caught his attention. Alarmed, he listened as it drew closer. His heart hammered in his chest when it ground to a stop on the other side of the lake.

Dropping the nail gun, he jumped into his truck and rushed to the Gallaghers' cabin.

Big Blue's rumble caught Vanessa's ear before she spotted the welcome sight. Chad's truck headed for them. The huge tires skidded across the dirt drive, halting in a cloud of dust.

Relief washed over her. She ran to greet him, falling into his arms before he slammed the door.

"Are you all right?" His warm hands held either side of her face. He searched her eyes, and then looked her over.

"I am now." She crumbled against him, clinging tight.

He held her. "Is your mom okay?"

"Yes, I think so," she said into his chest. Grateful for his warm comfort, she wanted to burrow into him and forget the scene behind her. As much as she needed to handle her own problems, it felt wonderful to lean on Chad.

"Why didn't you call me? I was working right up the road."

"No time. But I wanted to," she admitted.

"I'm glad you called the cops." He stroked her hair. "Are you sure you're okay?"

She nodded against his damp shirt, gritty with sawdust. He was always there for her – even when she didn't ask. She breathed in his sweat and loved it more than any cologne she could imagine.

Overcome with temptation to rely on him, her power to resist dissolved. If she allowed herself to depend on Chad, would he control her like her father?

She couldn't see him acting anything like her father. Yet that fear ruled her life.

Clyde still ruled her life.

That gave her pause. She wouldn't allow it.

Was it worth losing her independence to have this kind of love? At this moment, she couldn't imagine living without Chad's love. She trusted him implicitly and couldn't do this alone anymore.

If she believed in him, she had to take a leap of faith.

Chapter 10 – Rebel at Thirty

August sunlight shone through the stained glass windows of The Olde Methodist. Chad squirmed in a block of blue sunlight while Vanessa glowed beside him in a circle of royal purple. He hadn't anticipated her quick acceptance of his offer to pick her up for church before his birthday dinner. He fully expected her to balk at the invitation.

Who would have thought one of the Gallagher clan would seem so comfortable in church? His rebellious side was attracted to the cutie from the wrong side of the creek, but she turned out to be a good girl with a spiritual side. God was definitely looking out for him, despite himself.

Like a stately princess, Vanessa attentively followed his lead through the standing/sitting motions, caught each tune as she sang hymns with lusty enthusiasm, and listened intently to the sermon.

"The service was beautiful," she gushed in his ear as the pews emptied. "I really enjoyed the singing, and the sermon truly spoke to my heart."

"Oh, yeah, it was nice." Chad couldn't even recall what the sermon was about. He felt hopelessly inadequate compared with Vanessa's spiritual eagerness.

As several older women made a beeline his direction, Chad quickly led Vanessa out the door. He hadn't considered the onslaught of attention and questions about their intentions. He cringed when the town gossip snagged his sister Laura on the sidewalk before she could escape.

"I think Mrs. Winthrop wanted to talk to you." Vanessa chuckled, rolling her eyes. Paused at the door of his truck, she looked good enough to eat in an blackberry-colored sundress that played up the shine of her hair.

"Oh, did she?" Taking in Vanessa's beauty and astonishing lack of concern, his worries dissipated. Let Myrtle Winthrop say what she wanted. Proud to be with this sweet girl, he realized anyone who slandered her was the one with a problem.

"It looks like she caught up with my sister instead." He boosted Vanessa into the truck, careful to keep her modest in the dress.

"Off to the farmhouse," he said cheerfully as the truck roared out of the church parking lot. Anxious to return to his element, he looked forward to Mama's cooking of his favorite meal.

"Amen," Chad chimed in as his father finished saying grace.

Vanessa looked thoughtful beside him, soaking it all in.

"What a feast," she whispered as Chad passed her a platter of rib-eye steaks. "I've never seen this much meat in my life!"

Chad smiled as she pulled a steak onto her plate, piled her baked potato with butter, sour cream, bacon, and cheese, and slathered honey butter on a homemade biscuit. Then she heaped a bowl full of fresh-from-the-garden salad. Could someone so tiny eat all that?

"Save room for cake and ice cream!" his mother reminded them as groans filled the room.

"I have to work out twice as long on Mondays," Laura commented to Vanessa.

"Good thing I have a long walk," Vanessa replied. "Between this and the tea room, I'd be doomed."

"If I worked at the tea room, I'd be as round as Daddy's tomatoes," Laura said with a laugh.

"Did you grow these, Mr. James?" Vanessa asked with amazement.

"Yep." Chad's father beamed with pride.

"Yummy! Do you sell them?"

"Sure do. How many would you like?" John asked.

"Half a bushel if you have them. Julia and I created a tomato and basil tart and these would be wonderful."

"Oh, can I have the recipe?" Rachel asked.

"We have fresh basil too," Chad's mother piped up.

"Tomato tart?" Brett mouthed to Elliot with a puzzled

expression.

Chad's nieces, Jess and Amelia giggled.

Somehow Vanessa had managed to engage the entire family. Everyone loved Vanessa and she seemed perfectly at home.

What ever happened to the shy, reserved girl from the bait shop? He'd expected her to cower in the corner, bowled over by his boisterous family. Yet she fit right in, talking gardening and recipes like nobody's business, making *him* feel left out in his own family. On his birthday, no less!

He couldn't be happier.

After the meal, Chad opened presents before they could even think about dessert. He received a stylish outdoor thermometer from Rachel and Elliot, a couple of nice shirts for church from his parents, a goofy T-shirt from Brett, and Laura chipped in a gift card from an outdoorsman store since she didn't approve of the T-shirt. Finally he opened the box from Vanessa wrapped in silver paper with a bright blue ribbon.

Inside, a CD was carefully wrapped in tissue. It was a country music band with a muddy truck on the cover.

The room erupted in laughter.

"Perfect!" Elliot exclaimed.

Brett slapped him on the back. "Now you found a woman who understands!"

Chad turned the CD over in his hands. He didn't own this one, but had thought he'd buy it sometime. How did she know? And how was she able to fit so neatly into his family?

She was so perfect for him that he felt blindsided. His head was spinning.

While Vanessa helped serve cake as if she'd been part of the family for years, Chad went outside to sit on the front porch. He took a big bite of chocolate cake with butter cream icing and followed it with vanilla bean ice cream and chocolate sauce.

The screen door slammed and Laura sat beside him with a tiny piece of cake, but no ice cream.

"Happy birthday, big brother," she said, tasting a dainty bite.

He nodded thanks and swallowed his cake. "So did that old biddy at church ask you twenty questions?"

"She asked if you and Vanessa were serious, how long has this been going on – the usual. I was vague and noncommittal."

"Thanks. I knew I could count on you."

"I'm glad to see you dating her. I've always liked Vanessa."

"Me too. But she's so shy, I'm pleasantly surprised how she seems totally comfortable with you women, and only a little bit apprehensive with the guys."

"That's understandable, considering how she's been treated by her father." Laura scraped excess icing to the side of her plate. "But she's known Rachel and me for years. She's really come out of her shell since she's been working at the tea room. Mama's there all the time. Of course, who wouldn't be comfortable with Mama?"

Chad laughed in agreement.

"So much for your defiance," Laura teased.

"Vanessa has never been about defiance," his hushed voice vehemently denied the accusation.

"Okay, okay." Laura held up her hands in surrender. "But you gotta admit you still have that teenage rebellious streak."

"I'm thirty years old, little sister." Not the least bit offended, he enjoyed the sibling rivalry.

Laura laughed. "But you've always liked bucking tradition. From the names of your pets to spurning the family business to that monster truck in your driveway."

"What's wrong with my truck?" His voice rose a few octaves and his brows drew together.

"You mean the blue beast with no mufflers? Nothing, if you like stirring up trouble."

"Hey, it has mufflers. They just don't block the flow of exhaust that bogs down the engine."

"Whatever." Laura tossed her hair behind her and took a tiny bite of chocolate cake.

Brett pushed open the screen door and glared at his wife. "Are you giving my buddy a hard time on his birthday?" he accused with a smirk.

"Nah, just discussing his issues," Laura teased.

"Oh. Those." Brett smiled and took a seat, balancing a plate of cake on his lap and carrying a glass of milk. "I thought I heard something about the blue beast."

"Exactly." Laura finished off her cake with a flourish and bounded inside, laughing.

"Your wife just loves messing with me." Chad rolled his eyes.

"Hey, she's *your* sister. She certainly didn't pick that up from me." Brett grinned through his glass as he drank a swig of milk.

Early Monday morning, Vanessa descended the stairs to the police chief's basement office in the town hall. Along for moral support, Chad opened the door for her. He'd convinced her to file a report on Brian Daniels.

"Good morning, Chief." Vanessa walked to Hunter's desk to shake his hand.

"Mornin'" Chad followed suit.

"Good morning." Hunter motioned to two chairs. "How can I help you today?"

They sat. Vanessa fidgeted with her purse on her lap. Chad laid an assuring hand on her knee.

"I…uh…wanted to file a report," she said.

"Do you have further information on what happened Saturday?" The chief rubbed his chin.

"Yes. So much was happening, I didn't think to mention it at the time. Before you arrived, Brian Daniels came to the house."

Hunter's eyes widened. He pulled a form from his desk. Poised with a pen, he listened intently.

"He threatened Junior, saying he'd better lay off Brandy."

Hunter scribbled. "What exactly did he threaten to do?"

"Nothing specific. He said he had clout in this town and Junior better remember that. He shoved him and said 'Back off or you'll be sorry.'"

The chief furrowed his brow as he wrote the report. "You said he shoved him – did Junior shove back?"

"Well, that's when Clyde grabbed me. Junior shoved Brian out of the way and ran to help me. Brian said we were all crazy and took off."

"Okay. Why isn't Junior here?"

Vanessa shrugged. "He couldn't be bothered. Chad's the one who insisted we file a report."

"Good man." Hunter shot Chad a smile and scribbled some more. Footsteps sounded on the stairs. "Sounds like I've got company. That's all I need for now. Let me know if he shows up again."

"Okay." Vanessa stood with Chad beside her. They turned to leave, coming face to face with Brian Daniels.

"What are you doing here?" Shock registered on Brian's face

and his eyes darted. He nervously scratched red welts on his hand and arm. Redness on his neck appeared rash-like as well.

"You got poison ivy?" Hunter commented. He stared at Brian's sport coat. Burrs clung to the hem.

"Oh, maybe that's it." Brian looked befuddled. He stopped scratching but twitched with an obvious itch.

"How'd a city boy like you get poison ivy?" the chief asked. "And burrs?" He pointed them out.

"I…I'm looking at some land," Brian stammered, picking off the burrs.

"Awful early to be scouting out land," the chief commented.

"The builder wanted to come early, before he was busy with contractors all day."

"Builder?" Chief asked with surprise. "If you're building another house, why not have Chad here do it?"

Brian looked nervous. "It's a bigger project than that."

"Bigger than the mansion I built you last year?" Chad scoffed. "Where you gonna get the money for that?"

"I have a financial partner investing with me." Brian acted secretive.

"Why would someone invest in your house?" The chief went into interrogation mode.

"It's really none of your business." Brian grew defensive yet seemed to swell with pride. "But it's a development, not one house. My partner wants to increase her net worth for retirement."

Vanessa cringed. "You're building a development in Crystal Falls?"

"We haven't determined an exact location yet." Avoiding her eyes, Brian seemed uneasy. He held his head high, but his itchy twitch returned. Apparently unable to hold out any longer, he scratched furiously.

Vanessa stared at him in disbelief. Crystal Falls residents enjoyed its rural beauty and small town charm. That's why Chad built custom homes on acreage. Development on a grand scale would breed more development. Traffic problems and overcrowded schools and stores would ensue. Then highways, big box stores, and strip malls would move in. Her quaint hometown would be ruined.

Without giving that weasel the satisfaction of a response, she walked out. Chad was right there beside her.

Blowhard Brian didn't have a clue they had just filed a report on *him.*

Business at The Porcelain Teapot picked up dramatically by mid-September. This particular Friday, working women had shown up in droves for lunch. At two o'clock, twenty-five ladies in red hats appeared for their monthly get together.

Vanessa and Julia had never been so happy to run out of three types of desserts and deplete her gift shop inventory in a single day. Fortunately they stocked twelve desserts and did NOT run out of chocolate torte!

Both women were exhausted by closing time. Julia cleared a table and carried the half-empty teapot to the kitchen. She looked pale. She clumsily set down the teapot on the nearest table, sloshing tea on the linens.

Alarmed, Vanessa steadied her aunt. These episodes happened with increasing regularity and it frightened her that something serious could be wrong.

"Are you all right?" she asked.

"I think so." Julia laid a hand across her forehead. "I felt faint for a moment there. I'm just tired. Getting old, you know!" She laughed it off.

"Aunt Julia, sixty-five isn't *that* old!"

"I love hearing you call me Aunt." A smile lit Julia's face, erasing the wrinkles in her cheeks and accentuating those at the corners of her eyes.

"I love you being my aunt." Tenderly taking Julia's hand, Vanessa looked into her eyes. "The truth about my father was both a shock and a relief, but finding out you were my blood relation was the happiest news I ever received."

Julia patted her hand with a wan smile. "Thank you, Vanessa. What joy you're brought to my life."

Vanessa gave her a hug and poured her a cup of tea. "Let me get you a bite to eat. That always seems to help you feel better. I don't think you're eating enough to keep your energy up. And we're surrounded by food!"

Julia ate eagerly and recovered after a short rest. Vanessa cleaned up, torn between spending more time with Julia and her eagerness to run upstairs.

Excitement bubbled within her. As soon as they closed up, she enthusiastically climbed the stairs to her apartment and pulled the day's tips from the bulging pocket of her apron.

Now that Clyde no longer siphoned money from the bait shop, her mother and Junior handled the expenses without her tips. She'd been saving for over a month.

Counting the ones, fives, and a couple of tens, her excitement mounted. She finally had a down payment for a car!

She emptied the canning jar hidden behind the sugar in her kitchen cupboard and sorted her stash by denomination. She added the day's tips and counted the total.

Five hundred and fifteen dollars.

On cue, her doorbell rang. She threw open the door, knowing Chad would be on the other side.

"I have a down payment!" she exclaimed, running into his arms. "Over five hundred dollars with this week's tips."

"Woo hoo! That's my girl." He whirled her into the air and spun around the tiny living room.

Her heart floated with her feet. She clung tight until her feet hit the floor. Then she smacked a kiss on his lips.

"Hmm," he moaned with pleasure. "Gimme more." He pulled her close, way close, and her body thrummed with desire. His soft, hot lips covered hers, and she wanted to eat him alive.

Yet she dared not hope for more than a kiss. He controlled his passion – somehow. She felt his desire, strong and loyal, yet his impeccable morals kept him celibate.

They'd been dating for three months and the man was driving her crazy. She buried her head in his chest, breathing him in, wanting him from the depth of her soul.

Did he really expect to wait until marriage? She was nowhere near ready for marriage, but she was more than ready for a little hanky panky with Chad James.

He stroked her hair, took a ragged breath, and pulled back with sheer determination.

She felt cold and forlorn, wanting and unfulfilled. She leaned back against him, greedy for the comfort of his heat.

He hugged her tight, tension ebbing from him as he fought for control.

"So you wanna go car shopping tomorrow?" The subject sounded forced, yet anticipation filled his voice.

"Only if you come with me." She refused to raise her head, to let one inch of herself separate from him.

"Of course. I wouldn't miss it for the world."

"Good. Because I know nothing about cars."

He chuckled. Cupping her chin, he drew her face to look at him.

"Just think, soon you can run to Springfield for that special tea you like, go to the mall and buy your own blouses, see your mom this winter without walking four miles in the snow. And come visit me whenever you like." He waggled his eyebrows. "You'll be free as a bird!"

Catching his enthusiasm, she sprang from his arms and danced across the floor.

"I'm soooo ready!" She'd waited so long for this day. "Let's celebrate!" She pulled a bottle of lemonade from the refrigerator and two plastic cups from the cupboard. "Maybe I'll even buy real glasses!" she said with a laugh.

"I'm so proud of you." His smile emanated love for her.

The look in his eyes caught her unaware. In that second, she knew he'd fallen in love with her. Her heart ached with love for him, as it had for some weeks now. Desire raged full force again. If he'd let her, she would take him right there on the kitchen floor.

She desperately needed love, and Chad had given it to her. Now, what she needed most was his physical affection. She also yearned to show how much she loved him. Words failed her and she had no money for gifts. Affection was her way. But she had to resort to other means. Like cooking.

"Thank you, Chad." She busied her hands pouring the lemonade. "Are you hungry?"

"Am I ever!" His expression belied his hunger, like hers, was for more than food.

"Last night I made meatballs and sauce." She looked away. Hands shaking, she pulled a dish from the refrigerator. "I'll heat them and cook some spaghetti."

"Sounds good to me. But tomorrow night I'm taking you out. I'll buy if you fly."

"What do you mean, 'you fly'?" she asked, at a complete loss.

He chuckled. "You're driving. In your new car."

"Oh." Anxiety washed over her. She'd been so excited with the idea of freedom, she'd never actually thought about having to *drive*.

Amid her excitement, dread and fear crashed down on Vanessa. She slid behind the wheel of the compact Chevrolet for a test drive. Chad climbed into the passenger seat. The salesman waved them on, her barely used driver's license clipped to his pocket.

"I... I haven't driven in quite a while," she confessed.

"It's okay, just relax. I'm right here beside you," Chad assured her.

"No, seriously, Chad. I haven't driven in almost two years – Clyde's 'punishment' for working at the tea room. Before that I never drove further than the convenience store to buy him beer. I didn't get my license until I was twenty-one, and then I barely passed the test," she rambled.

He furrowed his brow. "You *are* sheltered."

"Yeah, no kidding." She stared at the dash and her eyes glazed over with confusion. "What do I do first?" she asked, fighting panic.

Chapter 11 – Like Riding a Bike

"First, relax." Chad patted Vanessa's knee, catching her eye. "You'll remember how to drive in no time. Just like riding a bike."

"I never had a bike."

"Great." He shook his head. "Okay, put your foot on the brake. Then turn the key and start the car."

She pressed the brake. The salesman stood watching them, puzzlement and apprehension all over his face.

"Just ignore him," Chad said. "This will be *your* car. What does he care?"

"Okay." She felt a hint of belligerence. She turned the key. The engine turned over and then roared, startling her.

"Let go of the key!" Chad cried.

"Oh!" She let go and the engine idled to a normal rate.

"This is gonna be a long ride," she warned him.

"Keep your foot on the brake and put it in gear." He pointed to the lever on the floor between them. "D – for drive."

Two hours later, Vanessa carefully backed her new car out of a parking space near The Parkside Cafe. The delicious meal left her belly full and her heart filled with love.

With Chad in her 'new' used car, she'd be a happy girl if only she could get this driving thing down.

"It gets easier with practice, I promise." Chad rested his hand on her knee, a gesture that warmed and calmed her. With sudden alarm, he cried, "Stop sign!"

"Oh, yeah." She spiked the brake, sending them both toward

the windshield. As they leaned back in their seats, she said sheepishly, "I'm so used to walking right around the corner. I don't have to stop unless I'm crossing the road."

"Uh huh," he murmured with a teasing tone.

As uneasy as Vanessa felt about driving, there was no one she'd rather learn from than Chad. The man had more patience than Job. At least from what she'd heard about Job at a recent church service. All her life, she'd never understood who that patient Job character was until now.

Her heart swelled with love for Chad, with pride for the new life she'd begun, and with hope for a happy future with this gorgeous, loving man.

Headed out Lake Road, Vanessa slowed to pull into the bait shop driveway.

"What's he doing here?" Chad growled, pointing to Clyde at the edge of the woods.

"I don't know. He's not supposed to be on the premises." Vanessa's stomach clenched. Every nerve in her body tensed with fear and dread.

As the gravel crunched, Clyde looked their direction. Skinny and bedraggled, he scurried into the woods, limping.

"Hopefully we scared him off. Thank goodness he doesn't know it's me," Vanessa said. "Or he'd be running over here to give me the third degree – restraining order or not."

Chad crossed his arms but remained silent.

Vanessa parked her car in the blissfully spacious area. Refusing to let Clyde ruin her special moment, she hurried inside with excitement.

"Mama! Junior! Come see my new car!" she called at the door.

Darla rushed out, followed by her son.

"Nessa, it's beautiful!" Darla exclaimed.

Junior whistled. "Well lookee there. Must be making the big bucks, Ness. First an apartment down town and then a brand new car." His delighted smile showed pride in her accomplishments, though she detected just a hint of unwelcome envy.

"It's not *brand* new," she explained. "It's two years old. I got a good deal, thanks to Chad." Standing tall, she tossed him a bright grin full of gratitude and love.

He returned a reserved smile.

Darla's enthusiasm seemed forced as she opened the car door to peer inside. Much as she wanted to ignore the bad vibes, Vanessa needed to know what was going on. She pulled Junior aside.

"Did you see Clyde?" she asked.

"He came begging for money."

"Did you give him any?" she asked with disbelief.

"No. I sent him packing," Darla piped up, sticking her head out of the car. Her chin rose in defiance.

"Thank goodness." Vanessa sighed with relief. "You should have called the cops. He's not even allowed on the property." She placed a hand on her forehead in exasperation.

"He didn't make no threats and he was starving." Darla frowned. "He begged me to take him back. But I gave him a sandwich and sent him on his way."

Turning to Junior, Vanessa asked, "Why didn't you stop him?"

Junior scrubbed his hands over his face. "I didn't know he was here 'til I saw him leaving."

"Great. Now he'll come back and terrorize you any time he needs food." Vanessa's voice rose in anger.

"No, he won't," Darla protested. "I told him in no uncertain terms this was the last time. I'm going through with the divorce and if he returns I'm calling the cops."

"And you think that settles it." Her voice filled with sarcasm, Vanessa shook her head as she stared at the sky in disbelief.

"You didn't see him up close," Darla defended herself. "He's a shell of a man. He looks like he hasn't had a meal since he left here. He's been out there a month, living in that shack. I felt so darn sorry for him. All he has is traps and it's been slim pickins this year, ain't it Junior?"

Frowning, Junior rolled his eyes.

"He wouldn't have come begging if he wasn't desperate," her mother argued. "He slunk off with tears in his eyes, totally dejected." She shook her head with sadness. "Pitiful sight."

"I can't believe you feel sorry for him," Vanessa gritted her teeth. "After how he treated you."

"He's gotten what he deserves," Junior growled.

"No matter what he's done, he's still my husband. The divorce ain't even final." Darla slammed the car door. "I can't let him starve."

Chad stood with his arms crossed over his chest and his jaw clamped shut.

Obviously ready for a change of subject, Junior walked around Vanessa's car and peeked inside.

"Real nice, sis. Looks like Brandy's ride. It gets thirty-some miles to the gallon." He motioned to the rusted pickup that he'd bought for five hundred bucks. "Beats that gas hog of mine, for sure."

"For what you're spending in gas, you could make a car payment," Vanessa suggested.

"Nah," Junior scoffed. "I ain't giving my money to no bank. Forget that."

"Your car's really nice." Darla ran a hand over the hood. "I may have to get my driver's license yet."

That made even Chad laugh.

Chad's laugh soon turned to a worried frown. An expensive sports car pulled in, carefully driving over the dirt and gravel.

"Someone else Clyde owes money, I suppose," Disgust filled Darla's voice.

"What do you mean, Mama?" Vanessa asked.

"His hoodlum friends were here yesterday, begging for money. I told them he was staying at his huntin' shack in the woods. He can deal with them hisself, and this guy, too."

The car's driver climbed out with an air of importance. The guy looked familiar, but Chad couldn't place him. Short and muscular, he sported a blonde buzz cut, a salon tan, and a thick neck. He looked like a middle weight on steroids.

Chad positioned himself between Vanessa and Darla. He wrapped a protective arm around Vanessa and felt her tremble. Junior looked like a pit bull but stood silent.

With one glance at Chad, the man's eyes registered sudden recognition. His arrogance ratcheted down a notch, replaced with nervous uncertainty. He cautiously approached Darla.

"Hello Ma'am." He pulled a cigar from his mouth. Rum-scented smoke circled his head as he reached out to shake Darla's hand. He ignored the rest of them.

"Hello." She shook his hand with a shy smile, seeming enchanted by the good-looking man's courtesy.

"I'm looking for Clyde. Is he your husband?"

"For now." She frowned. "He doesn't live here anymore and I'm filing for divorce."

"Oh. We're working on a business deal. Can you tell me where I can find him?" The guy seemed anxious to leave.

"In his hunting shack over on Rose Hill Drive." She shot a look to Chad. "Pass the nice big houses and then there's a dirt path on the right. Goes back in the woods a ways. Suppose the fancy neighbors appreciate that." She winked at Chad.

"Thank you, Ma'am." He puffed his cigar and high-tailed out of there heading toward town – or Rose Hill Drive.

"I'm glad he's gone." Vanessa snuggled to Chad's side. "And I'm so glad you were here."

He pulled her close and kissed the top of her head. He wished she didn't have to deal with this, but hopefully Clyde wouldn't come around again. "Before long, his 'business associates' will know where to find him."

"Business, my butt," Junior said. "That guy's a bookie and Dad probably owes him money."

A bookie? That didn't register with Chad. He knew the guy from somewhere, but never gambled. He worked too hard for his money to throw it away.

Friday night, Chad hurried home after work to shower and change. He had a date with Vanessa. He heard about a home and garden exhibition at the country club in Willow Pond, and he was anxious to surprise her.

Headed up Rose Hill Drive, he just passed Mr. Calvin's house when a shiny black sedan sped toward him up the middle of the road. The distracted driver tossed a wad of paper out the window.

"Get on your own side of the road!" Chad edged toward the ditch.

At the last minute, the car veered around him. Behind the wheel sat Brian Daniels, the mayor's son.

He put it out of his mind and pulled into his driveway. He had better things to worry about than some spoiled rich kid tossing litter into the woods across from his parents' house.

But what was Brian Daniels doing on Rose Hill Drive?

Anxious for Chad's arrival, Vanessa hurried to shower and change after a quick phone call to check on her mom. He said to dress up a little, so she wore black slacks and a light purple blouse – her only nice shirt that wasn't white for work. Time for a shopping spree soon – she'd have to take Mama.

She dried her long blonde hair and put her mother's troubles out of her mind, wondering with anticipation about Chad's big surprise.

Excitement ran through her with his knock. She threw the door open and rushed into his arms.

"Hey, good to see you too!" Chad's blue eyes lit up and he enveloped her in a warm hug.

"You look great!" She took in the button-down shirt and pressed slacks over his muscular physique. "So what's my surprise?"

He kissed her cheek. "You'll find out when we get there."

"I can't wait." She giggled with delight. "So where's dinner?"

"Willow Pond," he said with a smile. "The exact location is part of the surprise."

Floating on air, Vanessa grabbed her purse and headed for the truck.

As he drove past the intersection of Market Street and Route 3, an expensive car fishtailed around the corner and into their lane.

Chad swerved. The truck bounced up over the curb. Vanessa screamed. Her head hit the ceiling and she flailed around the cab.

They missed the erratic car by mere inches.

"Are you all right?" Breathing hard, Chad slowed to a crawl.

"I'm okay." She smoothed her hair from her face. "Are you?"

"I'm fine. Thank goodness for seatbelts." Chad shook his head. "The crazies are out in force today."

"What do you mean?" Anxiety filled her.

"Brian Daniels practically ran me off the road on my way home from work."

"Huh, that's strange. I wonder what's going on with him."

"I don't know. Has he bothered Junior again?"

"Not that I know of. I talked to Mama tonight, and she didn't mention anything. But speaking of crazies, Myrtle was over at the stable today."

Chad did a double take. "That was Myrtle who just ran us off the road."

"Are you serious?"

"Yeah." Chad laughed sarcastically. "I'd recognize that scowl anywhere."

"Great."

"Did she give your mom a hard time?" Chad asked.

"No, she just acted stranger than usual. She was snooping around when Mama spotted her. Myrtle acted all innocent and gave her the evil eye."

"Stirring up trouble – Myrtle's favorite activity." He shook his head. "Is your mom upset?"

"Yeah, but I think she'll be all right." Vanessa smiled. "She wants to know what my surprise is."

Chad laughed. He reached over to tap her on the nose. "You'll find out soon enough."

Antsy, she sat on the edge of the seat.

Chad pulled into the Willow Pond Country Club. The marquee announced "Garden Show." Vanessa bounced in her seat.

"You're taking me to a garden show? How fun!" Excitement filled her. Home improvement stuff was work to him, and he didn't care about decorating and flowers, but he knew how she loved them.

"I thought you'd like it." He beamed at her. "But first, dinner. The country club is known for its tender prime rib and signature chocolate silk pie."

She practically swooned. "You know how to win a girl's heart."

He was so considerate and loving. As much as she strove for independence, the temptation to rely on his strength and comfort became increasingly irresistible.

How would she keep her independence if she fell in love?

By the first Saturday in October, Rachel and Elliot's house was completed. Chad had hoped to finish by Rachel's birthday on September twenty-first, but the bamboo flooring arrived later than anticipated.

After moving in all the furniture, Chad pulled onto the stamped concrete driveway. Then he gathered the family on the front porch – Rachel and Elliot, Jess and Amelia, Mama and Daddy,

Laura, Brett and baby Kate, and their good friend, Max, who helped them move.

Vanessa had to work on Saturdays, but she'd hurried over after work. Finally getting the hang of the whole driving thing, she'd proudly parked behind Chad's truck and now stood beside him with a wide grin.

Chad made a show of pulling the keys from his shirt pocket.

"Congratulations!" he ceremoniously dangled the front door keys. Rachel kissed his cheek while Elliot nabbed the keys.

"Thanks, man." Elliot shook Chad's hand and then wrapped an arm around Rachel. "I can't believe I'm standing here, on my new front porch with my new wife and family." His voice cracked. "It's a dream come true."

Rachel's eyes grew misty as she hugged her husband.

Chad shot a meaningful look at Vanessa. He wanted all this for her. Her eyes hooded with uncertainty but her smile shone with hope.

"Let's go in!" Amelia yanked on the door handle, creating laughter all around.

The massive house dwarfed Rachel and Elliot's hodge-podge of meager furnishings.

"This is almost as empty as my house when I moved in," Chad commented as he looked over the great room.

"We need to do some serious shopping," Elliot agreed. "My bean bags were relegated to the attic playroom, and that flowery sofa is outta here next. The whole house needs furnished."

"Except the kitchen. It's perfect." Rachel's eyes glimmered as she ran a hand over the reproduction china cabinet Elliot had given her last week for her birthday. It matched the antique table and chairs from their grandmother. The hutch was even larger than the original one in Laura's kitchen.

Vanessa stood right there beside her, awed by the heirloom furniture and china.

After their grandmother died, Rachel had agonized over the choice between the table and the hutch. She coveted the hutch, but desperately needed a table and chairs. Laura had ended up with the hutch, and Chad had been happy with bedroom furniture for his spare room.

Leave it to Elliot to make things right.

Chad wanted to be that kind of hero for Vanessa. He caught

her eye and they walked toward one another as if pulled by invisible magnets. They met in the middle and embraced. The excitement of Rachel's special day rubbed off on everyone, but Chad was keenly aware of the effect it was having on his sweetheart.

Vanessa buried her face in his neck and he felt a touch of moisture there.

"This house is so beautiful, Chad," she whispered. "I can't believe how talented you are."

"Thank you." He held her tightly, stroking her silken hair. She shuddered with emotion. He moved her to an alcove out of earshot of the rest of the family.

"You okay?" he asked.

She nodded against his shoulder. "I don't know why I'm so emotional." She wiped her eyes and let out a self-conscious laugh. "I feel like some sentimental old lady crying at a wedding."

He chuckled and kissed away her bashfulness.

"Time for lunch!" Chad's mother appeared with a tray of sandwiches, fruit salad, and brownies. His dad followed her with a cooler of drinks.

As typical in their family, the women congregated in the kitchen and the men headed out to the porch.

Wolfing down a sandwich, Brett paused long enough to ask, "Was Vanessa working today?"

"Yeah," Chad replied. "Saturday's their busiest day."

"But she's made every Sunday dinner since your birthday," Brett said with a wink.

Chad just smiled. The guys laughed appreciatively, but his mind reeled.

"Vanessa's great," Elliot said. "Rachel and I really like her. The girls too. It's amazing how well she fits into the family."

Chad's father nodded, surprising him.

"So I noticed," Chad said.

"We like Vanessa too," Brett agreed. "Laura's already swapping recipes with her."

"She seems really nice," Max said with a reassuring smile. "Brett tells me she's independent as all get out – really making her own way in the world."

"Yep, that's her." Grateful for Max's encouragement, Chad gathered his courage.

"Are you getting serious?" Elliot asked.

Chapter 12 – Release the Hounds

"I've only been seeing Vanessa a few months," Chad hedged.

"Yet you've known her since you were kids," Brett reasoned. "Like Laura and me."

"Yeah, we've come a long way," Chad admitted with a smile.

Brett waggled his eyebrows.

"I didn't mean it like that." Chad grimaced. "Guess we'd better get back to the party." While the others laughed, he headed inside.

He found Vanessa in the kitchen, laughing happily with all his favorite ladies. He tossed his paper plate in the trash and bent to kiss her cheek. He longed to talk to her, but not here, not now. And he didn't want to disrupt their camaraderie.

"I'm heading up to the attic," he told her, anxious to be alone with his thoughts. On the top floor, he unpacked a box of toys and lined them carefully on the bookshelves he'd tucked under the eaves.

He and Vanessa *had* come a long way. They cared deeply for one another. Devoted and faithful, they spent every weekend together and spoke on the phone every day, longing for each other. The woman was hot, hot, hot and he didn't know how much longer he could hold back.

He couldn't imagine getting through the long, cold winter ahead without her by his side. Or in his bed. It wouldn't take much to entice her, but he wanted to do things right.

Were they ready to make that vow?

He still worried about Vanessa's faith. She attended church with him now but how much did she really believe? She relied on herself more than God.

Yet he'd been doing the same thing.

Praying for guidance, he realized he hadn't even declared his love. Maybe because the last time he vowed love for a girl, she'd dumped him. While he struggled with feelings of desire, that girl had apparently struggled with feelings for someone else.

He was over her years ago. Yet she had tainted his view of women – until Vanessa.

Frost covered the grass in early October. The next Sunday morning, Chad escorted Vanessa into The Olde Methodist, the third pew on the right. His family always sat there as if assigned. If someone new to the church took their spot, he felt misplaced and the girls were sent for a loop.

"Mornin' Jessica, mornin' Amelia." Vanessa patted their knees as she took a seat and removed her creamy suede jacket. Dressed in a soft ivory skirt and a sumptuous purple sweater, she looked prettier than ever. Now that she had wheels, the woman had learned the art of shopping.

She even wore a hint of mascara and a touch of lipstick. She certainly didn't need blush, although the new clothes did wonders for her confidence and those neck to hairline blushes were a lot less frequent.

Vanessa swung her long blonde hair over her shoulders and it bounced in waves down her back.

Her beauty took his breath away. Tonight was the night.

After the long day of moving and unpacking yesterday, Chad had no enthusiasm last night to tell Vanessa he loved her. The words had hung in his mind all night long – as she made him dinner, insisted on cleaning up herself, and rubbed his aching muscles until he fell asleep on her lumpy old sofa.

When he awoke past midnight with Vanessa at his side, it was all he could do to force himself to drive home. Her begging him to stay didn't make it any easier.

Lord, how he loved that woman!

And today he would tell her – as soon as he got through the church service and family dinner. He couldn't wait to get to her apartment and have her alone to himself.

Vanessa finished Emily's warm apple crumble with a moan of delight. Chad's mother made it with plenty of cinnamon and nutmeg and topped it with vanilla ice cream. Heavenly! Tossing her spoon into the bowl, she finished her glass of milk and waited for Chad to beg off early as promised. He seemed anxious to get her home alone.

Nervous and excited at the same time, she jumped sky-high when the doorbell rang.

Chad hurried to the front door and opened it.

Junior stood on the front porch, wringing his hands.

Vanessa's stomach churned. Was something wrong with Mama?

"Hey, Junior, come on in," Chad said.

Junior barely crossed the threshold before blurting, "It's Clyde."

Immense relief washed over Vanessa. She rushed toward her brother.

"He…he's missing."

"What do you mean 'missing?'" Skeptical, she narrowed her eyes. Clyde had pulled stunts like this before.

"I noticed his traps ain't been checked but I just thought he was on a drunk. Happens all the time, especially when he has a fight with Mama. I woulda checked on him if he hadn't been so hostile the last time I seen him." He lowered his ball cap over his face and looked at the floor.

"So what makes you think he's *not* drunk?" Vanessa frowned. Feeling sorry for her brother, she found it difficult to show concern for Clyde.

"If he is, he's out there missing somewhere. His moonshine buddies came looking for him 'cause he owes them money." Junior scrubbed a hand over the stubble on his face. "I checked his traps again and they ain't been touched in at least a week. Nothing but rotten coons and a fox full of maggots. A fox! You know what their skins are worth? He'd never let that happen."

"Oh no." Vanessa's hand flew to her face. Her eyes widened in fear.

"Something's terrible wrong," Junior muttered. "He ain't at the cabin and it's been ransacked. Guns are gone and his car's sitting right there. The hood's up and the battery's missing. The tires and wheels are gone and I don't know what else."

Had his moonshine buddies stripped his car because he owed them money? That couldn't be good. Vanessa began to sway. Chad's warm hands helped her into a chair.

"We'd better call Chief Hunter," John stated emphatically. "And organize a search team."

"We only have an hour or so of daylight left," Chad noted. He held a steadying hand on Vanessa's shoulder as Emily handed him a cool washcloth. He placed it gently on Vanessa's forehead and she squeezed her eyes shut. Her nostrils flared and her chest heaved as he instructed her to take deep, cleansing breaths.

"No disrespect, John," Junior said. "But he's been missing a week. With it getting dark, we should probably wait 'til morning."

"The sooner the better," John insisted, picking up the phone.

Chief Hunter appeared at the door. On duty since daylight, Deputy Warren looked a little worse for the wear, but excited nonetheless.

Vanessa couldn't understand how traumatic situations exhilarated some people. Thank goodness for emergency workers because she certainly couldn't be one.

"We'll start at the hunting shack and work our way out," the chief instructed. "I called some fellow officers from Springfield and Willow Pond to meet us there bright and early. As many as would answer on a Sunday night. No sense going out there now. I ran by for a preliminary check and sectioned it off with tape, but it'll be dark by the time we get organized. Let's go over the plan tonight, though. It'll save time in the morning."

Everyone nodded.

"How many men will be joining us?"

"I'm in," John piped up.

Looking alarmed, Emily motioned him into the mudroom.

"One here." Chad raised his hand for the count.

As the chief wrote down names, Vanessa couldn't help overhearing the hushed conversation in the mudroom behind her.

"John, I don't think you need to go." Chad's mother sounded worried. "Hiking through the woods, over rough ground and wet leaves, is not a good idea. You can't afford another knee surgery," she said softly.

A moment later, they came around the corner and blended in. John looked disappointed, but smiled appreciatively at his wife.

Amazed at the way Chad's family related to one another, Vanessa couldn't imagine her parents being civil and actually *loving* over a disagreement. Could she and Chad have a relationship like that?

Brett was on the phone, nodding to the chief.

"Okay." The chief tallied the names. "I've got Junior, Chad, Elliot, Brett, and your friend Max. That's five." He didn't look up at John.

"Count me in." Vanessa diverted everyone's attention. "I'm going too." She stood, unsteady on her feet.

"That's not a good idea," the chief said.

"But he's my..." she caught herself, but finished anyway. "He's my father. I have to help if I can." She struggled to stand tall, feeling light-headed and sick to her stomach.

Chad was at her side in a heartbeat. He kissed her cheek. "I'll go in your place, Ness. You should be with your mama."

Her eyes widened. "Mama must really be upset..."

"I'll run you home while Chad hears what the chief has in mind." John piped up, grateful for something he could do.

Vanessa only wished there was something *she* could do. She'd anticipated a special evening with Chad, but now she had to console her mama over a missing man she'd rather not find. She had to deal with Clyde Gallagher no matter how she tried to get him out of her life.

She swallowed the sickening taste of bitter resentment. How she hated that man. If only he were dead this time.

Guilt swept over her, yet the sinful hope hung on. She might regret wishing that, but it wasn't the first time. Once he was gone, she wouldn't have to face that thought again. Maybe in time, the remorse would lessen.

At least she wouldn't have to deal with him anymore.

Monday morning dawned cold and bleak, the first snow of the season in mid-October. Discouraged with the prospect of the day ahead, Chad slipped his hiking boots over his warm wool socks. He pulled the leather tops up the bright orange legs of his hunting pants and tied the high laces.

They were to meet at the shack and spread out. They had a lot of woods to cover today.

The sun peeked orange through the wooded horizon behind the cabin, giving the yellow police tape an eerie glow. Chad walked up to the patrol car as Chief Hunter marked plastic bags of evidence. One with mud scrapings smelled like manure. Another held a wet, muddy cigar butt. It hadn't rained and would have taken several days of dew to get that saturated. Hunter quickly gathered the bags and put them in his car.

"You're here early," Hunter said brusquely. "I'm just finishing up."

"No problem, I can wait." Chad got the definite feeling the chief didn't want him observing the evidence.

Several other police departments arrived. Squad cars lined up behind Chad's pickup on the rutted dirt path. Then Junior's pickup pulled in. Junior walked up to Chad, puffing on a slim cigar.

Chief Hunter left his clan of cops to join them. He eyed the cigar, and then his gaze fixated on the thin box in Junior's pocket. He shot Chad a look that said 'Keep your mouth shut.'

"Were you here before last night?" Hunter asked Junior.

"Yeah, a few days ago but I couldn't find him. Like I said, I've been pretty ticked at him and I just figured he was on a drunk." Junior rubbed the back of his neck and stared at the ground. He blew out a puff of rum-scented smoke and took the cigar from his mouth.

"That cigar smells interesting," the chief said. "Where'd you get those?"

Junior smiled. "They're hard to find but the rum is my favorite. Smoke shop over in Riverside sells 'em."

"Ah." Hunter nodded, seeming to make a mental note.

Chad cringed. Vanessa would be devastated to learn her brother was suspected in Clyde's disappearance. Thank goodness she was home tending her mother. He hoped he'd have an opportunity to break the news to her – before someone else did. Better yet if they found evidence Junior was innocent.

Chad would keep his eyes peeled.

Brett, Elliot, and Max walked up from the long line of vehicles. Several others congregated to help now that full daylight had broken.

Junior dragged Clyde's coon dogs from his pickup.

The chief frowned at the unexpected dogs.

"Clyde was their master," Junior explained.

Chad wondered if he was the only one who caught that Junior said 'was' as if Clyde were already dead. Did Junior know something the rest of them didn't?

"The trail's cold," Hunter argued. "No use hearing them baying hounds for no purpose whatsoever."

"It ain't rained," Junior insisted. "Smith and Wesson will find him." Smoke whirling around him held a faint scent of rum.

Hunter shook his head and paired them up – Junior with Deputy Warren to keep him and the dogs in line, Chad and Brett, Max and Elliot, other officers and volunteers with whomever they knew best. The chief paired with a stodgy old officer from Willow Pond who moved even slower than he did.

"No civilians inside the yellow tape. No exceptions," Hunter said. "The chief and I will search the cabin and the car."

"No sense in pushing himself," Chad muttered to Junior as they set off.

"Not that anyone really cares about finding my father."

Chad didn't know what to say, so he kept his mouth shut.

"Everyone in town knows how rotten he was."

Junior used past tense again. Chad looked over at Deputy Warren to see if he'd overheard. Behind Junior's back, the deputy raised an eyebrow and shot Chad a knowing look.

"It's just sad," Chad sympathized.

Junior nodded. "I wonder if my mama won't be better off without him. Vanessa, too."

"And you," Chad added as they headed into the woods.

"No matter about me." Junior shrugged. "Come along, boys." He pulled the dogs over to Warren and headed into the woods in the direction of an old moonshine still hidden back there. Growing up on the farm next door, Chad had known about the still since he was a kid.

Was Junior leading Warren to the still or were the dogs?

"What was that all about?" Brett sidled up to Chad.

"I'm not sure what to think about Junior's reaction," Chad admitted. "He was all worried last night, but today he seems resigned to the possibility that Clyde's dead." Chad stepped around some poison ivy growing up the side of a tree. "Can't say that I blame him, though. Lord knows I'd be relieved to be rid of someone who treated me that way."

"Clyde *does* treat you that way," Brett affirmed.

"Not as bad, not as long. And I'm not his son, thank God."

"True. My dad wasn't *that* bad, but I do have a clue how he feels." Brett watched Junior.

"You think he killed the old man?" Chad whispered.

"Hunter found a cigar butt," Brett said. "I heard him telling the deputy it was some uncommon rum-flavored brand."

"I saw him eyeing Junior's cigar," Chad said. "But even if he left that butt here, it doesn't prove he killed Clyde."

"Let's just keep our eyes open," Brett said.

Elliot and Max joined Chad and Brett as Junior went to his pickup and scrounged inside. He held an old flannel shirt under the dogs' noses to sniff.

"I take it Clyde Gallagher wasn't well-liked." Max said.

"No one will miss him," Brett said. "Least of all his son."

The friends nodded soberly as they reached the point where they needed to split up.

"Guess we're headed this way." Elliot pointed to the right. He and Max took their assigned territory while Chad and Brett headed for theirs. Junior and Warren took a left as the hounds dragged them down a trail into the woods.

After hours of combing the area, they'd found nothing. Chad and Brett neared the edge of a ravine over the creek bank – a dead end.

Then Junior, Warren, and the dogs appeared. Leaving Junior far behind, Warren looked stoic and angry, on a mission to see what the dogs would find next. The hounds meandered through the woods, sniffing from tree to tree as they followed Clyde's trail. Then they began howling, intent on a beeline toward Chad and Brett.

Chad's heart sank as he backed away from the cliff, not wanting to get in their way. Brett's eyes widened at their approach. He looked over the edge.

"Oh no." He froze, holding his stomach. "Not again."

Chad feared looking over the edge. He'd seen that shock and turmoil on his friend's face before...when Brett found Rachel's first husband's body riddled with bullets on the banks of this same creek.

Jake Santos had hurt Rachel, and Clyde Gallagher had hurt Vanessa. A combination of dread, horror, and guilty relief flooded Chad.

Chapter 13 – Broken Necklace

"He's dead?" Vanessa couldn't wrap her mind around the meaning of the words. She'd expected her *step*father to be found drunk somewhere – fallen in the woods, staying with his hoodlum friends, or holed up with some hooker. Darla had called everyone she knew, but Clyde led a secretive life.

Now he was *dead?*

Vanessa nestled next to her mother on the ratty sofa in Darla's front room. Chad stood at her side, caressing her shoulder as Chief Hunter relayed the story.

The portly man perched precariously on a metal kitchen chair from the fifties. He held a notebook on one knee, as his rounded belly covered most of his lap.

The surreal scene was so different than her past experiences with the police. No frantic screaming, no handcuffs, no blood. Vanessa wasn't six years old hiding under the table or behind the couch with her brother and sister. Her mother wasn't wailing in fury and pain. Most notably, Clyde wasn't wielding a weapon, shaking his fists, or bellowing drunken threats.

Chief Hunter sat calmly on a chair. Chad stood supportive and strong beside her with a hand on her shoulder. Junior wrung his hands at the edge of the room. Vanessa and her mother trembled dry-eyed on the sofa as shock waves quaked through them.

The nightmare was finally over.

Clyde was dead.

"…at the bottom of the cliff," Chief Hunter was saying.

On auto-pilot, she answered questions with no coherent memory of what she said. Her insides churned and her head spun.

Gradually, the shock subsided. The enormous burden of fear

lifted from her shoulders, replaced with tremendous, guilty relief.

How horrible to feel such liberating freedom that a human being was dead. He was never her real father, and he was finally gone from her life forever.

Adding to the guilt, she had no assurance he'd gone to heaven. In fact, she had serious doubts. Horrific as that was, she was too traumatized to dwell on it.

Was he really gone for good? The confusing combination of lingering shock, oppressive guilt, and pure glee overwhelmed her.

Suddenly nauseous, she leapt from the sofa and rushed into the bathroom. Without time to slam the door or reach the toilet, she hurled into the sink.

Once cleaned up and back in the front room, Vanessa sat squeamishly beside her mother. Chad furrowed his brow and rubbed her back.

"Are you all right?" he asked.

She nodded, but wasn't all right at all.

The chief cleared his throat and continued. "It's evident there was an altercation. Clyde's body has the markings of a beating, marks that are unlikely to be the result of the fall. There will be an autopsy, and we're investigating this as a homicide."

Goosebumps sprang up on Vanessa's arms. A creepy chill snaked down her spine. Chad wrapped his warm arms around her.

"One of his hoodlum friends probably pushed him. He owed them money." Her mother shivered violently, eyes darting. "Why don't you go ask them?"

"I'll do that." The chief watched their reactions. Darla wrung her hands. Her gaze darted to her son. Junior frowned deeply with hooded eyes. He retreated against the wall.

Vanessa's shoulders slumped. Why were they acting so nervous? Surely it was no surprise someone wanted Clyde dead. He had enemies all over the county – from renegade trappers and moonshiners to the bartenders and bookies he'd stiffed.

"I'd like you all to come in for questioning," the chief said, eyeing Junior and Darla. Surely he didn't suspect *them*.

Nausea overtook Vanessa again.

Chad escorted Vanessa to the station, but now she was on her own for the interrogation. The questions began routinely enough –

where was she the last time she'd seen Clyde, who all was present, date and time, stuff like that.

"When was the last time you were at the hunting shack on Rose Hill Drive?" Chief Hunter asked

"Wow. I don't remember." Vanessa thought back. "Not since I was a little girl."

He nodded, taking notes. Then he pulled out a plastic bag with a gold necklace inside.

Wide-eyed, Vanessa's heart thudded in her chest.

"You recognize this ma'am?" Hunter asked.

"Why yes. It's my mother's." Vanessa stared in shock.

"We found it tangled in Clyde's fingers," the chief said. "See the strand of hair twisted in the clasp?"

Terror ran through Vanessa like an icy wind. The platinum gray hair was her mother's.

"It's still fastened. The way the chain is broken, it appears it was ripped from someone's throat."

"It was." Vanessa trembled in fear. "Clyde grabbed her throat and ripped it off her, just like you said. It fell in the dirt. He and Mama were fighting – right before you came and hauled him away." She speculated. "He must have picked it up before you took him to jail." She wondered if it he'd been planning to pawn it or only took it to hurt her mama.

Hunter raised an eyebrow. "Where exactly was the necklace dropped?"

"Right outside the doorstep at Mama's house." She sat up straight to steady herself. Her hands were as shaky as her voice.

"Are there any other witnesses to that?" Hunter asked.

Insides quaking, Vanessa gathered her courage. "Junior was there."

"Anyone else?"

"I don't think so. Chad arrived after you did." Wishing he were beside her right now, she ran through that day's scenario in her mind. "Wait." She gasped. "Brian Daniels was there."

"Brian?" Chief Hunter croaked with surprise. He furrowed his brow and scribbled furiously.

In the waiting room of the police station, Vanessa leaned against the hard wooden arm of the chair to cling to Chad's side –

anything to soak up his comfort and strength.

"Aren't you uncomfortable?" She noticed how bent over he sat to wrap an arm around her shoulders.

"I'm fine," he insisted. "Your mother's interrogation should be over soon."

"Yeah, right." Junior frowned, sitting across from them.

A while later, Darla emerged from behind closed doors. She shook like the last leaf of autumn, clinging to a branch in a strong wind.

"Mama." Vanessa went to her and hugged her tight.

"He thinks I killed Clyde. I know he does."

"Sit down, Mama." Vanessa motioned to a chair.

"No. Get me out of this place while I'm still free to leave." Darla headed for the door on shaky legs.

In silence, Chad drove them back to the house. Once inside and settled, Darla looked at her children.

"Hunter said the property taxes are delinquent on the land by the lake. Clyde didn't pay 'em for three years back!"

"You didn't get notice?" Junior's hackles rose.

The county auditor was Brian Daniels. Vanessa's stomach churned.

"No." Darla scowled. "That property's in Clyde's name only. I was never privy to the finances. The only reason my name's on the deed to this house is because I had to get the loan for indoor plumbing. Clyde never got a W-2 in his life. He took *my* paycheck to pay the bills."

She clenched her jaw. "But apparently he didn't pay 'em. The lake property's going to tax sale in a few months."

Vanessa couldn't believe what she was hearing. The land was all her family had.

"Well Daniels could have mentioned it!" Junior snarled.

"He could have," Darla agreed.

"How am I gonna come up with that kind of money?" Junior's face reddened like he was about to burst an artery.

"They just want to get rid of us," Darla lamented. "We're a scourge to their high-society lake community. Now Hunter wants to see my stable boots. What does he think, he'll find my footprints up on that cliff?"

Chad groaned.

"What?" Vanessa eyed him. "What'd you see up there?"

He took her hand and shook his head. "It wasn't up there." He squeezed her hand but looked at Darla. "The chief had evidence at the shack that looked and smelled like manure."

Darla's eyes grew wide. Vanessa followed her glance to Junior's hunting boots by the door. Her brother tromped through deer feces and everything else out there in the woods.

Vanessa's heart pounded. She clung to Chad. Surely she'd faint if he wasn't holding her up. Although she hadn't eaten a bite, her stomach lurched again.

Despite sleeting rain, The Crystal Falls Cemetery held a certain aura of peace. What was it about funerals and rain? It almost wouldn't seem morbid enough if the sun were shining.

Vanessa's icy fingers clasped Chad's hand. She and her mother huddled beneath his umbrella.

Chad's pastor held a brief service over a standard box of ashes and a spray of waterlogged flowers, donated by Rosebuds.

In the downpour, John and Emily James stood with the family in macabre silence. Vanessa appreciated the respectful gestures of Chad's parents. None of Clyde's so-called friends showed up, nor one member of his estranged family.

But Chief Hunter stood on the sidelines, arms folded over his chest. Beneath his plastic-covered hat, his eyes seemed narrowed with suspicion at her mother and Junior.

No one shed a tear – not Darla, and certainly not Junior. Vanessa felt no sadness – just immense, guilty relief. Eager to get this over with, she was thankful when the pastor concluded with a meaningless prayer.

Junior traipsed to his pickup without a word of comfort to her or his mother. Not that they needed comforting, but his distance troubled her.

Both he and Darla had been stoic and silent since Clyde died. Vanessa had no idea what they were thinking or feeling, and felt too awkward to express herself.

She squeezed Chad's hand. Thank goodness for him.

Chief Hunter watched Junior drive away and walked to his patrol car without a word to anyone.

Chad's father hugged Vanessa. She greeted him warmly.

"I'm so sorry, Vanessa." He patted her shoulder and turned to

Darla. The woman stiffly returned his hug. "I'm so sorry," John repeated.

Darla nodded like a caged animal set loose – free but lost.

Emily issued similar greetings as her husband, and received the same responses.

Keenly ashamed, Vanessa's only grief was the possibility of her mother or brother going to jail for pushing the old man to his death. Her insides convulsed.

"Let me know if you need anything. Anything at all." Emily hugged Vanessa and looked into her eyes.

"Take good care of her," Emily said to Chad. "She'll need it." She kissed his cheek. "We're getting out of the rain. See you later." She ducked back under her husband's umbrella.

John thumped his son's back affectionately and they left.

Vanessa thanked the pastor and offered him a small envelope. Then Chad escorted her and her mother to Vanessa's car and held the umbrella for them to get inside.

Chad climbed behind the wheel of the tiny vehicle.

"I'm glad that's over," Vanessa said.

"It ain't over 'til it's over," Darla said morbidly.

"What do you mean, Mama?"

"I shoulda been careful what I wished for. Now it's come true and I'll get blamed," she predicted.

"No one's blaming you for Clyde's death," Vanessa said.

"I saw Hunter giving me the eye," Darla insisted. "He thinks I done it. I know he does."

"Mama, don't be paranoid." From the backseat, Vanessa reached over the console to pat her mother's shoulder. "No one's thinking this is your fault." The lie roiled in her gut.

She didn't even know what to think, and the look in the chief's eyes told her he suspected her mother. Vanessa's head fell back in the seat and she closed her eyes against any more horror. Chilled goose bumps ran up and down her arms beneath the wet sleeves.

Ominous dread settled over her. If Darla Gallagher had it in her to kill the husband she feared, she'd have done it long ago.

Vanessa fortified herself to ignore the Chief's suspicions. Nothing would come of them because her mother wasn't guilty, and she'd do all she could to prove her innocence.

Vanessa savored her last bite of homemade pecan pie and leaned back into Chad's sofa. "Hmm. It's nice to eat someone else's cooking for a change."

"My mama's quite a cook," Chad bragged. He leaned across his sofa and pecked her cheek. "As are you."

"Thank you," she said shyly. "And thanks for making me dinner. It was delicious. After the week I've had, I was in no mood to go out."

He rubbed her thigh. She fell into his arms, hungry for his touch. If only life were simpler. She'd never come up for air.

"The worst is over," he said. "It has to get better from here."

She frowned skeptically.

"How's your mom doing?" he asked, as if reading her mind.

"Not so good." Fending off a sense of dread and worry that surfaced unbidden, she sat up and fidgeted with the hem of her shirt. "She's convinced the chief thinks she pushed Clyde over that cliff."

"I don't understand her obsession with that," Chad said.

"I know. I wish she'd leave well enough alone." She fought back a yawn, but it emerged with gusto.

"You're tired. Here, lie down." He shifted to the edge of the sofa and plumped up a pillow. He touched her heart with how he doted on her all week. "Do you wanna talk?"

Right now what she needed was to be alone with her thoughts and sort out her confusing emotions.

Why was God allowing this? Hadn't she and her mother been through enough trauma, pain, and humiliation to last a lifetime? If God was so loving and kind, where was He when she needed him most? Angry, frustrated, and exhausted, she wasn't prepared to discuss this.

"Actually, I should get home, Chad." She stood to go, although she didn't want to leave him – not now and not ever. She'd love to curl up in his arms, but she needed a good night's sleep.

"Let me drive you," he offered. "I'll be picking you up for church tomorrow anyway. You can get your car after dinner."

"No thank you." She grabbed her purse. Driving in the dark still made her nervous, but she refused to succumb to dependency on Chad.

"Okay. Sorry." He bit his lip. "I'm not telling you what to do.

I'm just trying to help."

"I know." She shrugged sadly. "I'm just not going to church anymore." With a defiant frown, she tossed the purse strap over her shoulder.

"What? Why not?" Deep disappointment reflected on his handsome face. "Vanessa, you need God more than ever right now."

"No. I needed Him most when I was little but He wasn't there for me." Looking away toward the ceiling, she blinked away tears. "My mama needed Him. But now I have the worst feeling something awful will happen to her. She's so consumed with guilt she can barely function."

Overwhelmed with grief for her mother, Vanessa dabbed an escaping tear. She swallowed down her cracking voice and fortified her resolve. "I know she didn't kill him; it's just not in her. Yet she feels responsible for his death and is convinced she'll take the blame."

"Let God help you through this," he pleaded. Despair filled his eyes as if he might break down and cry.

She shook her head, refusing to let her emotions get the best of her.

"God doesn't care," she declared stubbornly. Turning her face into her shoulder, she seethed, "Where was He when I was twelve? I felt so dirty and alone when my father left my bed. My mother would scream at him, and I heard him slap her down. I hid under the blankets and cried." Fighting back tears now, she choked down the lump in her throat.

"But God didn't make it stop. And now, when we finally stand up to Clyde, all three of us, and make our lives right again, this happens." She waved an angry arm.

"Like we haven't been punished enough for Clyde's mistakes? I'm tired, Chad. It seems no matter what I do, it's like I'm being penalized for wanting a nice, normal life."

Chad's hand felt warm on her shoulder. "Vanessa, it says in the Bible that trials and tribulations happen so we can learn to be firm in the Lord and endure. It builds our character and makes us stronger."

"Well, I don't need God to make me strong. I already am. I'm a big girl now. I'll handle life on my own, like I had to all along." She stomped toward the door.

Feeling sheepish, she turned back to Chad, who certainly wasn't to blame. "I'll still come for Sunday dinner if you like."

"Of course." He rushed toward her but his words couldn't hide the uncertainty and fear in his voice. His eyes echoed love for her beyond her wildest fantasies.

"See you then." She kissed his cheek and hurried out the door before she thought about how wonderful it would be to collapse in his arms with sheer exhaustion.

As strongly as she felt about this, Chad's concern for her spiritual well being struck a chord in her heart. Sobs wracked her insides but she refused to break down.

At least until she got off the porch.

Chapter 14 – Some Kind of Woman

Carrying a bouquet of yellow mums, Vanessa gently knocked on her mother's door before pushing it open.

"Mama, we're here!"

Chad followed her with steaming chicken potpie and warm pumpkin bread from the tea room.

Darla looked up from slicing an apple. Fresh piecrust lined a tin on the old farm table. Flour covered the surface and an antique wooden rolling pin sat nearby.

"Hey, sweetie." Darla's eyes lit up. "You just missed your father."

Taken aback, Vanessa looked at her like she was crazy.

"Baldy stopped by," her mother explained.

Oh yeah, her *father*. The idea still felt strange. She shot a look at Chad and he was grinning.

"He brought apples." Darla tossed the last slice into the bowl with a flourish. "He wants to see me again." Her eyes sparkled. "For real this time. No more sneaking around, no more hiding from Clyde."

The words shattered Vanessa's composure like a rock hitting a windshield. Squinting through the cracked glass web of life as she'd known it, she tried to process the news. Her mother dating – the man who was her real father.

"I thought he was seeing Myrtle?" she wondered aloud.

"She wanted more than friendship, but he was never interested."

Vanessa could see that. Even in church, Myrtle always leaned close to Baldy and he scooted away.

"He's still in love with you, isn't he?"

"We never stopped loving each other." Darla sighed with a dreamy look. She stirred sugar and spices into the apples. Then she poured them into the crust, covered them with a second crust and fluted the edge. A smile graced her face as she... hummed a tune? With a bounce in her step she placed the pie in the oven.

Vanessa stared in disbelief. "You can have a wonderful future now. I've never seen you so happy, Mama. Ever."

"I never have been. Not since I was a young girl, anyway. I feel so liberated – so free!" She threw up her arms in joy.

"Wow. It's like I have a whole new mother." Floored, Vanessa stared in wonderment.

"And a whole new father too! Baldy wants to get to know you. He's missed that all these years." The old bitterness seeped into her face, but diminished quickly. "Now you can spend time with a father who truly loves you."

"I can't imagine him loving me. I barely know him." Vanessa wasn't prepared to deal with that.

"Ah, but he knows you." Darla smiled.

"Baldy's a good guy," Chad said. "I've lived next door to him my whole life. You should be proud to be his daughter."

Vanessa nodded. She'd much rather be his daughter than Clyde's. Yet he was a stranger. She felt invaded, like he'd been watching her all these years, knowing more about her than she knew herself.

Chad wrapped his arms around her. "How could Baldy *not* love you?" he whispered in her ear.

Heart warmed, Vanessa brightened. She hugged him, grateful he shared this odd moment. Somehow no matter what happened, she felt better with Chad around.

She reached for her mother and they hugged in a rare moment of affection. Vanessa held her tightly.

They heard a clang as Junior locked up the bait shop. He waltzed into the kitchen and looked at the mess.

"I'm baking an apple pie," Darla said with pleasure.

"Yum. You ain't baked in a while." He grinned ear to ear.

"How ya doing, Junior?" Chad asked.

His grin faded. "I don't want to be called that no more."

"Huh?" Vanessa and Darla asked in unison.

"I've been thinking on it, and I'm a grown man. My father's dead now so there's no sense in calling me Junior."

"You want us to call you Clyde?" Darla asked with horror.

"NO! 'Course not." He winced. "I like my middle name. Lee."

"Lee." Darla smiled, looking him over with a nod of approval. "Now that really suits you. Lee, it is.

"I guess I could get used to that," Vanessa said.

"Lee is a fine name," Chad agreed.

"You're the man of the house now," Darla said.

"Don't go getting all sentimental." He shook his head. "I ain't lived in this house since I was eighteen. My cabin on the lake suits me fine."

"I figured you'd say that." She kissed his cheek. It was the first time Vanessa had seen her do that in years.

"I saw Baldy hanging around here." His brows drew together in question.

"We're gonna start seeing each other," Darla admitted.

"As if you ain't been doing that all along," he teased.

Darla blushed and the two shared a knowing look, as if Junior – Lee – had caught them a time or two.

"You just hush your mouth." Darla swatted his arm.

Vanessa and Chad shared wide-eyed chuckles. 'Lee' laughed and peeked in the oven, inhaling a whiff of pie.

Vanessa felt a peaceful ease settle over them. It was a new beginning – a chance to make things right that had been wrong for far too long.

She leaned into Chad. Apprehensive as she felt, with him beside her, she felt empowered to handle anything.

Even getting to know a whole new father...and mother.

Wednesday evening, Vanessa pulled Beef Wellington from her tiny oven and set it atop the stove to keep warm. The tea room didn't pay much but the perks were awesome. Chad was coming for dinner. A beef guy through and through, he should be impressed.

She placed her two best plates on the tiny table and scrounged for matching silverware in the hodge-podge of utensils from her mother. Then she pulled out her newly purchased prized possessions – two beautiful cut-glass goblets. As she placed them alongside the plates, she heard footsteps on the stairway.

She threw open the door. Chad climbed the stairs. His face broke into a huge grin beneath those dark locks escaping his ball cap.

"Anxious to see me?" His deep blue eyes turned violet.

"Always!" She waited on the landing until he reached her and engulfed her in a hug.

"It's only been a few days," he teased.

"Feels like forever since you held me." She melted in his arms.

He pulled her into the apartment and closed the door. Then his lips met hers with a sizzle that had her heart pumping and her body yearning for more. Much more.

His hands roved over her back. He held her so close every inch of her body molded to his. Passion built between them. His hands gripped her waist and he groaned with desire.

"Vanessa, I need you." His gravelly voice pleaded.

"I need you," she said with her whole heart, realizing the depth of meaning and truth those words held. He said he'd wait until marriage. Face buried in his chest, she wondered if marriage would ever be something a man like Chad would consider with a girl like her.

If not, what were they doing besides driving each other crazy? There was no point for him to be here if he weren't considering her as a wife. Could it possibly happen?

Suddenly she realized how wonderful that would be. And how much she truly loved Chad James.

He pulled back, holding her arms.

Her body shivered with sudden cold.

Looking into her eyes, his face agonized over words. "Not yet, Vanessa." He gripped her arms as if for dear life. "Soon."

Her mind reeled with the promise.

"You look beautiful. As always." He slowly released her and swept a strand of hair from her cheek.

Self-conscious, she folded her hands.

"Something smells good. Besides you," he said.

"Oh. Dinner." She moved to the stove. "I hope you like Beef Wellington."

His face glowed. "My grandmother's signature dish." He grinned. "Actually, you remind me of her. A great cook, a tea lover, feisty and stubborn as all get out."

"Well!" She snickered, thinking of herself as a grandmother. "I hope you're not disappointed in my rendition."

"It smells heavenly." He helped her bring food to the table and they sat. "Do you mind if I pray?"

The practice made her uncomfortable – like it was some formal occasion. She and God weren't exactly on speaking terms. She was questioning God, and angry with Him. Yet she yearned to get past it. She wasn't ready to go back to church, but saying grace might be a good start.

"Sure," she said uncertainly.

Chad prayed short and simple as if he was aware of her struggle. He thanked God for *her* as well as the food.

Thank you for Chad. These were her first heaven-bound thoughts since Clyde's death. *And thank you Mama's better.*

After a thoughtful moment, Chad blurted, "Check this out!" He picked up his goblet. "You've been shopping," he said with approval. "Give a woman a car and you never know where she'll run off to."

"Just a little something I picked up at the antique shop," she said with an airy flair. "On clearance."

"A smart shopper, too."

His grin boosted her confidence.

"I want to buy a few pieces at a time." She looked down at the chipped plates. "I should be able to spare a few dollars from each paycheck, now that my mom's doing okay on her own."

"How is she?" he asked with concern, cutting the tender beef with his fork.

"You wouldn't believe the change in her."

"No kidding?" He sat back in his chair and stared at her.

"She and Baldy are discussing marriage."

Chad dropped his fork. "That was fast."

"Well, they've been in love forever. Actually, they've waited years and years."

"True." He fingered the fork as if considering the implications.

"They're going to wait awhile, out of respect. And he wants to get to know me first."

"Baldy?" Chad seemed to be wrapping his mind around that, much like she'd been trying to do.

She nodded, unsure what to say, unsure how she even felt.

"I hope it all works out," he said. At last he took a bite of Beef Wellington. He chewed thoughtfully and smiled.

"Delicious! Just as good as Grandma's." He tweaked her chin.

"You're some kind of woman."

"Thank you." Pride welled as she took a bite, too.

"I've been praying for you and your family," he said.

"You don't have to do that. Clyde's dead now." Shame washed over her with the long-awaited reprieve. "The worst is over."

"We don't just need prayer when times are tough. We need God all the time."

"Why don't you tell Him that?" Bitter memories skittered through her brain. "I needed God when I was little, and He wasn't there for me."

"He WAS there, Vanessa. He was there when you were little and he's there for you now."

"Right." Sarcasm filled her. "Then why didn't He help me?"

"Did you ask him?"

She stared at him, dumbfounded. "Well, no." Then she narrowed her eyes. "If God's so all-knowing and all-powerful, He should know when I need help."

"He does. Maybe you didn't call out to Him, but God still helped you get through it."

"People get through lots of stuff. That doesn't mean God helped them."

"It doesn't?" He let that sit a moment. "When you were in high school, the gym teacher saw your bruises, despite the fact you were trying to hide them."

She crossed her arms and stared at the floor. A small part of her regretted bearing her soul, yet she felt comfort in his knowing. He knew her dirtiest secret and loved her anyway.

Everything he said was true. In her heart of hearts, she knew she needed to hear it.

"If that teacher hadn't reported those bruises, would you have had the gumption to stand up to Clyde?"

"No." She shook her head adamantly. "Absolutely not. I was terrified. If it weren't for the counseling, I never would have confronted him."

"Do you think maybe God had something to do with that?"

She shrugged. "Why did I have to go through it at all?"

"Going through difficulties makes us stronger. Trials either make us better or bitter. It's our choice."

"My mother was bitter," she said sadly. "I don't want to be

like that. Do you really think those awful experiences can make me strong?"

"Look how far you've come already. You stood up to Clyde and made him stop. Then you left the bait shop to work at the tea room, against his wishes, and saved every penny to move out."

"That's true." She smiled at his praise.

"Now think on this. If God took care of you when you *didn't* ask Him, how much more will He take care of you when you *do*?"

Despite his rationale, she couldn't believe God really cared. Easy for Chad to say, he never dealt with an abusive father. He didn't have to hide under the covers, crying himself to sleep, and hoping no one would assault him in the middle of the night.

Yet the more she thought about it, Chad was right. By all accounts, she should still be traumatized by Clyde, or a mess like Layla, or even dead. If God hadn't helped her, she wouldn't be eating Beef Wellington with the sweetest guy in Crystal Falls. And he certainly wouldn't be looking at her with love written all over his face.

"Miss, miss." A lady in a red hat called from across the tea room, waving an impatient hand in the air.

Vanessa moved that way, gathering empty plates, stuffing check holders into her pocket, and pouring fresh water as she went.

"Yes, ma'am," she said cordially as she reached the woman.

"My tea is cold," the woman said disgustedly. "If I'd wanted iced tea, I would have ordered it that way."

"The quiche is cold too," her companion added. "There's no dressing on my salad and the tea bread is dry."

"I'm so sorry." Vanessa gathered the plates, piling them on top of the empty ones in her hand. "I'll fix it right away." Against every rule in the book, she set the pitcher of water on the one empty table in the room so she could pick up the teapot. It was cold to the touch.

Making a beeline to the kitchen, three other ladies hailed her on the way.

"I'll be right with you," she promised, not knowing how she'd ever keep the food coming in edible condition.

Why did Julia's doctor appointment have to be the same day as the ladies' luncheon? And why had Vanessa assured her it wouldn't be a problem?

She dumped the plates on the counter and filled a clean teapot with hot water. As the tea steeped, she heated quiche and tea bread and filled a tiny pitcher with dressing.

Grateful it was going on four o'clock, Vanessa was anxious to finish the crazy day at The Porcelain Teapot. After work, she'd quickly check on her mother and run over to Chad's open house at the model home.

He'd been a rock for her through all the trouble with Clyde. At last she felt heady, liberating freedom – even if she was still afraid to drive further than Springfield. Her life was her own and she couldn't wait to see Chad.

Making change for the checks in her pocket, she carefully put the right change with the correct receipts and pocketed the tips. She couldn't expect good tips when the service was terrible. Although she'd never worked harder in her life.

Then the door chimes tinkled. Swallowing a groan, she looked up with her professional smile. Joy filled her when Sarita Santos waltzed in, beaming at her.

"Vanessa! I haven't seen you in ages."

Vanessa quickly delivered the plates in her hands.

Rushing toward her, Sarita held out her arms for a hug. Vanessa gladly embraced her late sister's friend. They both missed Layla, and they had similar family issues that few people understood.

"I'm so sorry about your father," Sarita whispered. She pulled back to look at her friend. "But look at you, doing well out on your own. Layla would be so proud of you. *I'm* proud of you."

"Thank you." The kind words brought a measure of sadness. Vanessa swallowed a lump in her throat. She couldn't cry over her sister now. "I sure miss her, but thank goodness I have you." She hugged Sarita again.

As her friend sat down with two regulars, Vanessa distributed change with polite smiles and thank yous. "Do you need anything else?" she kindly asked the women who'd complained.

After appeasing everyone for the moment, she circled back to Sarita's table.

"So how have you been? All graduated and some big time interior designer now." Vanessa pulled out her order pad, torn between a friendly visit and doing her job.

"I love it." Sarita smiled. "I shop for expensive furniture and accessories with someone else's money. The clients fall all over me with appreciation." She smiled gratefully. "But nothing like my last job." Winking, she referred to her stripper days, when she worked with Layla.

Her tablemates, Angelina Mitchell and Margaret Hunter, shook their heads.

"Best of all, I'm not ashamed to tell my daughter what I do for a living and I'm making good money."

"*I'm* proud of *you*!" Vanessa gushed. She poised her pen, sorry that she had to move along. "Are you ladies ordering tea?"

"Yes, but we're just having dessert," Margaret said.

"Sarita's helping us design a garden store in the old Mitchell's Mill barn," Angelina added with excitement.

Sarita ribbed Vanessa. "But don't worry, we'll be done by closing in case you have a hot date."

Vanessa giggled. "How'd you know?"

Feeling giddy at seeing her friend, she took their orders and delivered three slices of pumpkin-chocolate torte.

"Oh my," Sarita gasped. She stared out the window as Chad walked past.

Hurrying past the windows, he looked handsomer than ever in a button-down shirt and pressed slacks. With his short dark hair combed into its Sunday style, he looked good enough to eat.

"It tastes even better than it looks." Angelina Mitchell said.

Vanessa felt a spurt of jealousy and stared at Angelina for a few seconds before realizing the woman was talking about her dessert, not Chad. She bit into layers of spicy pumpkin filling and fudgy chocolate cake frosted with chocolate ganache.

"No – look." Margaret Hunter, the police chief's wife, nodded toward the windows.

Chapter 15 – A Mean Apple Pie

Wide-eyed, Brett's mother almost choked on her cake. "Chad James?" Angelina whispered. "At the tea shop?"

Vanessa's heart stopped when he snuck up the back steps. She broke into a grin and set down the moss rose teapot before her shaking hand spilled it.

"What's *he* doing here?" Margaret teased.

"He ordered some pastries to serve at his model home open house tonight." Vanessa refilled Margaret's teapot and hurried into the back.

"There you are!" Chad greeted Vanessa with obvious relief and kept out of the dining room's line of vision.

"Hi Chad." Her face heated as she hurried to get his pastry tray. "Sorry I don't have much time. I'm on my own today. Julia has a doctor appointment."

"Okay. Did you include some of those yummy chocolate tarts?"

"Of course." She pulled out a beautiful display of pastries on a silver platter lined with doilies. "I hope it's not too fancy."

Chad raised an eyebrow with a wicked grin. "Looking good."

She wanted to melt into his arms. Although in a rush, she motioned him toward the back of the room, even further from her patrons' view, and reached up to whisper in his ear.

"Looking good, yourself, handsome devil."

He chuckled, low and sweet. "You gonna stop up and see me?"

"Count on it," she promised. "If I can ever get out of here. I'm not sure when Julia will be done at the doctor's."

Before he could respond, the timer dinged and the tea was

ready.

"I gotta run." She turned quickly toward the butler's pantry off the dining room. With two orders in her pocket, she filled a tray with food and two pots of hot tea.

Chad headed for the back door with his tray of pastries as if the dining room full of ladies were a quarantine zone.

Vanessa squeezed past as he opened the door, whirling toward the dining room when she ran smack into Julia, just coming in.

"Aaaack!" They both screamed.

Food flew into the air with a flash of flying limbs. Plates crashed, porcelain shattered, and lettuce floated down like confetti. Tea splashed ceiling to floor and everywhere in between, running to puddles at their feet.

The boisterous dining room fell silent.

Speechless, Vanessa burst into tears.

Chad set down his tray and rushed toward her.

"It's okay!" After a brief hug, he launched into action. He mopped the kitchen floor and wiped the cabinets and counters. He even brushed bits of food off Vanessa's clothes and landed a quick kiss as she struggled to overcome a meltdown.

Faster than a woman half her age, Julia brewed a new pot of tea and heated fresh meals.

Wiping tears, Vanessa gathered her wits and pulled out salad fixings.

Chad scrubbed his hands. "I can make salads. Show me how."

She started an assembly line of six plates and completed one salad. "Make them all look like this."

Julia loaded a tray with the hot meals and yanked the first two completed salads. "You'll remember." She shot Chad a wink and thrust four dessert orders at Vanessa. "Serve these," she commanded without missing a beat.

Still numb, Vanessa followed Julia into the dining room and served dessert to a group by the window. The ladies glanced at her face, red as their feathered hats, and never asked what happened. Their polite thank-yous assured her of their empathy.

Hushed conversation resumed.

"Are you okay?" Sarita asked as Vanessa passed her table.

She nodded. "We just had a pedestrian accident in the kitchen," she said with a smile.

"You need some help, dear?" Angelina rose from her seat in

mother hen mode.

"No, no." Vanessa patted her shoulder. "You sit and enjoy. Figure out your garden center so I can come shopping."

She and Julia took care of every guest as the day wound toward their four-thirty closing time.

Back in the kitchen, Chad loaded the dishwasher, and then ran a sink full of hot soapy water and tossed in pots and pans.

Julia looked faint again, then plopped into a chair, clearly exhausted.

"Aunt Julia?" Vanessa got scared. "What did the doctor say?"

"I have diabetes," she choked.

"Oh." With relief, Vanessa rubbed her aunt's shoulder. "That's not so bad. We can deal with it. I thought you had a heart problem or something, the way you've been getting faint."

"Doc says I need to eat little meals throughout the day."

"That shouldn't be a problem!"

"No desserts," Julia said sadly. "And I can't keep going like I've been. We need to hire some help. We could hire Chad, he does salads and dishes."

Vanessa gaped at her aunt.

At first Chad looked mortified, then he laughed at her expression and Vanessa realized she'd been had by Julia's quirky humor. Chad's appreciation of it endeared him even more in her heart.

"Hire Darla," Chad said. "She bakes a mean apple pie."

Julia wrung her wrinkled hands. She didn't have a prejudiced bone in her body, but Vanessa knew what she was thinking.

"How do you feel about hiring your mother?" her aunt asked.

"Mama's a simple woman with no restaurant experience, but she's been cooking and baking and serving food all her life. At the stable she works with all kinds of people's quirks and demands. She's a hard worker and a quick learner. She'd be a godsend."

"Then it's settled." Julia smiled. "If she wants the job, it's hers. She must be some kind of woman to raise a daughter like you."

"Vanessa, here, is some kind of woman." Chad grinned ear to ear.

Vanessa took one look at the man up to his elbows in suds. The sleeves of his button-down shirt dripped at the edges and his pressed slacks looked a little worse for the wear.

"Oh no!" Then it hit her. "What time is your open house?"

Eyes wide, he peered at the clock. "Five." He made a face.

"You'd better run, young man," the petite shop owner said weakly. "I don't want you to be late on account of me."

"Are you sure you'll be okay?" he asked. "I can't leave you in the lurch."

"Look." Vanessa motioned around the kitchen. "You've already mopped and cleaned and washed the dishes. And got my mama a job." She grinned. "I don't know what we would have done without you."

"That's for certain," Julia said. "Thank you so much, Chad. You're a good boy and Vanessa's lucky to have you."

Vanessa started to get teary eyed and Chad took her hand. Her heart warmed at his kind-hearted understanding.

"Now go take care of your business." She waved him off before she started blubbering and changed her mind. This emotional roller coaster wore on her. "Go."

He looked uncertain, but started for the door. Avoiding the ladies in the dining room, he headed for the back door.

"Aren't you forgetting something?" Vanessa hurried toward him with the platter of pastries. Her eyes filled with love for the most considerate man she knew.

After the open house, Vanessa and Chad stopped to see her mom. Vanessa couldn't wait to ask her to come work at the tea room. With excited eagerness, she knocked on the door before walking in.

"Mama, it's me!" She walked across the empty kitchen to set the kettle on to boil. Finding the tin of Darjeeling tea she'd given Darla for her birthday, she scooped some into a tea strainer while Chad gathered three mugs.

With the kitchen commotion, she expected her mother to appear at any moment. Yet all remained quiet. Darla looked forward to her visits. What was she up to?

"Mama, Chad and I have a surprise for you," she called.

Eerie silence engulfed the house. She and Chad exchanged a look.

"Maybe you'd better go find her." His words were casual but she caught concern in his eyes.

Vanessa walked down the hallway. A door hung open,

revealing the empty bathroom. Her parents' bedroom door was partially closed. With a shiver, she looked behind her for Clyde's ghost.

"Mama, are you all right?" she whispered. After no response, she pushed open the door. Her mother's figure lay on the bed, still as the cool air surrounding her.

Vanessa's heart thumped wildly. Why would her energetic mother be in bed on a Friday evening, when she knew Vanessa was coming? She tiptoed into the room, unsure if her mother was asleep, or ill, or something worse.

A shrieking sound pierced her ears. Jumping, Vanessa screamed. Darla bolted upright, eyes wild and gray hair standing on end.

"What's that?" she screeched.

Mind racing, Vanessa hid behind the door, listening. She groaned with realization.

"It's just the tea kettle," Chad called from the kitchen. The whistle stopped.

"You made tea?" Darla asked. "How long you been here?"

"A few minutes. Didn't you hear me calling? Are you sick?"

Darla shook her head, static hair swaying like a peacock's plume. Her eyes lost their wild fear, settling into a downcast stare. She dragged herself from bed and slouched into a threadbare robe and ratty slippers.

Vanessa led her to the kitchen.

"Evening, Mrs. Gallagher!" Chad set a mug of tea in front of her as she slumped into a chair. "Here you go."

"Thanks." Darla stared into the mug.

"And one for you, sweetie." He handed a mug to Vanessa.

"Thank you." His enthusiasm made Vanessa smile, yet her mother said nothing.

She was never rude to Chad.

"Are you okay, Mama?" Vanessa sat close, worried at her mother's sudden change. Like a pricked balloon, she had deflated to a shriveled shell.

Darla shrugged as Chad placed honey and spoons on the table. He pulled out a chair.

"What happened? Just days ago you were happier than I've ever seen you. Now you seem so depressed." Could she be bipolar? Or was Clyde's death just now sinking in?

"Its true. Hunter thinks I did it." The words came out emotionless and dead.

Vanessa jerked upright and Chad froze.

"Who told you that?" Vanessa grew defensive, angry that some gossip had destroyed her mother's new chance at life.

"He did."

"What?" Vanessa didn't want to believe this. "When?"

"Monday night after supper."

"Where did this happen?" Vanessa had been here right before supper. Her mother had been jollier than ever.

"He came to the house and grilled me."

"What did he want to know?" Vanessa bit back impatience. "He already questioned us at the station."

She shot a bewildered look at Chad. He shrugged and gingerly sat down.

"He asked if I threatened Clyde."

"Why would he think that?" Incredulous, Vanessa couldn't believe anyone would have implicated her. "Clyde's the one who threatened you."

"Apparently Hunter talked to Brian Daniels."

"Ohhhhh." She had forgotten what he'd seen.

"Exactly. I'm done." Darla slumped deeper into the chair, never moving her hands from her lap, still staring into her untouched mug. "Be careful what you wish for. If it comes true you might get blamed."

Stumped and speechless, Vanessa fidgeted.

Chad blew on his tea. Looking thoughtful, he took a sip. Then he set down the mug and sat up straight.

"We need to figure out how to fend off this trumped up investigation."

Darla's eyes rose to his with a glimmer of hope. "You don't think I did it?"

"Of course not." His face filled with caring and hope.

"We all know you didn't do it, Mama." Vanessa's heart warmed. She squeezed her mother's hand and gently kissed her cheek. Then she looked to Chad with a grateful smile.

She stirred honey into her tea. Moving with purpose kept her mind off the harsh reality. She handed her mother a spoon and slid over the honey jar.

"Thank you," Darla said with feeling, taking the spoon. "I

didn't think you cared. You ain't been here all week."

"I didn't know you were this upset, Mama. You were doing so well on Monday." Guilt stabbed her. "I wasn't as worried about you now that Clyde's gone."

"It's mighty peaceful around here." Darla shot a look between Vanessa and Chad. "You been off seeing this boy?"

"I didn't mean to take up all your daughter's time," he said sheepishly.

"Just Wednesday," Vanessa answered. "I've been working late. The tea room's swamped and Julia had doctor appointments."

The jealousy on Darla's face stopped her. The explanation only escalated the problem, as her mother thought she didn't care. Vanessa wouldn't let her mother suffer alone again.

"We had an idea, Mama." She touched Darla's hand.

"We?" she asked skeptically.

"Julia and I need help at the tea room. She's ready to hire someone to cook and bake. Chad suggested you."

Darla blinked – her gaze shifting from Vanessa to Chad and back. Her mouth fell open and her hand went to her throat. "Me? Working at that fancy place?"

"You'd be in the kitchen, baking and cooking to your heart's delight. And it would get you out of that stable."

Her face lit up like a child being handed a lollipop.

Saturday night, Chad took Vanessa to dinner. Thrilled with the heart-to-heart conversation, he listened as she bared her soul.

"Mama accepted the job offer at the tea room!" she triumphed. "I feel so happy and liberated." She grew thoughtful. "Yet guilt and grief over Clyde's death dirty it. I still can't believe he wasn't my father. And the prospect of getting to know my real father scares and delights me at the same time."

"You have a lot of emotions to work through. One day at a time."

"Yeah." She poked at her chocolate silk pie.

The waiter stopped by their table and she asked for a box.

Surprised that she didn't finish her favorite dessert, Chad asked, "Do you still want to go to the home center?"

"Definitely." She visibly fortified herself and slid the pie into the promptly-brought box. With a deep sigh, she seemed to set aside her problems and prepare to move on. She smiled, eyes sparkling with anticipation. "Ready when you are."

He escorted her to the big blue beast in the parking lot.

During their excursion to the home center, he watched in amazement. Sucked into the excitement, she helped him choose hardwood floors, ceramic tiles, and paint colors, flitting from one department to the next.

He guided her from cabinets and counters to light fixtures and faucets, explaining the requirements. She seamlessly coordinated colors and finishes throughout the floor plan. For someone who lived in abject poverty, Chad mused that she had a natural eye for interior decorating.

"This house will be beautiful," she gushed with enthusiasm. "Can we use this one?" she begged, pointing out a gorgeous vanity.

"Why not?" He liked her choices better than his, which tended toward more basic.

Her taste would have a positive effect on sales. And no surprise, she was an expert at budgeting – finding a bargain here to splurge a bit there.

With a quick smile, she pecked his cheek. She took pride in the coordinated decorating plan. He'd rarely seen her so elated, except when he was kissing her, and that was entirely different.

But later, during a quiet moment waiting at the contractor's desk, she scowled at the floor in deep thought.

After signing for the merchandise, he walked her out of the bright store. In the dimly lit parking lot, he held her hand.

"Did you enjoy this?" he asked.

"Yeah, that was fun." Her zeal seemed strained.

He let it go for now. Driving her home, he interrupted bouts of awkward silence with small talk. He walked her up to her door, ready to get to the heart of the matter.

He kissed her tenderly, and then looked into her eyes.

"Can I come in for a while? We can talk," he suggested.

Her eyes darted. "About what?"

"Anything you like." He stroked her cheek reassuringly.

"Sure," she said with a shrug, leading him inside.

Her small apartment was unusually messy. A plate of half-eaten toast, a tea mug, and a pile of unread mail littered the rickety end table. The sheet covering her old sofa pulled off the cushions and colorful throw pillows mashed into a corner. Lint and crumbs dotted the floors. Dirty dishes filled the kitchen sink, and tea dribbled over the eighteen inches of counter.

Hiding his surprise, Chad pulled her to the sofa.

Color rose to her cheeks. "I'm sorry about the mess. It's been a rough week." She bent to smooth the wrinkled sofa.

"I imagine so." Chad took her hands, folding his over them. "Please don't worry about it. I honestly don't care." He stared into her eyes. "*You* are all I care about – how what's happening affects *you.*"

She squirmed, averting his gaze. He pulled her into a hug and held her. She relaxed in his arms like a woman starved for comfort. They sank into the sofa, clinging to one another.

Running his hand down the length of her hair, he felt her shiver. He whispered in her ear. "Talk to me."

She stilled, and then clung tighter. She shook her head. "I don't want to talk about it. Just hold me."

For a long time, he did. He rubbed her back and stroked her hair. Pressing against him, her body begged for more. Desperately tempted to give her what she wanted, he considered chucking his morals. But later he'd regret it.

Chapter 16 – Poison Ivy

"Vanessa," he breathed. "I want you. You know I do."

"Hmmm," she sighed with pleasure.

"We're ready physically, but we're not ready for real commitment." The words poured over them like cooling rain.

She leaned into his warmth, her head on his chest. She sighed with, he hoped, understanding.

"Our relationship can't get to that point until we get to the heart of our feelings. As much I want to comfort you physically, that won't heal your hurt. You're suffering, struggling. To get through it, you need to talk about it."

She lifted her head and rubbed her hand over his chest. She didn't know when to quit, and he loved it.

"It's too hard to talk about." She stared at his shirt. "I don't know what to say. I don't even know where to begin."

"Just tell me how you *feel*."

She met his eyes with a naughty grin. "I *feel* like making love." Her voice lilted like the song.

He groaned. "It's all I can do to resist you, you know. And you're *not* helping." He feigned a scolding.

"I know, I know. But you asked." She smiled wickedly.

"Vanessa." Sorely tempted to carry her into her bedroom, he drew her close and held her tight. *Why was it so difficult to do the right thing?*

"My only good feelings are the ones about you."

She always made him smile. "Wanna start there?" he teased.

"Okay." She ran her fingers over his chest.

He squeezed his eyes shut. Unable to endure the enticement, he stilled her hand. Her jaw moved against his chest with her smile.

"When I'm with you, I feel happy and excited and beautiful. I feel appreciated and respected and not at all like a poor girl from the wrong side of the creek. I'm a better, stronger person and I like myself."

She pulled back to look at him. "Most of all, I feel loved." She searched his eyes. "I love you, Chad."

"Vanessa, I love *you*." He felt so good to finally say it. He held her face, stared into her eyes, and kissed her for all she was worth.

She kissed him with intensity and he met her passion. Breathless, he kissed her face, her hair, and her neck.

"I love you," he whispered in her ear.

She burrowed her face into his neck. His skin grew moist, and he knew she wept with joy. He held her tight, never wanting to let go.

There had to be hope for them, because he loved her so much. God couldn't possibly give him this beautiful gift of her love, and strip it all away. Vanessa had God's spirit in her. He knew she did. Somehow, he'd help her realize that.

Then he'd marry her, because nothing else could stop him.

For a long time, they held each other and reveled in their breathtaking love.

"This is all I want to feel," she said at last. "Everything else is overwhelming, complicated, and sad. It's easier to forget those feelings than deal with them," she admitted.

"I know." He stroked her hair.

"But they won't go away. I don't think they will until I deal with them, but I don't know how."

"Do you want to talk about it?"

She shrugged. "Mostly, I feel guilty, you know?"

He didn't know, not really. He'd read books since discovering her father's abuse, in an attempt to understand. And he knew from his study that she needed to realize he would never treat her with less than the respect she deserved.

It wasn't her fault. Not ever.

But she was finally opening up and he dared not interrupt.

Huddled to his chest, she spoke softly. "It's so confusing. I was supposed to love Clyde because he was my father, at least I thought he was." She picked at the pocket of his shirt. "He raised me as his child."

She pulled away and threw her head back against the couch, staring at the ceiling. Biting her lip, she turned to look out the window across the room.

Chad waited patiently for her to continue.

"I tried to love him, like a good little girl. But I hated how he treated us." Trembling, she wrapped her arms over her belly.

He draped an arm over her shoulders.

"When I found out he wasn't my real father, I was too shocked to respond." She shrugged, blinking back tears. "I think I was still in shock when he died. Now I have this tremendous guilt and I don't know what to do with it."

She needed God's peace. But Chad held his tongue. She wasn't ready to understand the meaning of God's redemption and if he mentioned forgiveness now, she'd think he blamed her, too.

Heaving a sigh, she continued. "On top of that, there's shame, hurt, and anger for how he treated me." She pounded a fist on her thigh.

"He thought I was his daughter, his own flesh and blood, and he treated me that way." Gritting her teeth, she scowled. "Finding out he wasn't my father makes it not as bad, yet he didn't know it at the time, which makes it even worse."

Shaking her head, as if confused, she muttered, "I'm talking in riddles *I* can't even understand."

"Shhh." He smoothed her hair down her shoulder. "Don't beat yourself up. Emotions don't always make sense. We have to acknowledge them to work through them. Just let it out."

With a deep breath, she relaxed. "Thank you for understanding."

"I'm here for you, honey."

He hugged her close and she stilled in his arms. He'd never called her honey before. Heartfelt, it just popped out of his mouth. A warm wet spot spread over his shirt.

Again, he made her cry.

"My mother is the only one who's ever called me that."

What feelings had he conjured?

"Is that good or bad?"

"Good." She pulled back. Wiping her cheeks, she finally looked into his face. "But I don't know who I can trust anymore. My own mother lied to me – for years. She let me think Clyde Gallagher was my father. She gave me his name. As if I was the spawn of that...that monster!"

Burning resentment ignited her eyes. Tears evaporated as her face hardened like heat-tempered steel.

"She was trying to protect you," he said. "Wasn't she afraid of how he'd treat you if he found out you *weren't* his daughter?"

"What could have been worse? He belittled me, he beat me, he raped me!" she cried. "He treated me no differently than Layla and he knew she wasn't his."

Chad didn't know how to react. Vanessa's anger was certainly justified, and he didn't know how to squelch it, or even if he should. Yet he didn't want to add fuel to the fire either. Blinking, he listened as she vented.

"I can't trust my own parents. There's no one I can trust," she vowed adamantly.

"You can trust God." He paused. "And you can trust me."

"God? Frankly, Chad, I have a hard time trusting a God who let me and my mother suffer like that."

"But you believe in God, don't you?" he asked.

"Of course I do." She squirmed from his arms. "But I don't trust Him. I rely on myself alone."

She stood abruptly and stalked toward the kitchen.

"Vanessa, wait." His feeble response did nothing to stop her.

In a flash of running water and flowing dish soap, she clattered dirty dishes in the sink to the point he thought they'd break. Seeing her pain, he didn't challenge her assessment of God. Nor did he get in the way of those flailing elbows and flying plates.

He walked calmly to the kitchen and stood a few feet away.

"Okay, you don't trust God. What about me?"

Rinsing a fistful of silverware, she stopped mid-air. She glared at him for a long moment. Then she shoved the faucet to off and stuffed the silver into a cup on the dish drainer. She grabbed a towel and purposefully dried her hands before placing them firmly on her hips and turning to him.

"You think I can trust you, huh?"

"Y...Yes." She had him so befuddled he stammered.

"Humpf." She leaned against the sink, crossing her arms over her chest. "So you've never lied to me?"

"No. Absolutely not." This time he was steady and firm.

"Okay. So you're honest. I'll give you that because I have no proof otherwise. But your word isn't all there is to it."

"What else is there? Do you think I'm going to cheat on you or something? I'd never do that, Vanessa."

Her gaze bore into his soul. "Good to know, but that's not what I meant. I can't trust someone who doesn't believe in me."

"I believe in you!" He thought they were past this. Why was she bringing up old baggage? "You amaze me, Vanessa. I believe in all your talents and abilities. You're a strong woman."

"But not as strong as you, right? Not as smart either. I still need you to take care of me, look after me, tell me what to do so I don't make bad decisions and screw up my life."

She had him there. He couldn't deny it, not in honesty. Dumbfounded, he stood staring at the dripping dishes. Where had he gone wrong? He'd finally gotten her to share her feelings – and when she did – wow. She bomblasted him.

Maybe those feelings were best left buried.

Yet that wasn't working, either.

"I'm sorry, Chad." Her tone softened. "I feel vulnerable with you and that scares me. I can't deal with it right now."

"I'm just trying to help in the only way I know how." He searched her eyes, his heart heavy with defeat. He wanted so badly for her to turn to him, turn to God, to trust them both.

"I know." She took a step toward him. She stopped before she touched him, shoving her hands into her pockets with determination. "But I need to deal with this on my own."

He'd gotten so close. Then she shut him out.

"It's important to me that you trust me," Chad said sadly.

Her eyes hardened, confirming his fear that she didn't.

"I'm sorry you don't." With that, he tucked tail and turned to the door because he had no idea what else to say without making things worse.

Rumors spread like poison ivy. Climbing vines and creeping tendrils of gossip grew from insidious roots in Crystal Falls.

Vanessa ignored them. Despite an icy October rain, she determined to make her mother's first day at the tea room a delightful one.

Half an hour early, she unlocked the back door of The Porcelain Teapot. She checked the food inventory and started a shopping list. Then she pulled out recipes for cinnamon pecan scones, cream of pumpkin soup, chicken pot pie, and spinach bacon quiche.

As the back door rattled, Vanessa expected to see her mom. Chad walked in instead.

"What are you doing here?" Knowing he was hurt, she couldn't get into their personal affairs at work.

Looking sheepish, he wiped his feet vigorously and shoved his hands into the pockets of his coat. "It's raining. Remember, you asked me to install some shelves next time I needed indoor work?"

"Oh. Yeah." She felt like a heel. Yet she wondered if he would have shown up if they hadn't argued. "Chad, I'm sorry I hurt you. We need to talk. But not here, okay?"

"Of course not." With beseeching eyes, he asked, "When?"

She wanted to hug him but didn't dare – not here, not now.

"I'll call you tonight."

"Okay." His anticipation seemed strained. "What time do you open?"

"Eleven."

Looking nervous, he checked the clock on the wall. "I should be done before then."

"Let me show you where the shelves go." All business, she led him to the gift shop. "Thanks for coming early, before it gets crazy around here."

"I'm sure not coming when this place is full of women." He looked uncomfortable as they walked through the dainty dining room, and in the gift shop filled with china, he held his arms close and seemed to scrunch his tall body as small as he could.

She showed him the alcove where they wanted the shelves and explained how far apart they should be. Then she heard her brother's truck in the alley behind the building.

"Mama's here." She hurried to greet her. Darla appeared with freshly-dyed blonde hair twisted in a neat bun and a hint of blush on her cheeks. She nervously smoothed her new white blouse over crisp black slacks. Her polished black shoes sported rain drops.

"Mornin' Nessa." She grinned from ear to ear. "Do I look all right?"

"Mama, you look beautiful!" Vanessa hugged her tightly. Then she handed her a white chef's apron. "Here. You don't want to ruin your new clothes."

"Wow. I feel so professional." She put on the apron and

looked herself over.

"You *look* professional, Ms. Darla." Chad came through like he was walking on eggshells. He smiled at Darla's new look. "And downright pretty too." With a wink, he was out the door.

Darla beamed. She tilted her head in question with a mischievous look in her eyes. Vanessa knew that teasing look, but wouldn't allow her feelings for Chad to sidetrack her at work.

"Chad's putting up some shelves in the gift shop. Let's get you started."

Darla looked around anxiously. "Where's Julia?"

"She'll be here soon. You're a little early."

Chad returned with an encouraging smile at her mom. He uneasily laid a long sheet of plastic to cover his path across the hardwood floors. Careful not to touch anything, he worked quietly and scooted back out.

Vanessa showed Darla the eight-burner stove, four convection ovens, and enormous refrigerator. Impressed, her mother adored the large triple sink with a window overlooking Crystal Creek and the patio where they set up tables in the summer. The pantry stocked with giant containers of food made her gasp.

"I'm in over my head."

"Nope, it's the same as cooking at home. Everything's just bigger," Vanessa assured her. "If I can do it, you can do it. Mondays are slow. You'll have time to get the hang of it. By the end of the week, you'll be a whiz." She tried to boost her mother's confidence but Darla's only reply was a worried smile.

Chad came back through. He tiptoed over the plastic, holding an armload of wood close to his chest while carrying a toolbox at arm's length in front of him as he traveled the narrow path.

"Let me show you what he's up to." Vanessa led her mother through the butler's pantry that separated the kitchen from the public areas. The dining room lay before them in all its splendor.

Darla sucked in a breath. "This is like I've died and gone to heaven." With a hand over her gaping mouth, she stared at the antique tables and chairs, gorgeous paintings, and lush ferns filling each corner. Lacy curtains framed floor to ceiling windows glistening with raindrops.

Vanessa particularly appreciated the hunky carpenter in the corner, although she wished he didn't look like he wanted to bolt. She stepped through a wide doorway toward the gift shop out front.

Her mother froze. "Look at that." She stared at an antique buffet and hutch displaying every manner of teapot, teacup, and accoutrement. "It's beautiful." Darla touched the carved wood, eyeing colorful tins of tea, jams, curds, and scone mixes stashed on the bottom shelf.

"As you can see, we could use more shelf space." She grinned at Chad.

He raised an eyebrow but kept on working.

"If you want to buy something, you get a twenty-five percent discount," Vanessa said.

"I can't believe I work here," Darla croaked. "I feel like a bull in a china shop."

Chad laughed. "How do you think I feel?"

Vanessa shook her head. "Then let's start baking," she said to her mom. "You'll feel at home in no time." She motioned to Chad. "I'm not sure that guy will ever be at home here."

He chuckled. As they entered the kitchen, Julia slipped in the door.

"Darla! It's been ages." She walked briskly to greet her with a hug. "Vanessa assured me she learned everything about cooking from you. And Chad raved over your piecrust."

"Thank you." Darla looked pale.

Hammering sounded from the front room.

"I saw Chad's truck out there," Julia said. "Is he building our new shelves?"

"Yes."

"Good." With a smile, she turned to Darla. "Vanessa will help you with everything you need to know." She turned to Vanessa. "So what's on the shopping list?"

Vanessa produced the lengthy list.

"Be back in a jiffy." Julia breezed back out the door.

"What now?" Darla's voice grew high and thin. Worry in her eyes belied her lack of confidence.

Vanessa walked her through baking scones, starting soup, and preparing pot pie and quiche in large quantities. They baked desserts and frosted chocolate tortes.

When Julia returned, they helped carry in groceries. Then Chad's sister Rachel delivered the teacup centerpieces from Rosebuds Flower Shop.

Darla set the tables and then helped Vanessa cook while Julia prepared salads, created garnishes, and answered the phone.

Chad completed the shelves, cleaned up his mess, and emerged from the restroom with washed hands, combed hair, and a smile.

"Okay, I'll get out of the way before you open." He seemed anxious to leave.

"Do you have time to fix a broken drawer in the kitchen while you're here?" Vanessa asked.

"Oh." His eyes shifted. "Sure, if I won't be in the way."

"I'm thrilled to have you stick around." Tempted to kiss his cheek, she settled for a flirty wink.

At eleven o'clock sharp, they opened.

A typically slow October Monday, patrons trickled in.

In her element, Darla adorned salads with sugared grapes and garnished plates with fresh parsley. She decorated desserts with chocolate curls and saucy swirls.

Julia seemed much less anxious and Vanessa wasn't running a hundred miles an hour. The tea room's entire atmosphere felt calm and peaceful. Chad looked handsome and thoughtful, though cramped, working on the broken drawer in the kitchen.

"The scones are particularly delicious today," Angelina Mitchell complimented Vanessa.

"Why thank you." Vanessa said. "Julia hired help with lots of biscuit baking experience. My mom."

"Your mother!" Margaret Hunter looked surprised.

"May I give my compliments to the cook?" Angelina asked.

"I'm sure she could spare a moment," Vanessa said proudly.

In the kitchen, Darla sprinkled toasted pumpkin seeds on top of a steaming bowl of pumpkin soup.

"Some of our patrons want to compliment the cook."

Darla's jaw dropped.

"Come on, time to meet your loyal fans." Julia led a stunned Darla into the dining room. The hum of conversation quieted and all eyes looked up.

"This is our new cook, Darla Gallagher," Julia introduced her as the front door jingled.

Myrtle Winthrop marched through the doorway indignantly. Julia placed a protective hand on Darla's arm.

"What's *she* doing here?" Myrtle screeched.

"She's my *fabulous* new cook!" Julia bragged.

Glaring, Myrtle scrutinized Darla from the hair falling from her bun to the pumpkin stains on her apron to the flour sprinkled on her shoes.

"Just look at that lowdown tramp from the underbelly of society, trying to act all respectable after she killed her husband and stole my man!"

Chapter 17 – Pumpkin-Stained Apron

Chad appeared, standing tall and authoritative. "Ms. Gallagher did no such thing, and that kind of talk is not welcome here."

The elderly woman paled. He seized her arm and marched her back outside in the rain.

"This is far from over!" Myrtle vowed as the door slammed in her face.

A collective gasp rose from the small crowd. Tea sloshed, mouths gaped, and all eyes stared at Darla.

She froze. Wild-eyed, she blushed tomato red. As she turned to run, Vanessa reached for her arm but she was too fast.

Hand to her forehead, Julia's eyes rolled up in her head.

Chase Mama or catch Aunt Julia? Vanessa flew to Julia's side and buffered her fall. Darla bolted from the room. The back door banged on its hinges with striking finality.

On the front step, Chad released Myrtle with a reprimand.

"Go home and don't come back. And leave Ms. Gallagher alone!"

"Like I said, this is far from over." She tipped her pointy nose into the air and stomped off to her dress shop next door.

Chad turned to go back inside when he spotted Darla huffing down the sidewalk in the pouring rain. Torn between running after her and going back inside to check on Vanessa, he really didn't want to face those women inside again. Yet his concern for Vanessa made him stick his head inside the tea room door.

Albino white, Vanessa fussed over Julia, slumped in a chair.

Holy cow. Three women in crisis and which one to help?

He rushed to Vanessa. Hushed murmurs and wide eyes surrounded them.

"Your mom's walking home in the rain," he whispered. "Should I give her a ride or do you need me here?"

"Oh, Chad, please go after her. You're a lifesaver." Her color returned and her eyes filled with love. Fresh hope welled in his heart as he ran out the back to his truck.

One way streets circled Crystal Falls Square. Darla headed the opposite direction. Chad drove slowly around the square, catching up to her coming at him. Tears streamed down her red face.

He pulled to the side of the road. Traffic backed up behind him, but he didn't care. He cranked down the window and stuck his head out in the rain.

"Ms. Darla, let me give you a ride."

She walked right past as if she didn't hear him. Cars honked. He stuck an arm out to wave them around. As soon as traffic cleared, he backed up to her. She knew he was there but she kept walking and neared the corner.

Chad stopped, shifted into forward gear, and pulled the truck to the edge of the road with the four ways on. He hopped out and ran through the rain, chasing a fifty-year-old woman in a soaking wet apron covered with pumpkin stains.

Looking ridiculous, he only cared about helping Darla. He caught up to her.

"Come on, Ms. Darla. Let me give you a ride home."

She looked up at him. Her pretty blonde hair dripped in her eyes. "Home? You'd take me home?"

"Yes." He wrapped his arm around her shivering shoulders. "Let me take you home." She let him turn her around. They walked back to the truck in no hurry. They were already drenched. "You'll be lucky if you don't catch your death of cold out here," he said.

She sputtered a laugh. "You sound like somebody's mother."

"Well, everybody needs a mother sometimes." He looked down at himself. "Don't know if I qualify, though."

She looked up at him and smiled. "Chad James, my daughter is right lucky to have a man like you." Then she sobered. "But she doesn't need *her* mother. She has Julia Calvin," she said bitterly.

"That's not true. Vanessa needs you. But Julia fainted and Vanessa can't leave the tea room. She asked me to come after you."

Darla stared at the ground. "She probably wanted you to take me back there." Her face contorted with shame. "I'm *never* going back there."

By closing time, patrons were stopping in to ask about Julia.

No one asked about Darla. Her non-existence in this town plagued Vanessa like an itch she couldn't scratch. Chad and his family seemed the only ones who didn't feel that way. Thank goodness Chad was always there for her.

Vanessa was anxious to check on her mother after work. Chad called to let her know Darla was home safe and sound. He'd asked if she needed help, but Vanessa and Julia had it under control.

Julia was fine once she drank some orange juice and ate a slice of quiche. She'd forgotten to eat again. Coupled with Myrtle's outburst, she simply fainted.

Thankfully, Chad dealt with that wicked woman. But Vanessa heard her parting words. *This is far from over.*

She cringed, thinking what Myrtle would do next to get revenge on Darla.

Glad when the day was over, Vanessa vacuumed the dining room as Julia composed a letter to Myrtle, warning her not to return or she'd call the police. She signed it with a flourish.

Julia was adamant. "I won't have that nonsense in my shop. My patrons don't appreciate it and my health can't take it."

"Amen." Vanessa hugged her boss, her friend – her aunt!

As she finished closing chores, Chad popped in the back door. Her insides fluttered and she felt her face glow. She rushed into his arms.

"My hero." She laid her head on his chest as he wrapped his arms around her. "Thank you so much."

"You're welcome." He ran his hands up her back and stroked her long hair. "How are you doing?"

"Much better now," she said into his rain spattered coat.

"Good. Do you need some help?"

"No, I'm about done." She looked up at him. "I really want to see you but I need to check on Mama."

"Want me to come?" He smoothed hair from her face.

"I'd better go alone. She might need some undivided attention."

"I understand." He smiled. "How about later? Can I get some

undivided attention, too?"

"Of course." She kissed his nose. "I should be home by nine."

"See you then." He bent to kiss her, long and sweet. Then he was gone.

On the doormat of her mother's house, Vanessa was greeted by Darla's once shiny black shoes, tossed aside and smudged with rain-spotted flour. The pumpkin-stained apron hung over a kitchen chair.

Huddled in a corner of the sofa, her mother stared mindlessly into the darkened room. The curtains were drawn against a gray sky.

A cold mug of tea sat beside her with the teabag still steeping. The microwave blinked unused seconds. Lee must have checked on her. Darla never made tea in the microwave and neither did Chad.

The television droned some ridiculous teenage "reality" show her mother would never watch. Vanessa snapped it off.

"Myrtle won't be back. You don't have to worry about that ever happening again." Vanessa pulled warm chicken sandwiches from a bag.

"I won't be back, either. So you don't have to worry about me shaming you ever again."

"Mama, you didn't shame me. We need you."

Darla narrowed her eyes without focusing. "You don't need me. You're better off without me."

"No, we're not."

"We?" Darla screeched. "I'm talking about *you*, girl. You got Julia, you got Chad, you don't need me."

"But Mama – " Vanessa stopped, realizing this wasn't about the job. "Of course I need you. You're my mama."

"Don't matter. You have Chad now. And you have *Aunt Julia*. They're more important."

"Why would you say that?"

"You don't have time to spend with your man if you're here worrying over your mama all the time. You don't need this." Darla waved an arm at the shabby surroundings. Then she turned with an eerie glare. "As for Julia, today you made your choice. You started after me, then turned to Julia instead."

"You mean when she fainted?" Incredulous, Vanessa couldn't

believe the accusation. "Mama, I was afraid Julia would lapse into a diabetic coma. As much as I wanted to run after you, her condition was urgent. With her health problems, she's ready to quit. She needs rest, but she won't leave me hanging. She was delighted to have your help at the tea room. I can't tell you how happy and relieved she is that I'll be working with someone we can trust."

"Don't gimme that act. It ain't the first time you chose her over me. Nobody loves me best. Story of my life."

"For crying out loud," Vanessa mumbled under her breath. "I'm here now, Mama. I came to spend time with you."

"You should be with Chad, going out and having fun. Not fussing over your old mother. You don't need to waste your time with obligatory visits like some duty."

"Mama, it's not a duty. I love you and care about you."

"You can't honestly tell me you wouldn't rather be with Chad right now." Darla read her eyes. "And I don't blame you."

Frustrated, Vanessa couldn't deny it and grew tired of arguing. Her nerves were already raw from the brutal day.

"Mama, here's a sandwich. Why don't we eat something?"

"Don't patronize me! I don't need your leftover food or your leftover time."

Vanessa couldn't take it any more. "Suit yourself." She packed up her own sandwich and headed for the door. "See you in the morning."

"I won't be there." Darla crossed her arms over her chest and stared at a spot on the wall.

"I hope you change your mind," Vanessa spoke softly. She left the apron hanging in the kitchen and walked out.

Although it wasn't quite nine that evening, Chad was grateful to see the little Chevy parked behind the darkened tea room instead of over at the bait shop. He bounded the steps two at a time and banged on Vanessa's door.

It cracked open.

"I could recognize that banging in my sleep," she muttered.

"Can I come in?" He pushed the door wider, tentatively awaiting an answer.

Her shrug was all he needed. He closed the door behind him and removed his work boots. Little clumps of mud fell on the floor.

"Sorry. Got a broom?"

"Don't worry about it." She rubbed her red, puffy eyes. "What's up?"

Plopped on the couch with the remote in her hand, she made no offer of food or drink. At least she turned down the volume on her cooking show. The apartment was neater than the last time he was over, smelling of air freshener and fabric softener.

Usually the epitome of hospitality, she silently watched television.

"I take it things didn't go well with your mom."

She didn't even smile. Just another shrug.

He took the liberty of sitting at the opposite end of her sofa. She eyed a steaming mug on the table in front of her. Sprinkled with cinnamon, a dollop of whipped cream swirled into the creamy brown liquid.

"I'm sorry about what happened at the tea room today," he offered.

"The talk of Crystal Falls." She fiddled with the belt of her old purple robe.

"You had a pretty rough day." He laid the bait but she didn't bite.

It was half past eight and she looked ready for bed. With her hair pulled up in a clip, blonde tendrils on her neck dripped as if she'd just taken a bath. She smelled like flowers and soap. He wanted to grab her and kiss her into oblivion.

"Vanessa, please talk to me."

She blinked several times, crossing her arms over her belly as if comforting herself.

"Your whipped cream is melting."

Apparently so was her heart. She nearly leapt across the sofa and enveloped him a bear hug. He held her tight, relieved the tension was gone at last. She hugged him a long time before coming up for air.

"Would you like a cup of chai?"

"I thought you'd never ask."

She grabbed her cup and bustled off to the kitchen. In no time she hurried back to his side with a whipped cream embellished mug for him and a fresh dollop of cream on her own. Hands wrapped around the warm cup, she sank into the sofa pressing her soft thigh against his.

"Mama's really upset," she said into the mug.

He savored the sweet spicy tea, waiting for her to talk.

"You know, it's bad enough Myrtle accused Mama of killing Clyde, which is a lie, but she has a lot of nerve saying she stole her man. Baldy was never her man. Myrtle dated Baldy back before he met my mama, but Myrtle left Baldy for Clyde."

Chad nodded. The Gallagher/Calvin feud was legendary, starting with the parents fighting over land and culminating with their sons, Clyde and Baldy, fighting over women.

Yet he got the feeling a lot more was bothering Vanessa than Myrtle. But he let her deal with it her way. "I heard Clyde and Myrtle broke up, and then he stole Darla from Baldy."

"Yeah." She nodded. "Myrtle fired up the feud, instigating Clyde to go after Mama to hurt Baldy. She figured she would get Baldy back, but he was in love with Mama and heart broken. After what Myrtle did, he wanted nothing to do with her."

She stared into her cup. "Meanwhile Clyde got Mama pregnant. She was ashamed and they didn't talk about it back then. They got married right away before anyone figured it out."

"Wow. That's really sad." Chad hadn't heard that side of the story. "I can't believe she stayed with him all those years."

"She was completely traumatized and afraid. Her only reprieve was sneaking to see Baldy."

"So he never got back with Myrtle?"

"No. That's why she married that rich banker."

"Poor Winthrop never knew what hit him," Chad said. "She manipulated him for money, refused to give him children, and drove him to his grave."

Vanessa made a face. "Now she's old and lonely, and wants Baldy back. He finally forgave her and needed a friend, but he still loves my mama. Myrtle wants more than he can give."

"And she's not happy about it," Chad concluded.

"All these unhappy people who never did what they wanted," Vanessa concluded. "Everyone is so bitter. Myrtle tried to ruin everything and may have succeeded. Now Mama refuses to come back to the tea room."

"Do you think she'll come back eventually?"

"I hope so. Julia can't work like she used to," Vanessa lamented. "It's all falling on me and I can't do it alone."

"Why not hire someone else?"

"If we do, Mama won't ever come back. She'd probably go back to the stable and never get out of there."

"Uh, I don't think that'll happen," Chad said.

"You don't know Mama. She's always said horses are easier to deal with than people. She's stubborn."

"Unfortunately, so is Myrtle. She went to the horse farm today."

"What?" Vanessa's head spun toward him. "What was she doing there?"

"Getting her revenge." Chad hated to break the news, but better this way than have Darla run back with her tail between her legs and get pushed down in the dirt.

"She wouldn't..." She set her mug on the table and turned to face him. With narrowed eyes, she asked, "What did Myrtle do?"

"She told the new owner what happened at the tea room – from her unique point of view, of course. Right in front of the kids taking lessons – and their parents – she spouted off that your mother abused her own kids and shouldn't be trusted around children and animals. Basically, she made sure your mother wouldn't have a job to go back to."

Vanessa brought a hand up to her mouth. "I can't believe this. If the old owner hadn't died this never would have happened. He'd have known better than to believe Myrtle."

"Heard she was pretty convincing. Guess for good measure, she made a hefty donation to the Ponies for Palsy program."

"The nerve of that woman!" Growling, she clenched her fists. "My mother started that program."

"Really?"

"Yes!" She gritted her teeth, and shook her head.

"Tell me about it." He took her hands and pried them open. Her jaw relaxed a bit.

"One of the neighbor boys had cerebral palsy." She frowned at the floor. "He came to the farm everyday, watching other kids take lessons as he leaned on the fence. Mama felt so sorry for him, she asked the trainer to let him ride just once."

"Good for her!"

"Kid took to riding like a bird in the air." She smiled. "Pretty soon half the kids at the special needs school were taking lessons."

"No kidding?"

"Yeah. They honored my mom for starting the program."

"Impressive. Darla's a smart woman. She'll be all right."

Vanessa scooted away, arms crossed and silent. He saw her anguish and frustration, but she clammed up and shut down.

"There's more to it, isn't there? Talk to me Vanessa."

Bunching her fists, she scowled. "She's not all right, Chad." She pounded a fist on her thigh. "You don't know how depressed she's been. This will crush her."

"I know it's been rough." He reached over to take her hand but she pulled away. "Your mom will get past this."

"Ha. That's what I thought." She hung her head. "She was doing so well after the funeral. Last week I figured she'd be fine now that Clyde's gone. By Friday night when I finally showed up, she was dragging bottom. Her husband just died, Chad. And I totally ignored her. She thought I didn't care."

"She knows that's not true." Chad touched her face. "I know your mom is hurting, but please don't blame yourself."

"I need to be there for her and I let her down. I just don't know what to do. I don't know if I'll be able to spend so much time with you."

"I understand. Your mom needs you right now." Chad fought disappointment. They had very little time together already. The idea of spending even less time alone upset him.

"I'm going to spend evenings with her again. Just to make sure she's all right."

"Every evening?" He couldn't hide his surprise.

Vanessa nodded. "Yeah, for a while."

"How long is a while?" he wondered aloud.

"Well, I don't know Chad. Until she's better." Her voice took an edge of irritation.

"That could be a long time," he said sadly.

"I know." She looked apologetic but determined. "I'll spend the weekends with her, too."

"We won't be able to see each other at all?" Shocked, he fought frustration but it came through his voice.

"You're welcome to visit her with me. And she goes to bed early, we can see each other after nine."

"You should be able to live your own life," he blurted.

"This *is* my life!" Angry exasperation filled her voice. "Don't tell me what to do!"

"Vanessa, come on." Not that slippery slope again. "We've

been here before. I'm simply hoping to spend more time with you, yet lately, it's been less. If you spend every evening and weekend with your mom, what about me?"

He raked a hand through his short hair, unsure whether to voice his thoughts yet convinced she needed to hear them.

"If you allow it, Darla will be running your life, much like Clyde did. Don't let her manipulate you."

"Why not," Vanessa exploded, "so you can?"

The words hit him like punch in the stomach.

"I finally have freedom from my controlling father – " She shook her head. "Stepfather – that monster who raised me – and I refuse to let you take over where he left off."

Chapter 18 – Forbidden Love

Stunned, Chad backed away. He stood speechlessly, refusing to sit there and take her insults. He strode to the door and let himself out, boots in hand.

On the bottom step, he thumped down to put his boots on. As he laced them, he second-guessed himself. Again.

Was she right? Was he really trying to run her life? He didn't mean to. He just wanted her to…to what?

Taking a long hard look at the situation, he recognized the pattern. Darla didn't *expect* Vanessa to be at her beck and call.

He did.

Chad drove slowly, not eager to face his empty house alone. On Rose Hill Drive, he passed Old Baldy's house. The TV glowed through a window. Ironic if the old folks worked it out with all that baggage, yet he and Vanessa couldn't seem to.

How did *he* get so much baggage? He was supposed to be a normal American guy from a stable family, a hard-working, successful businessman, not some Neanderthal that needed to pull a woman around by the hair of the head.

Windows on the first floor of his parents' farmhouse glowed with warm light. Just inside the front porch, his father's head rose above an open newspaper. He could bet his mother was either in the kitchen baking something yummy or by the fire with her nose in a book.

Chad pulled in their driveway. Bounding onto the porch, he caught his dad's glimpse over the paper.

A bright smile filled his father's face as he pushed up from the recliner. The door burst open.

"Chad! Good to see you, son!" John gripped his shoulder with affection and pulled him inside. "Come on in."

A heavenly cinnamon aroma wafted through the house. His mother sat in a cushy armchair near the crackling hearth, a colorful hardback in her hands and bifocals perched on her nose.

"Hello, Chad." With a wide smile, she rose, not as quickly as she used to, and hugged him tight. "I have apple crisp in the oven," she whispered in his ear like it was some secret. Then she kissed his neck. "It should be ready in ten minutes or so but you'll have to wait for it to cool a bit."

How comfortably predictable.

Chad made small talk about business and the weather until the oven timer dinged. Emily shuffled off to the kitchen.

On cue, his father asked, "So how's Vanessa?" The man could read his mind.

"She's having a rough time," Chad answered. "I suppose you heard what happened at the tea room today."

"Yes. And at the farm."

"News travels fast. Word is, Myrtle's out for revenge."

"Big surprise." John scratched his jaw. "How's Darla?"

"She's a mess. Vanessa's trying to help her as much as possible." Tight-lipped as he was, Chad was desperate for advice and he had no time for games. Thanks to Vanessa, he knew how it felt to badger information from someone. So he spilled his guts. "Which means we don't see much of each other right now."

"How are you handling that?" John asked with compassion.

"Not well," Chad admitted. "We had an argument tonight."

His dad nodded knowingly. "I knew something was stewing."

"How do you do that?"

John chuckled. "Reading people comes with age, my boy. 'Specially with your own kids. I've known you from birth and you're just like me, I can surely read you by now."

Dad wasn't the only one. His mother puttered in the kitchen far longer than necessary to remove a pan from the oven. Now she was sweeping her spanking clean floor.

"I just want to help her. I offer suggestions, but she says I'm controlling."

John belly-laughed.

"You're such a big help." Chad felt miserable.

His dad's laughter subdued to a chuckle. "Sorry, son. But I

always did say you were just like your grandma. Bull-headed and tough as nails."

"Thanks a lot, Dad. But that has nothing to do with being controlling."

"When you force those bull-headed ideas on someone else it does."

"I'm not trying to do that," he defended himself.

"Apparently the jury's still out."

Chad huffed a sigh.

"Look, son, I admire your determination. You run a successful business and your male friendships thrive. But the drive that gives you strength and ambition can drive a woman away if you're not careful."

"Then what do I do? How do I help her?"

"Vanessa's a delicate little girl, not a construction worker. Oh, she's tough. Being brought up by Clyde Gallagher she's had to be, but under all that bravado she's a dainty young woman. Win her heart softly."

Softly wasn't part of Chad's description of himself. Soft was for bunnies and pillows and vanilla ice cream.

"You look confused," John said.

"Women and children are soft, not grown men."

"But you can have a soft heart, an understanding attitude."

"I'm trying to understand, but you need to stop talking in riddles. Give me something concrete, Dad. What the heck does 'win her heart softly' mean?"

John smiled. "Keep in mind the way Vanessa thinks and works. Surely you've seen her at the tea room in all her feminine glory, full of elegance and grace."

"Well, I ordered some pastries. I help her out, work on the place, but no self-respecting male would actually eat there."

"I eat there!" John puffed out his chest. "I took your mother for her birthday. The quiche is delicious."

A low chuckle emanated from the kitchen. That sneak was listening in!

His father glared at her and she disappeared onto the back porch.

Chad was still processing the news. His father, the man he respected most in the world, not only ate at the tea room, he ordered *quiche*.

"What a guy," he said sarcastically.

"I do what I can to support my woman and see her point of view. If you want to win Vanessa, you will, too."

"Yeah, but eating at the tea room?"

"If you want a serious relationship, you'd better get comfortable with what she does for a living. She certainly takes an interest in your line of work."

"Hey, she likes helping me choose fixtures and flooring. She's good at it too."

"Sure, but she's willing to tromp through muddy jobsites, too. You like eating, but you're not willing to get past the dainty china to get the food. Not to mention Vanessa's heart – and all her other parts." He blushed.

Chad had begrudgingly turned down all her other parts, no matter how available they were. At this rate, he'd never get the chance to appreciate them.

Maybe he'd better listen and try to keep an open mind.

"Do you really think I'd understand her better if I ate at the tea room?" He knew how much she loved it, and the pastries were delicious. Someday she'd own the place.

"Don't you think her interest in your work helps her understand you better?"

Vanessa had practically begged to help decorate his model home out at the lake. While he'd helped her at the tea room and ordered pastries, he was embarrassed and uncomfortable there.

"Yeah, I guess you're right. So do they serve something other than quiche?"

"Why don't you go down there and find out?"

"Okay. There's always dessert and a cup of tea. Suppose they'd serve it in something other than a porcelain teapot?"

John laughed. "The very name of the place defies that."

Chad sighed miserably. "Okay, okay. I'll win her heart 'softly.' Hopefully I won't turn soprano by trying."

Tuesday morning, Darla didn't show at the tea room. Vanessa rushed to the bait shop as soon as she got off work, determined to persuade her to come back. She hoped her mother hadn't gone back to the horse farm.

Junior's – check that – *L ee's* pickup truck sat in the driveway with Brandy's little sports car beside it. They didn't usually hang out at Mama's.

Something was wrong.

Vanessa's senses tingled with alarm. She ran inside.

"Nessa, I'm glad you're here." Lee sighed with relief. Deep creases lined his forehead as he paced the kitchen.

Looking distraught, Brandy shifted her weight from one foot to the other, back and forth, as she leaned against the sink.

Vanessa scanned the front room. "Where's Mama?"

"Sleeping. She couldn't take it anymore."

An ear-splitting crash reverberated from the bedroom.

Flying down the hallway, Vanessa felt a chill course through her. She nearly fainted at the sight of her mother. Covered in blood, Darla slashed at her wrist with a shard of glass.

Lee grabbed the glass shard and tossed it to the floor where a mirror lay broken.

Frantic, Vanessa ran for towels. Wide-eyed and shaking, Brandy dialed 911 on her cell phone. They couldn't afford an ambulance but Vanessa was too traumatized to care.

"Why Mama?" she cried for answers as she wrapped a tourniquet around her mother's trembling arm. "Why would you do this to yourself?"

"Hunter thinks I killed Clyde," Darla moaned.

"You didn't kill him," Lee said adamantly.

"It's my fault Clyde's dead. If I hadn't kicked him out of the house..." Her voice trailed off with misery.

"No, Mama." Lee clenched his fists. "This is nonsense. Those hoodlums at the pool hall probably pushed him. He had gambling debts, you know."

Darla's eyes hooded as she looked at her son with tremendous sadness.

"Hunter will find out who killed him." Vanessa stroked her mother's hair. "This will all be over soon, and you have so much to live for! You and Baldy have a bright future ahead of you."

Darla shook her head. "Baldy has always loved me, but that doesn't change my reality. They want to condemn the house and close down the bait shop. What about Lee?"

"Who wants to condemn the house?"

Her brother held up an official-looking pink notice. "The county wants her to put on a new roof, new siding, fix the gutters, and remove the outhouse!" He wadded the paper into a ball and hurled it at the wall.

"This is Myrtle's doing, sure as you're standing here," Lee's voice boomed in the tiny room. "She started some petition with the lake homeowners to shut down the bait shop. 'Cuz it attracts 'undesirables.'"

"Revenge," Darla murmured. "Myrtle swore she'd get revenge."

Vanessa gasped. That woman had hit Darla's livelihood and now her home.

"You can live with me and work in the tea room." Vanessa offered hope. She'd wanted that all along.

"I won't be a burden to you, an embarrassment. Thanks to Myrtle, I can't even show my face in this town."

"You are *not* a burden, and you've never been an embarrassment." Anger swelled in Vanessa. How dare Myrtle shame her mother that way.

"How will Lee make a living?" Darla wailed. "My son – " She fell to his feet and wrapped her arms around his legs like a woman begging for mercy. "I'm so sorry. It's all my fault."

Lee's face turned hard as he fought emotion.

Vanessa's thoughts whirled. There was more to this than on the surface.

She blamed herself for Clyde's death and everything she did made her look guilty.

The autopsy proved he'd been beaten. Mama had no strength to get the best of him, no marks indicating she'd been in a fight.

Why would she draw attention away from finding the real killer?

Realization dawned. Mama was too worried about Lee. He'd made his own way for years and she'd never been an obsessive mother. Vanessa froze, horrified.

Her mother thought Lee killed Clyde.

"I can't live with this," Darla wailed. "I might as well be dead!"

"Mama, don't let them stomp you into the ground. You gotta stand up and fight," Lee told her.

Vanessa blinked. She couldn't believe he'd quoted his father.

Darla stared at him with an incredulous expression.

"Don't look at me like that," he said. "That's one thing Clyde was right about. Maybe the only thing, but you gotta stand up and fight."

Darla went limp and her eyes rolled back in her head.

"Mama, nooooo!" Vanessa screamed. "Where's that ambulance?" She tightened the tourniquet as sirens wailed in the distance.

At the hospital, Vanessa, Lee, and Brandy found a quiet corner of the lobby to sit away from everyone else. With an unopened magazine on her lap, Vanessa stared out the window into the dark. Lights twinkled throughout the city of Springfield, but the light in her heart had nearly gone out.

She'd just lost the man she grew up thinking was her father. As much as he mistreated her, he'd been a part of the life she'd left behind. Reeling with loss, she couldn't bear to lose her mother.

The foundation of her life was crumbling and she had no control over it. When would the doctor come out and tell her Mama was okay? She wanted to see Darla, to tell her how much she loved her, and how life was worth living.

Beside her, Lee's sniffling turned to full-fledged sobs.

In horror, she watched her brother break down. Lee never cried. Even as a child, she'd never seen him cry. He stood up to Clyde, and stuck around the bait shop to protect his mother. He'd been strong every day of his life.

To see him cry now was Vanessa's undoing. Tears, long held at bay, now tumbled forth without restraint.

Brandy scooted closer to Lee and wrapped her arms around him. She calmly placed his head on her chest and kissed his hair. Tears spilled freely as her embrace muffled his sobs.

Uncomfortable with her brother's pain, Vanessa looked away. Her gaze scanned the deserted darkness outside as she wiped her tears. Banning all thoughts from her brain, she forced herself to open the magazine. She mindlessly turned pages but the pictures wouldn't focus and the words were just a blur.

Finally she sensed movement beside her. His tears spent, Lee sat up straight. Brandy handed him a tissue.

Seeming embarrassed, he said, "I'm supposed to protect her. She's my mother. But I don't know how to protect her from this."

"She's my mother, too," Vanessa said. "I didn't protect her

either."

"It's not your fault," Brandy spoke softly but adamantly. "All you can do is love her, and you've both done that. The grief and loss she's feeling has nothing to do with you."

"I thought it'd be better now that he's gone," Lee admitted. "But Clyde still haunts her." He ground his teeth and looked at Vanessa. "Be glad he's not your father. You're not tainted. That shame rests on me alone."

"That shame rests on Clyde alone," Brandy corrected.

One corner of his mouth turned down, but he didn't argue.

Vanessa touched his arm. "I'm still your sister. We're in this together."

"Thanks, sis." A smile lit his eyes but didn't quite reach his mouth. "Mama married him because of me. Clyde told me he got her pregnant on purpose to force her into marrying him."

"What a horrible thing to tell your child!" Brandy hissed. "How dare he dump that guilt on you."

Lee shrugged. "I can't really blame Mama for resenting me."

"She does *not* resent you!" Vanessa insisted.

"Don't let him haunt you, too," Brandy warned. "Your mother loves you very much. I've seen it in her face and heard it in her voice. Any resentment she feels is toward your father alone."

Lee looked into her eyes, as if reading their sincerity. Then he nodded. "I've carried this guilt for years and it's not going away overnight." He stood. "I need some air. Come get me if the doctor shows up, okay?"

Brandy and Vanessa both nodded as he headed outside.

As the waiting room doors slid closed, Vanessa realized how much her brother had grown since he met Brandy Kennedy. With her gentle teaching, he was learning to love.

"You're really good for him," she praised the redhead beside her.

"Thanks," Brandy said. "He's really good for me, too."

"Oh yeah?" Vanessa smiled. "So how'd my brother wind up with a woman like you?"

"We met at Brian's office," Brandy said with a chuckle.

"You're kidding!"

"Nope. Lee came in to ask about permits for a campground."

"He did?" Vanessa was impressed. "He's been talking about that for years."

"Yeah. Well, Brian blew him off, angry to be disturbed during his lunch break. I only had a half hour to spend with him and had to get back to work."

"You work for Chad's brother-in-law, don't you?"

"Uh huh. Elliot's great. You know, he warned me about Brian's dark side. I'd never seen it until I broke up with him."

Vanessa remembered how he threatened Lee that day at the bait shop. The day he'd witnessed her mother threatening Clyde.

Brandy's face turned dreamy. "The minute I met your brother – I knew there was something genuine about him. He's unlike anyone I've ever met – mild-mannered, shy, unassuming. I was fascinated with that country bumpkin."

"I'm sure he felt the same way. You have a caring heart and a generous soul." Vanessa glanced at Brandy's trendy blouse. It fit in all the right places. "Not to mention a great sense of style. I wish I had the guts to dress like that." Maybe if she were more blatantly sexual, Chad would forget that moral code of his.

"That's not why I asked her out." Lee approached from behind them. "Not that I wasn't smitten," he said with a grin.

"Oh really?" Brandy crossed her legs with a natural air of sensuality. "So it was my charming personality?" she said with beguiling eyes.

"Actually, it was your interest." Lee took a seat beside her. "No woman like you ever looked twice my way, let alone treated me like an intelligent human being."

"Your entrepreneurial spirit impressed me, along with the idea of living off the land. I'm tired of pretentious, snooty politicians. For all their judgmental talk about living green, I've never met one who practiced what he preached."

"Brian was ticked when you asked about my plans," Lee said with a laugh.

"All the more intriguing. So I jotted down the bait shop address and decided to take up fishing."

Vanessa laughed for the first time in days.

Lee put his arm around Brandy. "So you gonna quit that job in town and come run the campground with me?"

Surprised at her brother's serious tone, Vanessa awaited Brandy's response.

"I don't know." Brandy shrugged. "We might need the extra income and the health insurance."

Health insurance? Were they talking *marriage*?

"I'd miss my high heels. And Elliot's a great boss."

Lee bristled and pulled his arm away.

"Don't be getting all jealous." Brandy put his arm right back in place and he let her. "You know the guy's hopelessly in love with his wife. And I'm hopelessly in love with *you*. You're never boring and nothing like a politician. I like you a little rough around the edges."

Lee laughed and pulled her close. Vanessa's heart warmed as he talked about the campground, expanding the bait shop into a camp store, and building a secluded log cabin in the woods.

"It'd be a fine place to raise a family," Brandy agreed with excitement. "But I warned him," she said to Vanessa, "I'm not living out there unless there's a master bath and a dishwasher. No clotheslines, either!"

Vanessa watched her brother's face beam with pride. Lee with a master bathroom – what a surprise. Yet not nearly as surprising as Lee talking marriage and babies.

All joviality vanished when their mother's doctor appeared.

Chapter 19 – Not in a Coon's Age

Worry crashed down on Vanessa as she remembered why they were here.

"Darla Gallagher's family?" The doctor walked toward them.

"Yes, doctor," Lee's formal voice sounded unfamiliar as they stood in unison, anxious for the news.

"Darla is sleeping peacefully. Don't worry, she'll recover. We'll discuss treatment after her evaluation. But she'll be out for the night. She should be alert in the morning and you can see her then. Go home and get some rest." One by one, he shook their hands with authority and no one dared question him.

Devastated, Vanessa realized she had to work in the morning. She wanted to stay at her mother's bedside, tell her she loved her, and reassure her everything would be okay.

Yet at the doctor's insistence, she left her, again, when her mother needed her most.

Cold rain pelted Chad's windows as dark clouds swept across the late October sky. He wouldn't be roofing today. With toast and a cup of tea, he settled in to watch the weather channel. Rain was expected to last all day and into tomorrow.

After breakfast, he drove to the far end of the county. The shingles on that house were so far gone, he needed to make sure the elderly lady was doing okay. Thankfully, she had plenty of buckets.

Today was the perfect opportunity to eat lunch at The Porcelain Teapot, a thought that made him cringe. Yet he headed there at noon, wearing his best button-down shirt and a pair of khakis. Wanting to observe Vanessa without her knowing he was there, Chad snuck in quietly and hung back in the corner of the gift shop.

No wonder his mother loved this place. Oozing femininity, the shop overflowed with all things Emily James: teapots, teacups, tinned tea, scone mixes, antiques, flowers, and lace.

Vanessa bustled into the dining room carrying four plates at once. Without needing to ask, she placed each one in front of a delighted patron. Then she efficiently refilled their water glasses and asked if they needed anything else or would like a fresh pot of tea. Carrying teapots, she hurried into the back. As the kitchen door swung on its hinges, he saw her simultaneously grab the ringing phone off the wall, drop tea strainers into the teapots, and check meal tickets clipped to a shelf.

He glimpsed Miss Julia in the background, pouring steaming water into those teapots and readying plates of food.

Impressed, he wondered how women juggled so many jobs at once. His mother and grandmother, and now his sisters, had the same abilities and teamwork.

Vanessa reappeared within seconds. Carrying two plates of steaming chicken potpie, she delivered them to a table near him. Taking in the delicious sight and smell, he knew what he'd order without seeing a menu.

Another patron walked into the gift shop and selected a cup and saucer. When she approached the cash register near the door, Vanessa hurried in from the dining room to ring up her purchase. With great care, she wrapped the delicate teacup in tissue and placed it in a pretty paper bag.

Chad realized how much she loved pretty things, and how much she belonged in this place. Yet she owned nothing pretty or frivolous of her own – just basic necessities.

He spotted a porcelain teapot with violets on it, along with matching cups, saucers, and dessert plates. He'd call Miss Julia later to buy the entire set for Vanessa's Christmas gift. Then he'd build her a shelf to put it on.

When Vanessa completed her sale, he stepped out of the shadows. She looked up with surprise.

"What are you doing here?"

"I wanted to see you, so I came for lunch."

"By yourself?"

"Well, my girl had to work, so yeah, I'm alone."

Vanessa's face glowed with pleasure. She proudly took his arm and led him to a quiet corner table and handed him a menu.

"Chicken pot pie." He didn't take the menu. "I saw you serving it. Reminds me of my grandma."

Flustered, she tucked the menu under her arm and pulled out a notepad and pen. "What accompaniments would you like?"

"What's that?" He asked with a playful grin.

"Soup, salad, breads."

"You mean side dishes?"

"Yes." Laughing, she rolled her eyes. "Today's specials are butternut squash soup or corn chowder, and pumpkin bread or apple cinnamon swirl. Our salads are the garden salad, ambrosia, or cranberry walnut gelatin." She poised, pen above the pad.

"Corn chowder, apple cinnamon, and the garden salad."

"You get either soup *or* salad." She raised an eyebrow with a sassy grin.

"Well I want both, so just charge me for it."

Looking perplexed, she scribbled on her notepad. "Do you want tea?"

"Make it iced tea. No dainty little tea cups," he whispered under his breath.

As he watched her up close doing her job, he gained a whole new respect for her. With friendly efficiency and boundless patience, she never rushed the patrons or appeared bothered.

To his surprise, the fabulous food filled his belly. Of course, he'd ordered extra and suspected she'd given him 'man-sized' portions as the plate overflowed. He chose the infamous chocolate torte for dessert and was not disappointed. With his manhood intact, he left a twenty-dollar tip, pushed in his chair, and took the check to the cash register.

Vanessa met him there. "Did you enjoy your lunch?"

"Delicious." He patted his full belly. "The chicken potpie rivaled my grandmother's and the 'accompaniments' were superb. You're a great cook, as usual." He waggled his eyebrows.

"Is that what brought you here, my cooking?" she teased.

"I came here for lunch because I wanted to see you. To understand you better and take an interest in what you do." He whispered in earnest. "I care about you and I want our relationship to work. You take an interest in my career without hiding in the back room."

A tear glistened at the corner of her eye when she saw his sincerity. "I love this tea shop."

"And it shows." But her eyes were dim and she wasn't smiling. He dabbed the tear. "So what's this all about?"

"It's Mama, Chad. Last night she tried to-" Fresh tears sprung to her eyes. "To commit suicide," she choked out a whisper.

Horror and sorrow struck his heart. No wonder she was upset. How could she even handle doing her job? He couldn't believe she'd actually come to work.

"I...I'm so sorry," he said. "I didn't know...or I would have been there for you."

"We'll talk later, okay?" she asked.

He nodded, pulling her further into the shadows. Hugging her, he tried to infuse her with his strength. He held her tight, kissing the top of her head, hoping he was doing the right thing to make her feel better.

"Be still, and know that God is near," he whispered. He swiped a finger across her cheek to blend away the tear tracks. "Want me to stay and help with dishes or cleanup so you can go see your mama sooner?"

"No!" She stared at him in shock. "Work is helping me get through the day. Mama is safe in the hospital and she needs to rest without me hovering. I'll spend time with her after work."

"All right, then. See ya tonight." With a kiss on her forehead, he squeezed her shoulder. His hand trailed down her arm to her fingertips, touching her as long as possible before walking quietly to the door.

Friday after work, Vanessa drove to the hospital. Lost in her thoughts, she appreciated Lee's silence in the passenger seat.

After several days of observation, Darla hadn't spoken a word, but she was being released.

Vanessa pulled into the hospital drive. When she bent down to hug her mother, Darla's eyes shone with love.

"I love you, Mama."

"Love you too." Darla uttered her first words in days!

"Oh, Mama, it's so good to hear your voice!"

Her shy smile reminded Vanessa of her confession of love for

Baldy. Too quickly, the smile faded back to lethargy.

Desperate to bring her mother back to the living, Vanessa hatched an idea. Conniving maybe, but how better to jumpstart a heart than forbidden love?

"Now that you're home, Mama," Vanessa said with an eye on Darla's listless face. "Would you like to see Baldy?"

Darla's gaze sprang to Vanessa. "I thought you were mad at me about him." The words rolled off her tongue as if she hadn't spent the last three days mute.

"I never said that. How did you know?"

"Mothers know these things." Tears fell to her lap. "I feared what Clyde would do if he found out. But I always wanted to tell you Baldy was your father."

Love emanated from Darla's face, with passion she couldn't deny. Heartfelt emotion was bringing her back – overriding unsubstantiated grief for a husband who never loved her.

"I dared not let a single word slip – even to Baldy. He knew and understood. Since your conception, we'd kept our distance for fear of what Clyde might do to you. It was safer that way. We were both relieved you were the spitting image of me. Clyde had no clues that way – unlike Layla's telltale dark eyes and cleft chin." She swiped at unrestrained tears.

Wow – Vanessa had wanted to get her talking, but hadn't expected the dam to burst. She'd better get all the info she could while words were gushing forth.

"Didn't Baldy ever want to see me?"

"Oh, but he did," she cried. "When we passed on the street, he and I were careful not to show any emotion. But when he looked at you, I caught the warmth in his eyes. That look was enough," she choked out. "It had to be."

"Now you can have a real relationship, Mama."

Her eyes twinkled as she looked into space with a hopeful smile. Vanessa wanted a relationship too – with her real father.

Then someone banged on the door. Darla's eyes darted back and forth as she cowered in a corner of the sofa.

"It's okay, Mama." Vanessa patted her knee. "No one will hurt you anymore." She stood. "I'll see who it is, okay?"

Retreating into her shell, Darla brought her knees to her chest.

Vanessa tamped down disappointment and anger as she went to the door, hoping to heaven it wasn't Chief Hunter.

"Hi." Chad stood on the doorstep. Again he had impeccable timing. With a grin, he held out a pot of flowers.

"Violets?" Did he remember she was picking violets when they met on the road that day?

"What else? Violets for Vanessa." He searched her face. "I thought they might cheer up your mom, too."

Gazing into his deep blue eyes, she longed to step into his arms and kiss him.

He stood holding the violets like a peace offering.

"I'm sorry I didn't call." His sincere words came in a desperate rush. "I was afraid you'd say no and couldn't bear not to see you."

His pleading eyes shot straight to her heart. Taking the flowers, she grasped his hand.

"Come in, Chad."

He bent to remove his work boots.

Then she led him to the living room where ratty rugs camouflaged the worn linoleum. "Mama, Chad's here to visit."

Darla peeked over her knees. "Cops with you?" she asked.

"No, ma'am," he said gently.

She visibly relaxed, but kept her knees tucked close.

"He brought violets." Vanessa set the flowers on a table near her mother and motioned for him to sit. She resumed her seat on the sofa beside her mother.

Darla glanced at the flowers.

"Don't worry, Darla." Chad spoke softly from a chair across the room. "I know you didn't do it, and I'll find out who did."

"No, don't!" Her body quaking, Darla rocked back and forth.

He squinted at her. "Why not?"

"Let me to take the blame. I can't bear to lose my son."

"You think Lee killed Clyde?" Vanessa scowled at the absurdity. "He'd never do this to you."

"He did it to protect me." Rocking in a fetal position, Darla hid her head beneath her arms and sobbed.

"But Lee reported him missing," Chad reasoned. "If he killed Clyde, he never would have called Chief Hunter."

Vanessa smoothed her mother's hair. "Mama, Lee would never let you suffer this way if he was to blame."

Nothing they said made an impact. Darla continued rocking, crying, "No, no, no – "

Chad waited on the sofa while Vanessa took her mother to bed.

"Mama's asleep, at last." Vanessa sank down beside him and rested her head on his chest.

When he wrapped an arm around her, she embraced him. He lifted her chin. At first hesitant, her kiss quickly turned passionate, stirring him to the core. Physical affection seemed his only way to reach her.

No complaints there, but he longed to touch her heart, to tap into her essence. He wanted to know and understand her, to further their relationship to the next step emotionally, not just physically.

Yet she felt so good. Before he could stop himself, he leaned back, pulling her on top of him. She happily obliged, more willing to share her body than her soul.

"Vanessa." Breathlessly, he eased back from the kiss, cradling her cheek and looking into her eyes.

She dropped her head to his shoulder, refusing to meet his gaze. Her body melded to his; her hot kisses trailed along his throat. He prayed silently for guidance, asking for strength to withstand temptation.

Her lips burned a path to his chest, setting him on fire. His hands ran up her sides. Her blouse bunched, exposing warm, soft flesh. She writhed on top of him, pressing in all the right places. Of their own volition, his hands slipped beneath her blouse. She moaned with pleasure.

There was no stopping now.

Groaning, he pressed against her.

Then came an approaching rumble.

"Lee's here." Vanessa leapt from him, straightening her blouse and smoothing her hair.

"Lee?" He couldn't keep the annoyance from his voice, yet knew this was an answer to prayer. He shook off dizzying desire and sat up.

"He's here to take over with Mama. So I can go home."

"This late?" His watch read almost eleven o'clock.

"That's the arrangement."

The rumble grew louder, closer.

Chad wanted to talk to Vanessa about God tonight, to encourage her that God loved her, that he was praying they'd find the real killer. Now his time was up.

"Can I see you tomorrow?"

"I have to work. Then I promised Mama I'd spend the night. That's the only way I could get her to calm down." Headlights shone in the window and crossed her face.

He grimaced. "Can I pick you up for dinner on Sunday?"

She shook her head sadly. "I'll be here with Mama most of the day. Then I have to get groceries and catch up on laundry."

"I can help," he offered as the rumble outside stilled.

"I'm sorry, Chad." She looked down at his chest. He could almost feel the heat in her intense gaze. "I can't deal with my emotions for you and take care of Mama, too."

He wanted to understand, but feared he was losing her. The back door banged open. He was out of time.

"You need a break," he insisted. "How about next weekend?"

"I don't know." She shrugged, looking more defeated than eager to see him.

"Hey, Chad." Lee stood in the kitchen. "How ya doing?"

"Okay." It was the best he could muster. "I'm just going home." He stood with a longing look at Vanessa.

"Good night." Staring at his chest, she never met his eyes.

"Good night." He turned to Lee. "See ya, man."

"Drive safe," Lee said as if Chad was drunk.

He must have looked bad. Drunk on love, that was about it.

The door banged behind him with a conclusive thud.

She might be willing physically, but emotionally he was losing her. They'd made such progress before all this happened.

He'd touched her heart; he knew he did.

The last Saturday in October, The Porcelain Teapot brimmed with customers for their Costumed Victorian Tea. Vanessa and Julia had spent untold hours planning, promoting, and preparing this fun event. Yet they had no idea how popular it would be.

Patrons of all ages showed up in costume. Young mothers and grandmothers brought costumed little girls. A group of widowed friends dressed to the hilt with excited grins.

Julia bustled by wearing a Victorian dress similar to Vanessa's costume, accessorized with cameos and antique hair barrettes.

By one o'clock, Vanessa rushed to prepare more 'spooky' spinach quiche and 'chilling' chicken salad for the late crowd. Squash bisque and corn chowder simmered near the bottom of the pots and the toasted leaf-shaped garnishes were gone. Salad greens and fixings ran dangerously low. The pumpkin tarts and chocolate black cat cupcakes had been wiped out. They'd stocked up on chocolate torte, but even that was in short supply.

At the end of the day, Julia collapsed into a chair.

"I can't do this anymore." With shaking hands, she pulled out her blood sugar test kit.

Vanessa brought her a glass of juice and two chicken 'bones' – the last finger sandwiches in the house.

"Are you ready to take over? To be the boss?"

Vanessa's heart thrilled at the offer, at Julia's confidence in her. Yet her personal responsibilities nearly drained her. How would she handle it all? But she couldn't say no. Julia was right – she couldn't do it anymore.

"Sure," Vanessa answered.

Visibly relieved, Julia wolfed down a sandwich in two bites. Vanessa gathered fresh linens to reset the tables.

"Never mind that," Julia said. "We'll get those Monday morning. It's a slow day."

Vanessa gratefully set down the pile of napkins.

"Grab whatever's leftover and get home to your Mama." Julia waved to the door. "I'll lock up."

There was nothing leftover.

Traveling up Lake Road, the gravity of her situation weighed on Vanessa. Seeing Baldy's pickup in the driveway offered brief gladness – maybe he'd cheer up her mother. Reality quickly replaced the optimism. He was another person to feed.

She grabbed her bag of groceries and headed inside.

Sitting close to Darla, Baldy hung his head. She stared out the window. He looked up with a furrowed brow.

"Hi Vanessa." His voice lacked any sense of happiness, yet he seemed relieved she arrived.

"Hi." She didn't know what to call him. 'Baldy' seemed disrespectful, yet 'Mr. Calvin' was too formal.

"Hello, Mama." She bent and kissed her mother's cheek.

"Hello." The hollow words rocked Vanessa to the core. Gone were the days her face lit up to see her daughter.

"I see you have company. Have you had a nice visit?"

Her mother looked over at Baldy and shrugged. Over the course of a few days, she had deteriorated drastically. A shell of a woman, Darla was finally able to spend time with the man she loved and she barely acknowledged him.

"I'm making your favorite, Mama. Biscuits and gravy."

No response.

"Would you like to stay for dinner?" she asked her father awkwardly, still unsure how to address him.

"Thank you, I'd like that." His eyes shone at her. "I love biscuits and gravy. Haven't had 'em in a coon's age." His faint smile cheered her heart, ever so slightly.

Vanessa gratefully headed to the kitchen and began cooking. As she pulled the biscuits from the oven, Chad's pickup pulled into the drive.

Chad bounded to the door, wearing holey jeans, a worn flannel shirt and a beat up hat. Black makeup smeared across his face. She opened the door as he reached the step.

"What are you supposed to be?" she asked.

Chapter 20 – Trick or Treat?

"I'm a bum." Chad beamed. "Same as every Halloween."

"Not much of a stretch, is it?" she teased.

"Gee, thanks." He grinned from ear to ear. "Wanna go trick or treating? I'm taking my nieces."

"It's my turn to stay with Mama." Disappointment filled her heart. She loved trick or treating, and wanted to be with Chad.

"When will I be able to see you?"

"Probably not any time soon." She leaned against the door with sheer exhaustion. "Julia asked me to take over the tea room. She's struggling with diabetes and can't handle it any more. With the added responsibilities there and caring for my mom, I just don't know when I'll have time."

"How can I help?"

She smiled. "Right now I need to get supper on the table. Can you stay a minute?"

"Sure can. I allowed time for you to figure out a costume."

"I wish." She led him inside. Baldy looked awkward sitting with her unresponsive mother.

"Hi Chad," he called across the room.

"Hi Baldy." Chad motioned to his outfit. "I'm going trick-or-treating with the girls later."

"Ah." Baldy nodded with understanding and turned back to Darla. "Do you remember when you brought Vanessa to my house for trick-or-treating?" He rested a hand on her knee.

Darla gave him a blank stare.

Memories of Baldy offering homemade cider and cinnamon doughnuts came to Vanessa. She'd always been surprised at the town hermit's hospitality on Halloween – and her mother's insistence not to tell Clyde. Now it made sense.

She looked at Baldy, so gentle with her mother. Had he really loved them all those years? Grief settled over Vanessa at what she'd missed.

Chad rubbed her back. She leaned into him and he held her for a long moment. She never wanted to leave his arms, but the gravy needed stirring. With a heavy sigh, she picked up the wooden spoon.

"Can I set the table?" he asked.

She handed him four plates and pointed out the silverware drawer. As she stirred gravy, Chad set the table and poured iced tea.

"Are you hungry?" she asked.

"Unfortunately, I ate at home." He eyed the steaming biscuits. "But I might nab one of those."

"Help yourself." She smiled, enjoying how Chad loved her cooking.

He got out the butter and quietly bowed his head for a brief prayer, although no one seemed to notice but her. "What else can I do?" he asked as he buttered his biscuit. "Run errands, grab groceries, help at the tea room?" He took a large bite. "Mmmmm," he moaned.

"All of the above?" She scrunched her face, hating to ask.

"You got it. I'll stop at the tea shop after closing tomorrow. You tell me what to do and I'll do my best – dishes, clean up, whatever. I'm not too bad at fixing things either." He polished off the biscuit.

"That would be awesome." She sighed with grateful relief. "How'd I ever deserve a man like you?"

"Just by being you." He tweaked her nose and put his plate and butter knife in the sink. Then he washed the biscuit pan.

She ladled gravy onto split biscuits on the remaining three plates.

He took the empty skillet from her and scrubbed it clean.

"I'm sorry, but I have to go trick-or-treating now." He made a funny face, like a big kid.

She kissed him full on the lips right in front of her parents. That was weird in more ways than one.

"You've done enough. Thank you." She hugged him.

"See you tomorrow." Her goofy, dressed as a bum, knight in

shining armor walked out the door and rode off in his big blue beast.

Vanessa peeked into the living room. Darla stared out the window into gathering darkness. Baldy held her hand, eyes full of love and worry.

She set the plates of steaming food onto the table. With the sausage gravy and flaky biscuits, she served buttered green beans and canned peaches. The best she could do with her limited resources, the simple meal looked delicious.

Baldy prompted Darla to the table. She sat staring at the plate in front of her but wouldn't touch the food. He wolfed down his portion and helped himself to seconds.

He prodded Darla to eat but she refused to open her mouth or even acknowledge the love of her life.

She was shutting down. First it was endless tears, now numb nothingness. Barely breathing, it seemed too much effort to even chew food. She'd completely withdrawn from life.

Slouched in a chair and poking at her own plate, Vanessa began to understand. Weighed down with burdens, she had no desire to eat, no energy to deal with the problems around her.

No one cared. Baldy gave up feeding Darla. He looked anxious to leave this awkward situation.

She tried praying, but God didn't know she existed. It seemed that God just didn't care. Lost, groping for meaning and answers, she had to find her own way.

Sunday morning, November first, dawned cold and frosty. Vanessa had spent the night on her mother's sofa, too drained to even drive home. Depression threatened to engulf her as she looked at the shabby surroundings and remembered her mother's plight and not being able to have Sunday dinner with Chad. She had nothing to look forward to but another grueling day.

Then she remembered – Sarita was coming! She sprang from the couch and prepared breakfast. Darla refused to eat, but Vanessa managed to slip some eggs down her throat. With her mother settled on staring out the window, she scrubbed until the place looked as clean as she could get it.

Shortly before noon, Baldy stopped by, carrying grocery bags. Vanessa greeted him at the door with a cheerful hello.

"Lunch is on me this time." He handed her the bags.

"Bless you!" She took the bags and spontaneously hugged him. Both surprised at her sudden affection, they pulled back quickly. "What'd you bring?" She acted casual.

"Roast chicken and potato salad." His chest puffed out.

"Yum. You know what I like." She doled out food on plates.

Baldy tried to feed Darla, but she clamped her mouth shut. Discouraged, he didn't stay long after that.

Vanessa wondered how long he'd keep coming over. She wondered how long Chad would stick around, too. She didn't have the time or energy for a relationship right now, and she couldn't accept his offer to help with her mom. She relied on him far too much and wouldn't lose her independence altogether.

Besides, it wasn't fair to dump her problems on him. She couldn't bear to see him turn into a sad shell of a man like Baldy had become, waiting for a woman who couldn't be with him.

Mid-afternoon, Sarita pulled up in her little SUV. Vanessa met her and Gracia at the door.

"I'm so glad to see you!" Vanessa hugged her friend.

"Remember my friend?" Sarita asked her daughter. "Gracia, this is Miss Vanessa."

Gracia nodded with a broad smile. Vanessa hugged her too.

"And there's her mama." Sarita led the child to greet Darla. "Hi Mrs. Gallagher. I haven't seen you in a long time."

Unflinching, Darla stared out the window.

"What's wrong with her?" Gracia jabbed Darla's leg, getting no reaction.

"Don't poke her like that." Sarita pulled the child's hand away. "She's not feeling well, honey."

Shrugging, Gracia toddled off to inspect the kitchen.

"It's time for Mama's nap." Vanessa pulled her silent mother to her feet. "Let's go lie down, okay Mama?" Thankfully, Darla cooperated. "I'll be right back." She gave Sarita a sad smile.

When Vanessa returned, Sarita gave her a look that said, 'We need to talk.' Gracia was playing with her toys on the rug.

"How long has she been like this?" Sarita asked.

Vanessa sighed. "Since Clyde died, but it's gotten worse."

"I can't imagine how you're caring for her yourself. Maybe

you should consider serious counseling. What if she attempts suicide again?"

Vanessa's head spun. The social worker's pamphlet burned into her brain – the classy building, the pretty landscaping, the fancy letters screaming: *Riverside Mental Health Center.*

"Vanessa? Are you okay?"

"No." She heaved a sigh. "The hospital suggested a mental health center, but I just can't do that to Mama."

"If she commits suicide, you won't have your mama," Sarita said gently. "The way things are, what kind of life does she have?"

Vanessa nodded, unwilling to face the truth.

"And what kind of life do you have, Vanessa? I admire your determination to care for your mother, but you could end up sick yourself if you don't get help."

"You sound like Chad. He wants to help but she's *my* mother. It's not his responsibility." Her dependence on him frightened her and she couldn't ask any more. She already considered breaking it off with Chad so she could take care of her mother.

"Rachel says he's crazy about you. I'm sure he really wants to help or he wouldn't have offered."

Vanessa shook her head stubbornly.

"Whatever you decide, I'm here for you," Sarita promised. "I'll be praying for you too."

Chad said he prayed for her, yet the situation only got worse. God wasn't coming down to write a check for that fancy place – nor was he helping her mother.

"We don't have insurance to pay for care."

"There are programs to cover you. The hospital has social workers who should be able to direct you." Sarita took her hand. "I had to do this for my mama, too. For her alcoholism. I understand how you feel. But Mama would be dead if I hadn't done it."

Vanessa appreciated Sarita's concern, but wasn't convinced. Darla wasn't an alcoholic. She was grieving, that was all. She just needed time and it was Vanessa's responsibility to care for her. If she put off her mama on someone else, she'd get worse. Just like she'd been upset the day when Vanessa helped Julia instead of chasing after her mother.

Besides, she didn't have time to deal with social workers and all their questions and forms. Overwhelmed, she felt like she'd go crazy herself if she had one more responsibility, one more person making demands on her.

By Wednesday morning, Chad missed Vanessa something fierce. She'd been staying with her mother every night after work. She refused his offer to help, and he figured they needed this time alone to deal with the grief. So he prayed for their healing and for Chief Hunter to solve the case. Maybe that would help them find closure. Meanwhile, he'd let her know he was there for her.

Right now, he had work to do. Dumping his tea down the sink, he readied for a chilly day up on a roof.

Old Miss Green's rooftop soared above the surrounding area. On a hill, the shingles took a beating with winds whipping over the trees. Chad had replaced the roof a few weeks ago and noticed chimney work needed done as well.

Despite deep discounts that barely covered his costs, the elderly spinster had tapped out her bank account on the roof. He agreed to throw in the chimney work for free after completing a few bigger jobs. So here he was on a rooftop in the cold November wind, hoping it didn't knock him to the ground.

He'd already been knocked for a loop by Vanessa.

He smiled. He'd waited so long to find her, and she'd been right under his nose all along. He longed for a loving wife, and a family of his own. He didn't want to live like the lonely Miss Green. She inherited this house from her parents, but had no one to pass it on to.

He finished the flashing and stood. Clinging to the chimney, he looked over the landscape. Two weeks ago, the view was spectacular – red, yellow, and orange leaves covered the rolling hills. Today the trees were bare.

A movement caught his eye. In the woods on Gallagher property, two men walked toward a black pickup. He recognized the logo of Riverside Developers on its door. An expensive black sedan parked behind the truck.

What was a developer doing on Gallagher property?

Junior wanted to build a campground, but the taxes had to be caught up first. Chad got the distinct feeling he didn't call these guys. Otherwise, he'd be here with them.

Anxious to question the trespassers, Chad climbed down the ladder and meandered over to meet the competition. The men spotted him walking across the field between Miss Green's house and the wooded Gallagher property. They paused at the truck, but made no effort to brave the windy, open meadow. Then he recognized them, and apparently they recognized him.

One of the men was the guy who had shown up at Darla's looking for Clyde. Chad knew he looked familiar – of course, Riverside Developers. They ran into each other all the time at the home center in Riverside.

The other man was Brian Daniels.

Neither looked happy to see Chad.

Tossing his cigar, the developer jumped into his truck. Brian hustled to the car and they both took off in a cloud of dust.

Chad reached the Gallagher property and smelled rum smoke. A cigar butt lay smoldering on the ground. It seemed mighty fishy that the land was going to tax sale and the county auditor was out here with a big bucks developer.

Then Chad remembered seeing Brian speed up Rose Hill Drive like a maniac.

Coming from Clyde's hunting cabin?

He pulled out his cell phone and called Chief Hunter.

Pulling into the alley behind The Porcelain Teapot, Vanessa could not believe the big blue truck was waiting there under the street light. Chad bounded out with an unstoppable grin.

Exhausted, she couldn't deal with one more person, not today. She just wanted a shower and her nice warm bed.

He didn't understand what she was going through.

Slowing her car to a crawl, she readied herself to break it off with him, once and for all. She needed space and she needed time and right now the last thing she needed was Chad James with that ridiculous smirk.

Parked in her usual space, she shut off the engine and resolutely dragged her tired body from the car.

"Don't." She slammed the door and held up a hand to ward off his approach. "I can't do this anymore, Chad."

The crushed look in his eyes broke her heart. Beneath that macho mask was a sensitive soul. He always had her best interests at heart. This time, she had his at heart.

"I'm sorry. I didn't mean to be so harsh." She stared at his chest, unable to look into his sorrowful eyes. She yearned to lay her pounding head on that broad chest, to feel his comforting arms around her. Her heart fluttered, but she kept her resolve.

"My mother is getting worse. I need to take care of her. I need to run the tea room." She released a weary sigh. "I need to rest."

He sucked in a breath as if about to say something.

"I don't have the energy for a relationship right now," she rushed on. "And frankly, I don't know if that's going to change any time soon. I need space and I need to figure this out on my own. I feel like I'm losing myself to everyone else and their demands on me."

"I'm so sorry." He whispered on a shaky breath. "Vanessa – "

"Maybe if my life weren't such a mess, we'd have a chance." She stared at the ground, which was so much safer than looking at that enticing chest or those caring, deep blue eyes. "But right now, I can barely take care of my own problems, let alone figure out a relationship."

"We can work this out, Vanessa – together. I'm willing to help you, to do whatever I can."

She held up a hand to stop him, but he kept on talking.

"I know you don't believe it right now, but God is with you and He'll work this all out."

The mention of God simmered her blood. She narrowed her eyes, stepped forward and glowered at his startled face.

"I'm tired of waiting for God to come to my rescue," she growled.

Her mind exploded with the horror of her father's menacing scowl while he unzipped his pants, the gym teacher's concerned grimace when she saw the bruises, her mother's tortured glare as she slashed her wrists.

"God's never been there for me and He certainly isn't now." Vanessa could taste the whiskey breath, smell the locker room Lysol, and feel the sticky, blood-soaked towels.

Boiling over, she bellowed, "I don't want to hear another word about GOD."

She stormed up the stairs, leaving his dropped jaw and puppy dog eyes far behind her.

"Mama's agitated today," Lee warned Vanessa. "But at least

she's not staring into space. I think she's coming around." He hugged her tightly. "If you got it covered, I'm off to see Brandy after I check the traps."

"Tell Brandy I said hi." Vanessa kissed his cheek, grateful for their new closeness. "Is she coming over this weekend?"

"Sure, we can hang out. Are you cooking?" He lifted an eyebrow hopefully.

"How does BBQ sound?" It was his favorite.

"We'll be here!" He smiled broadly and shot out the door.

"Off to see his girl." Darla commented without emotion.

Relief flooded over Vanessa to hear her mother speaking.

"I have some nice salmon bisque for supper, Mama."

"I'm not hungry. I keep telling you that and you keep trying to shove food down my throat." Darla picked up the TV remote and turned up the volume on her favorite talk show.

Too bad the episode was about workaholics – one of the few dysfunctions Mama and Clyde never experienced. Most anything else might have been helpful.

Vanessa warmed the bisque, prepared a small salad, and baked cinnamon biscuits to entice her mother.

"That's what you are, a workaholic," Darla hollered from the living room as a commercial came on.

"Oh really?" Vanessa figured as long as her mother was talking, she'd go along.

"Work all day, then rush over here and try to force feed me. Clean this house, wash clothes, run home at bedtime and then get up in the morning to do it all over again. I don't know when you clean your own house."

"It doesn't get too dirty since I'm rarely there."

"Ought to be taking care of your own self, not here breathing down my neck day and night."

"I'm just trying to help, Mama. You've had a rough time."

"I don't need your help! I'm a grown woman."

"I know." Vanessa refused to argue with her. Fortunately the show came back on and Darla focused on that.

The cinnamon biscuits smelled wonderful. Vanessa ladled salmon bisque into her mother's prettiest bowl. She arranged it with the salad plate, a steaming biscuit, and two pats of honey butter on a large tray with silverware and a napkin.

Carrying the meal into the living room, she set it on the coffee table in front of her mom.

"What would you like to drink, Mama?"

"I told you I'm not hungry." She bent to one side to see the TV past her daughter. "Get outta the way," she barked.

With a sigh, Vanessa returned to the kitchen to eat at the table. Her very presence seemed to agitate Mama even more. Vanessa's appetite waned and the food lost its flavor. After a few spoonfuls, she gave up trying to eat.

Darla went to the bathroom, so Vanessa cleared her dishes. She covered the untouched food with plastic wrap and refrigerated it. She put the clean spoon back in the drawer. Hadn't she given her mother a knife for the butter? She checked the coffee table, the sofa, and the floor. No knife.

She heard grunting in the bathroom.

Please, God, no!

Chapter 21 – Sweating Torpedoes

She ran down the hall and burst into the bathroom.

Darla sat on the floor, sawing a dent in the scar on her wrist. Blood seeped from the dull butter knife. With a glance at Vanessa, she sawed harder and faster.

"No! STOP!" Vanessa seized the knife and threw it toward the hall.

Darla kicked and screamed, but Vanessa held her arm above her head to prevent as much blood loss as possible. Weak from lack of food, her mother collapsed into a bawling heap.

Grabbing a towel, Vanessa wrapped the wrist tightly and then held her mother to her. Rocking and holding her, she kept the arm high above her head.

Finally out of tears, Darla gave in to exhaustion and curled into a ball.

Vanessa checked her wrist. The mangled skin was deeply bruised but the cut was shallow. She applied antibiotic cream and a strong bandage. She gave her mother pills the doctor had prescribed and a cup of water.

"That's gotta hurt. Please take these."

Resigned, Darla placed the pills on her tongue and swallowed them with a sip of water.

"Mama, talk to me," Vanessa urged. "Why are you doing this? Don't tell me you don't want to burden me. As if this behavior isn't a burden, how much guilt do you think I'll be carrying around if you kill yourself?"

"I…don't know…how else to fix it…" Her voice trailed off in misery.

"How will your suicide fix anything, Mama?"

"It makes me look guilty so the cops will stop looking at Lee. I thought about killing Clyde, more than once. I'd gladly take the blame to spare my son."

"Lee didn't kill him." Vanessa knew it in her heart.

Darla shook her head. "He already suffered so much, I can't let him lose everything. Now that Clyde's gone, I've never seen him so happy. He's even got a wonderful girl who loves him."

"Mama, this is not the way to fix things."

Darla was so worn out, her head lolled to the side.

"Let's get you to bed." Vanessa lifted her mother to her feet. "The medicine will help you sleep. We'll talk later."

She tucked her mother in with a kiss, made sure nothing sharp was in the bedroom, and left the door open. Completely spent, Darla was snoring in a matter of minutes.

Desperate and needing to talk to someone, Vanessa called Julia. Insurance or not, her mother needed help.

"Take the day off to handle this," Julia said.

"You can't run the tea room by yourself."

"I've been talking to friends about working part time. One's already coming in tomorrow, and I'll round up another."

"But they're not trained yet."

"They're mature women. They know their way around a kitchen, and I'll light a fire under their butts. You take care of your mom."

"Thank you so much, Julia."

"Take care, Vanessa. I'll be praying for you."

Julia prayed for her?

Vanessa wasn't so sure God was the one who would help her. Why would some elusive God out there running the universe be bothered with her?

As much as she wanted to take care of herself and her mom and her career on her own, independence seemed impossible.

Julia was independent. She ran her own business and never married. Yet she couldn't run the tea room alone. Vanessa's mother finally pulled free of Clyde Gallagher, yet she needed help more than ever.

Vanessa would spend the night with her mom and take her back to the hospital the next day. She'd stay there until she was better this time. The social worker said there were programs to help with the cost. They'd figure it out later.

Right now her mama needed help.

It seemed that everyone needed help to survive in this world. Vanessa found security in her Mama and Lee. She found strength in her cherished relationship with Aunt Julia, and took solace in her friendships with Sarita and Brandy. Despite being jaded by Clyde, she yearned for the father she never had in Baldy.

The stronger her connections became, the less independent she was. Yet like ropes entwined together, those ties made her strong. The bond with her mom and brother could never be broken. No matter what, they loved each other.

Chad said God loved her like that – no matter what. Could she have a bond with Almighty God like she had with her family – a bond that could never be broken?

With a connection to the all-powerful God of the universe, how would she ever be independent? Wouldn't a love that strong encompass her, taking over and controlling her life?

That sounded like someone else she knew. Did she need God – and Chad James – more than she cared to admit?

Hard-won independence was hard lost.

Chad poked at the reheated chicken he hadn't been able to eat last night. What made him think tonight would be any different? He scraped the meal into the garbage and parked in front of the TV. Mindlessly clicking through channels, he rubbed his sore red eyes.

He wanted to help Vanessa but what was he supposed to do? And if she wanted nothing to do with God, should he continue pursuing a relationship with her?

Yet he had to believe she'd come around. She'd professed her faith. She was just angry with God right now – *really* angry.

With a huge yawn, he leaned back in his recliner. He might as well settle in for another long, sleepless night.

Hours later, the late show droned on. Chad could barely keep his eyes open, but he couldn't sleep either. He clicked off the TV and pulled out his Bible. He should have done this hours ago. After a few comforting chapters of Psalms, he snapped off the light and let the verses flow over him.

Visions of Vanessa permeated the green pastures and quiet waters in his mind. She was always there, yet never *here*. How could he sleep when she never left his mind?

He heard a car outside and went to the window. Anything to get his mind off Vanessa. The car pulled to the side of the road and cut its headlights. Just what he needed – a reminder of teenagers in love. How odd they'd stop right across from his parents' house. Past Laura's there was nothing but woods on both sides of the road.

And the Gallagher hunting cabin.

The car's dome light came on and a single figure got out. A flashlight spot moved over the road, through the ditch and into the woods. The patch of light scanned the ground. Somebody was looking for something.

A creepy feeling washed over Chad. On a hunch, he threw on a jacket and grabbed his cell phone. Silently, he headed out the front door where he wouldn't alert the dogs sleeping out back. Moonlight lit the way as his eyes adjusted to the darkness. Halfway across the front yard, he recognized Brian Daniels' car.

After a quick text to Chief Hunter, he crept closer. Maybe he could apprehend Brian before the approaching police scared him away. Creeping low, he moved from tree to tree across the dark yard and slunk across the road.

From the ditch, he watched the telltale flashlight slice through the dark. Fortunately, he knew these woods like the back of his hand. He and his sisters played here as children and he hunted here often. He stepped over the gnarled roots of an old maple. Crickets and tree frogs chirped in the distance.

He waited for Brian to turn his back before sneaking closer. Careful to step lightly, Chad hid behind a tree as the light swept his direction. An owl hooted above him.

Brian jerked in alarm. His head snapped around nervously as critters skittered through the undergrowth. He shone the light toward Chad. It lit on something white in the wet leaves. Brian brought the light back to the white object about four feet from Chad and stepped quickly toward it.

Chad's breath came fast. The light focused a wad of paper. Was it the litter he'd thrown from the window that day? When Brian bent down to examine it, Chad jumped him.

Brian screamed like a girl. He threw up his arms and hurled the flashlight through the air.

Chad knocked him to the ground and pinned him.

"Get off of me!" Brian kicked and screamed, struggling to

grab the paper just out of reach.

Blue and red lights lit up the woods. The squad car skidded to a stop behind Brian's car and the door flung open.

"Over here, Chief!" Chad called.

Brian hyperventilated beneath him.

Chief Hunter hoisted his pants up under his potbelly and jumped the ditch. Clearing his throat when he reached them didn't camouflage his huffing and puffing.

"Hey, chief." Breathless, Brian fought to get up.

"Stay where you are." The chief held a boot on his back and promptly cuffed him.

Getting up, Chad pointed out the wad of litter. "I think that's what he's looking for."

"Don't touch it. It's evidence." The chief wrestled Brian to his feet.

"I don't know what you're talking about." Brian glared at Chad. "I lost a hubcap and I was just looking for it."

"In the dark, in the middle of the night." Chief Hunter shone his flashlight on Brian's car. "Your car doesn't have hubcaps."

"It wasn't me!" Brian wailed. "It was all Myrtle's idea. She told me to get rid of the note."

Realizing what he'd said, his eyes widened to the size of golf balls and his breath came in short bursts. His red face puffed up as if his head might explode.

"What's Myrtle have to do with it?" The chief asked as a cold wind whipped through the trees.

Chad scrunched his neck down into his collar and thrust his hands into his pockets. Yet torpedoes of sweat jetted from Brian's brow.

"I was notifying Clyde of the tax sale, that's all." Brian lifted his chin. "Myrtle wants to buy the property so I told her about the suicide note."

"Suicide?" The chief and Chad exclaimed in unison.

Chad couldn't believe it. Clyde Gallagher was too all-fired stubborn to rid this town of his evil.

"Who would be banging on my door at six thirty a.m.?" Vanessa threw down her hairbrush and looked out her bedroom window. Chad's big blue truck parked next her car. On the other side was a police car.

Her stomach roiled.

"No, Mama, no." The hospital was supposed to *prevent* suicide. Frozen in place, she stared into the alley.

The pounding on her door resumed.

In a daze, she straightened her white work blouse and walked to the door. With great trepidation, she turned the deadbolt and inched the door open.

"Morning, ma'am." Chief Hunter's solemn face belied nothing. "May I come in?"

Unable to speak, she opened the door wider. Her breath came fast but her body moved in slow motion.

The chief took off his hat and held it over his belly.

"I'm sorry to inform you, ma'am – "

Her stomach lurched. Vomit rose to her throat.

"We found a note that suggests Clyde Gallagher committed suicide."

Suicide. The word stuck in her brain.

"Clyde?"

"Yes ma'am. We believe it's his signature on the note. With a lack of evidence that anyone else was on that cliff – no other footprints and no dragging marks – we're ruling his death a suicide and closing the case."

"Mama? Is my mama okay?"

Hunter's head jerked back with surprise. "Well, yes, I believe so. I just notified her and she seemed fine. Quite relieved, actually."

Vanessa released a huge calming breath. She swallowed the bile taste and it burned all the way down.

Hunter patted her arm. "You let it all sink in, and let me know if you have any questions." He plunked his hat back on his head. "Someone's anxious to see you."

The chief turned to leave and she popped her head out the door. Chad stood at the bottom of the stairs with that unstoppable grin.

The chief passed him with a pat on the back and Chad bounded the stairs in practically a single leap.

"Your problems should be over soon." His blue eyes deepened to violet, filling with hope and purpose.

Her eyes locked with his and right then she knew. Chad James loved her, and she'd fallen head over heels for him.

Not running straight into his arms took every ounce of restraint she could muster. And it was waning.

A draft brushed her hair across her line of vision. She pushed it aside impatiently, needing to see his face.

"Come in." She motioned to the living room but her eyes never left his.

Blinking back tears, Vanessa steeled herself. An onslaught of emotion assaulted her as words gushed forth.

"All those years I thought he was my father. I was so ashamed. I hated him so much. Yet because he was my father, in some dysfunctional way I loved him and I knew he loved me."

Chad's eyes filled with empathy. How could he possibly understand, when she didn't understand herself?

"Then I found out he wasn't my father at all. I didn't know whether to be ashamed or relieved. I was illegitimate, but I wasn't Clyde Gallagher's child." She shrugged with resignation.

"And then he was dead. I didn't know what to think or how to feel. I was overwhelmed with guilt because I was so relieved. Yet I knew someone pushed him over that cliff and I was scared to death it was someone I loved."

"No one pushed him." Chad's gentle voice whispered.

Her body relaxed as fresh relief washed over her, only to be replaced with regret and more guilt tightening to a knot in her gut.

She covered her face with her hands.

"He ruined my life and my family. Yet I feel so sorry for him." Overwhelmed, she couldn't believe all that happened.

Chad listened patiently as she poured out her heart.

"So he killed himself." Even as she said the words, they weren't quite sinking in.

Her knees buckled. Chad rushed to her side and steadied her. She leaned into his warm, comforting chest. He wrapped his arms around her and she never wanted him to let her go.

"Let's sit down." Chad led her to the sofa.

She looked up into his kind, loving eyes. Desperately in need of his love and affection, she wanted to kiss him and never come up for air. She touched his cheek. The smooth skin felt as if he'd just shaved. A muscle in his jaw twitched.

His mouth lowered to hers. Her eyes drifted shut. Their lips touched and undeniable chemistry radiated between them.

On a breath, she moaned his name. He pulled her to him

hungrily, burying his face in her hair.

"Vanessa..."

Her body screamed for him, yet something pricked her consciousness like a thorn in her brow. There was something she had to do.

Right now.

Pulling back, she looked into his eyes. Filled with desire and passion, what she recognized most was fear.

She couldn't hurt him again. This gentle bear of a man truly loved her. And she loved him.

"Chad, I – "

With two fingers he stilled her lips. Panic flickered across his face.

"Vanessa," he pleaded. "I can't bear to lose you. Please don't tell me it's too difficult to work out. It's too difficult not to." He paused, searching her eyes.

Not daring to interrupt, she nodded ever so slightly.

"I love you, Vanessa. I can't live without you."

Tears welled in her eyes. "Oh Chad, I love you too."

Their eyes locked until their foreheads touched. When their lips met, jubilation filled her heart.

He loves me!

Peace and joy washed over her. It didn't get any better than this. Chad loved her, and her mother was cleared. Suddenly she broke the kiss.

"My mother," she blurted. "I have to see her. Right now."

Elation filled Chad at the excitement in Vanessa's voice. He helped her to the truck and they hurried to the hospital.

In Darla's room, Baldy leaned over her hospital bed. Were they kissing? Vanessa and Chad backed out of the room and kept walking down the hall.

"He's here awful early," Chad said.

Vanessa took his hand. "What's with these men showing up at the crack of dawn?"

"Must be love." He gave her a goofy grin.

They rounded back to the room. Red-faced, Baldy sat in a chair acting like nothing happened. Darla beamed.

"Hello Mama!" Vanessa rushed into her mother's room. In a

robe and slippers, Darla sat by the window staring out into the darkness.

"Good morning," she said to Baldy, pausing as if she was still unsure what to call him.

He nodded nervously. "Good morning, honey." His eyes filled with love. He was her father – her dad! Could she learn to call him that?

Vanessa had confessed – she hadn't called Clyde "Dad" since was fifteen, since Layla left home and the infamous day he first assaulted her. She'd called him Clyde since then.

Vanessa looked away from Baldy's loving gaze. She fidgeted a moment before greeting her mother with a kiss on the cheek and a tight hug.

"Hey, Mama." Lee walked in then, indescribable joy on his face.

"No one pushed Clyde, Mama," Vanessa's gentle voice belied her excitement. "He jumped off that cliff."

Darla's face brightened to full rapture. "We're free." She looked up adoringly at her son. "This proves we didn't kill him." Her voice filled with relief.

She reached to her night stand and handed Vanessa a photocopied note.

Chapter 22 – Stupid Vengeance

Intrigued, Chad peered over Vanessa's shoulder as she read the note aloud.

"Darla, Jr, and Nessa, Im sorry I dun you rong and made you hate me. Im sorry Layla ran off cuz of me and got herself killed. I coudnt even pay the taxes and keep are home. Sell to them develipers if you want. I never thot Id do this but I cant live with mysself after what I dun. Yer beter off without me. I love you. Clyde"

"The writing and wording are his." Vanessa looked up at Chad. "Clyde killed himself."

"I just came from the police station," Lee said. "I guess *Mr. Daniels* got scared and spilled his guts."

"Really? So what's the story?" Vanessa asked.

"Apparently this whole thing was Myrtle's idea to hurt Mama, beginning with denying the campground permit," Lee explained. "Brian went along with it to get back at me. He thought Myrtle would be happy, but apparently there's no pleasing that woman."

Baldy grunted. Chad tried to muffle a chuckle, yet it escaped.

"Brian went out there to give final notice on the tax sale." Lee scowled. "He knocked on the door and it pushed wide open. No one answered, so he let himself in. He found the suicide note but swears he never saw Clyde. At least that's his story," Lee sneered. "Chief's still investigating Clyde's beating and the missing guns."

Vanessa hadn't heard about missing guns, but that would be a sore point with Lee.

"Personally, I think it was that loan shark bookie." Lee shot a look toward Chad that begged understanding.

"You mean the Riverside developer?" Chad commiserated. "I don't trust that guy."

"Me either," Lee said. "He was in cahoots with Brain and Myrtle. They wanted to buy our land at tax sale. Myrtle and the developer had the money, Brian had an in with the county and access to info about the sale."

"Nice to know our county officials are on our side," Vanessa said.

"Oh yeah," Lee agreed with sarcasm. "Anyway, I guess it's not every day you find a suicide note. Plus the place was ransacked and Clyde's car was stripped. Apparently Brian freaked. Told the chief that he called Myrtle and she went off the deep end. Brian says she told him to rip up the note. He took off outta there and tossed the note into the woods."

"That's what he was looking for when I found him in the woods that night," Chad interjected.

"Yep. He swears it was Myrtle's idea to frame me and Mama." He looked to his mother. "If we went to jail, there'd be no chance of us coming up with the tax money to save the land."

"I can't believe even Myrtle could be so evil and vindictive," Vanessa said. "Let alone the mayor's son."

"Plus Baldy and Brandy would both be free," Lee added.

"Don't mean I'd wanna see that old bat," Baldy scoffed.

"That wicked witch." Darla gave him the eye.

Chad couldn't help laughing. He wrapped an arm around Vanessa. She seemed bewildered by the whole turn of events.

"Oh, and Brian blamed Myrtle for the horse manure too," Lee said.

"That's why she acted so weird at the stable." Darla's eyes widened. "She was collecting manure to frame me!"

"That's planting false evidence," Lee said.

"A serious offense," Chad agreed. "So is withholding evidence and altering a crime scene. Looks like they'll both serve time in jail."

"Wow." Vanessa looked shocked.

"Stupid vengeance," Chad muttered under his breath. He imagined how humiliated the mayor would be. Brian had been handed money, power, and fame in this small town. But he threw it all away.

Chad could only imagine what Vanessa could have done with

privilege like that.

Myrtle would lose her business – everything she'd worked for all her life. How sad. Despite everything Myrtle had put their families through with her vicious lies, he couldn't help feeling sorry for her.

"I'll be jiggered," Baldy said.

"I'll tell you what I'll be jiggered about." Lee smiled at Chad. "Why are two women fighting over this old fart?"

Vanessa giggled and Baldy grinned.

Chad chuckled to himself. Baldy's life had sure taken a turn. So had Vanessa's. He hadn't seen her this happy since the first time he kissed her.

The room grew quiet while everyone seemed lost in their own thoughts.

"Well, Mama," Vanessa broke the silence. "At least Clyde was finally sorry for what he did. He lost his arrogance, realizing how much it hurt to lose you."

Suddenly deflated, Darla looked down at her wrists, then around the hospital room. "All this was for nothing. A waste of time and money." She brought her hands up to her cheeks, her mouth forming an O. "How will we ever pay for this?"

"Don't worry, Mama." Vanessa rubbed her back. "We're applying for help. You just get better." The soothing words couldn't erase the worry lines around Vanessa's eyes.

Chad decided then and there. He needed to do two things: raise funds to pay Darla's hospital bills, and help her daughter understand Christ's love.

The first part was easy. Chad stopped at the hospital again the next day. Fortunately the whole family was in Darla's room. He wrapped an arm around Vanessa and kissed her cheek.

Darla looked better and had an encouraging report from the doctor. Baldy and Lee stood at opposite ends of the room, seeming unsure of one another's acceptance.

"Hey, honey, I have an idea," Chad said. "I just want to make sure it's okay with all of you." He looked in turn to each of them.

"Okay..." Vanessa sounded leery. "Shoot."

"What do you think of putting donation cans around town to raise money for the hospital bills?"

The room fell silent.

"It's just an idea. If anyone's opposed, no problem."

"It's a wonderful idea, but I don't – " Vanessa looked perplexed.

"You don't have the time. No problem. I can wrap the cans and do the footwork," Chad assured her. "You need to concentrate on your mom and the tea room right now."

"You're not doing all that alone," Lee said.

"Does that mean you like the idea?"

"It isn't like the whole town doesn't already know what's going on." Lee grinned. "Might be interesting to see how many friends we really have around here."

Baldy snickered. "I have scores of coffee cans stashed in the barn, if you need 'em."

"That'd be great." Chad looked to Darla, who remained silent. "What do you think of the idea, Mrs. Gallagher?"

"Please Chad, call me Darla." Brow furrowed, she twiddled her thumbs. "I appreciate the offer. Really, I do. But I don't want you going to all that trouble for me."

"No trouble at all – Darla. I'd be honored to help."

She looked troubled.

"Maybe you can help, Mama," Vanessa piped up. "We can bring the cans here and you can help wrap them."

Darla's face brightened. "It'd be nice to have something to do besides sit here and try to convince everyone I'm sane," she said with a laugh.

Lee insisted on helping Chad deliver the wrapped cans to every business and government office in Crystal Falls and a few in Springfield and Willow Pond as well.

Over the next few days, Chad met with the few wealthy citizens he knew well enough to beg a donation: Max Carter, Elliot's parents, and Mayor Daniels.

The mayor frowned at Chad's request. Then he pulled out his checkbook.

"I'm sorry for my son's part in this tragedy." He handed Chad a sizable check.

Just a few days after learning of Clyde's suicide, Vanessa picked up her brother and father and Chad and headed to Riverside

Mental Health Center.

"Congratulations on a speedy recovery, Darla." The sweet nurse patted her mother's shoulder, and then looked to all of them. "Family support means everything. Keep up the good work and I don't expect to see her back here."

Heartened by her mother's beaming face, Vanessa gathered Darla's belongings. Chad and Lee grabbed the heavy stuff and Vanessa carried the flower arrangement from Rosebuds. Baldy took her mother's arm.

"I have a note here asking you to stop in the financial office on your way out – for some good news." The nurse's eyes smiled at them.

Vanessa and Darla popped in the hospital office while the men waited just outside.

"Hello," Vanessa said to the clerk. "The nurse said we needed to stop in for good news."

"Yes." The administrator's face beamed as she read the paperwork. "This says your bill is paid in full."

Darla's mouth fell open. Vanessa couldn't imagine Chad collected that much in coffee cans.

"There must be some mistake," she whispered to herself.

"No mistake." The lady apparently had bionic hearing. "A man named Chad James brought in a few large checks and several coffee cans filled with donations." She read the bottom of the paper. "Then an anonymous donor paid the balance."

"An anonymous donor?" Vanessa puzzled.

The administrator just shrugged and wished them well.

When Vanessa told the guys, Lee and Chad looked equally aghast. But Baldy had a smug expression on his face. Surely he didn't have that kind of cash. But the man knew something.

"Well, then let's go home." Baldy reached out to take Darla's hand, suddenly anxious to hit the road.

More comfortable with city traffic than Vanessa, Lee offered to drive Vanessa's car.

Chad sat in front with his long legs.

Vanessa sat in the back with her mother and father. Darla sat in the middle. Once settled in her little car, they headed toward Crystal Falls.

"So who's the anonymous donor?" Darla rested a hand on Baldy's knee.

"What makes you think I know?" Baldy's voice rose with surprise.

"You used to be so good at keeping secrets," Darla teased. "Now you're as transparent as that windshield."

Chad turned to Vanessa with a knowing look. He'd learned to read her like that, too. At first disconcerted, she now felt comforted that he knew her so well. He understood her and loved her anyway.

Baldy huffed a breath and looked down at his fidgeting fingers. "Myrtle paid those hospital bills."

Lee laughed out loud. "Isn't that old biddy in jail?"

"She's out on bail," Baldy replied.

"No way," Darla argued. "You're just assuming that because she paid *your* bills. Myrtle hates me, remember? She got me fired and tried to get our house condemned."

"She did it for me," he confessed. "She told me to never tell you, but I can't keep secrets from you. All my life..." He looked at Vanessa. "All of Vanessa's life I've kept secrets and they've eaten me alive. I can't do it anymore."

His face looked worried. "Never let on that you know, but Myrtle paid those bills."

Secrets – Vanessa didn't have secrets from Chad anymore either. He knew her darkest, most embarrassing secrets.

And again, he loved her anyway.

He'd even arranged to repair Mama's house for free. She'd comply with the town's orders and stay in her home.

"Myrtle Winthrop doesn't do anything just to be nice." Fear flickered across Darla's face as she looked at Baldy. "She wants you back."

"Now that makes sense," Lee said. "She's trying to guilt him into it." Looking up from the road, he glanced at them in the rearview mirror.

Chad turned and shot a compassionate look at Vanessa.

Baldy shook his head. "I already told her, I'm not interested. She respects that. Jail has changed Myrtle. With a little misery of her own, she realized how much everyone has suffered.

"Being deprived of luxury with few provisions, the barest essentials, and demeaning treatment, a few days in jail forced her to face the reality of what she'd done." His voice wavered.

"Darla has suffered more than anyone because of Myrtle's manipulation." Tears glistened in his eyes. "Then she tried to condemn Darla to prison for no reason. Myrtle actually hit rock bottom in that jail cell. She's ready to turn her life around."

"I don't believe that," Darla seethed.

He sighed. "It's penance. All these years you assumed Clyde schemed to take you away from me as revenge. In truth, Myrtle put him up to it. Clyde wanted Myrtle, they're two of a kind. But she loved me. Since I was in love with you, Myrtle decided if she couldn't have me nobody could." Baldy's face contorted with pain. He continued on a shaky breath.

"Myrtle knew Clyde would rise to the bait if he could hurt me deeply. She told him I wanted to marry you. Seeing how pretty you were, and the fact that Myrtle didn't want him, Clyde's revenge came easily."

Darla stared at him, flabbergasted.

"How could you be friends with her after what she did to you?" Lee scowled in the mirror, looking into the backseat with disdain.

Baldy sighed, long and deep. "I've lived a bitter, lonely life for many years. When I had the stroke, I thought that was the end." He wiped escaping tears. "My sister Julia visited me in the hospital, but our relationship is strained. At the end of the road, I had no one."

"I wanted to come – " Darla choked out, rubbing his knee.

"Clyde would have killed you," Baldy said matter-of-factly.

Darla snatched her hand from his knee, crossing her arms stiffly. He looked into her face as he spoke.

"Then Myrtle came to see me. She poured out her soul, and sincerely apologized." His voice shook with emotion.

"It wasn't easy, but I finally forgave her. It was like a burden lifted from me. I'd been carrying a heavy load of hate for a long, long time. It was wonderful to make peace. And pretty nice to have someone to talk to."

Darla stiffened, her eyes narrowed.

"I believed her," he continued. "I couldn't imagine the evil she'd plan. And I never dreamed she'd want to get me back. At this age!" He patted Darla's leg.

"Don't worry. I made it clear that would never happen." His eyes brimmed with tears. "You are the love of my life. I've waited all these years to be with you, and I'm sure not giving you up now."

Then he set his jaw. "And don't pull no more of your stunts neither. Do you know how it made me feel, you wantin' to kill yourself like that?"

Darla dropped her head as her expression softened.

"I'm sorry." Taking his hand, she held it a moment before she continued. "At the time I didn't realize what I was doing to all of you."

She looked into his eyes, and then into Vanessa's. She caught Lee's gaze in the rearview mirror.

Chad faced the windshield, apparently understanding this was a family matter.

"I'm so sorry," Darla said. "I didn't see how any of you could love a loser like me. I'd let you down my whole life, without enough backbone to even protect my dear children." She turned to Vanessa. "How could you love me after the suffering I let you endure?" Her eyes begged for an answer.

"You're my mother," Vanessa said. "I've always loved you, and I always will." She looked at the back of Lee's seat. "It's not your fault what Clyde did. He treated you even worse."

Lee stopped at a red light. "You didn't see a way out," he added. "If you fought back, he would have killed us all." He turned to face his mom. "If we ran, he would have hunted us down. You handled him the best you could until we grew stronger and he grew old and weak."

Darla nodded sadly. "I should have found a way to get out."

"But Mama – " Lee sighed with exasperation and faced the road.

"I'm the one who should have stepped in," Baldy said. "I stood idly by and let him terrorize my family."

The words jolted Vanessa like an electric shock. He considered them his family?

She stared past her mother at her father. She had a real father and the chance to have a relationship with him. This sweet, gentle man was her *father.*

"You had no more options than I did," Darla said emphatically. "And I asked you not to war against him. That feud had gone on long enough." She squeezed his hand. "There would have been fall-out, and the children would have suffered most."

He stared out the window. "I love you so much, but I couldn't show it. So many mistakes, so many lost years."

At last Vanessa realized she was worth loving. She'd been loved all these years by a man she didn't even know.

Chad turned. His caring, loving gaze caught hers. He loved her, warts and all.

He'd talked about her *heavenly* father. She didn't know him either.

Maybe God truly loved her too.

"Let's not waste another minute," Vanessa whispered with emotion. She reached across her mother's lap and touched her father's hand.

His gaze shot up at her and he grasped her hand tightly. Tears glimmered on his cataracts as his eyes filled with love.

She had a real live father! Not a man who abused her, raping or beating her at whim, but a father who *loved* her.

Darla rested her hand on their joined ones. She placed her other hand on her son's arm. Baldy placed his free hand above hers, squeezing Lee's shoulder.

Reaching up, Lee spread one hand over both of theirs, blinking away tears and keeping his eyes on the road. In the passenger seat and the back seat, tears flowed freely.

The sense of family Vanessa felt was unlike anything she'd ever experienced. She felt whole, accepted, *loved*. Not for how she looked or performed or what benefit she could provide, but simply for whom she was – daughter, sister, family.

Even Chad made her feel a part of his family. And she wouldn't mind sharing families with him.

Chad had succeeded in part one of his plan. The second part was harder.

Darla's hospital bills were paid. But Vanessa's family never had much to do with God.

On Sunday, he went to church with his family. His mother met him with a warm hug.

"No Vanessa again?" she asked.

"No, she's spending the day with her mother."

"Darla's doing better, isn't she?" Emily was concerned.

"Yes, we're hoping she can go home soon."

"Good. I miss Vanessa. She really seemed to enjoy coming to

church."

Chad smiled. "But I think she liked your Sunday dinner even better."

"Sacrilege!" Emily said with a laugh.

She didn't seem to notice his past tense. He didn't dare mention his greatest fear.

Did God and church really mean anything to Vanessa? Or did she just enjoy dressing up, singing, and the comforting words? He even wondered if she went simply to please him.

After dinner, he would visit Vanessa and talk to her about God. He had to know where she stood before he took the next step.

Chapter 23 – Beef and Chocolate

The weather finally warmed. Vanessa loved Indian summer – one last burst of sunshine before the blustery winter ahead.

After lunch and a lengthy visit with her Mama, she met Chad at her apartment.

"How about a walk?" he asked.

"Sure, let's enjoy the weather while we can." She grabbed a sweatshirt and they headed outside.

With an arm wrapped over her shoulders, he walked her toward the bridge over Crystal Falls and began talking about philosophical stuff.

And God.

Talking about God made her uncomfortable. Her beliefs were nobody's business but her own.

"Do you believe in God?" he asked.

"Of course I do." If he weren't so genuine, she might have been offended. "I wouldn't be so angry with Him if I didn't believe in Him. Besides, how could I not believe in God while enjoying all this?" She waved an arm toward the sparkling falls, moss-covered rocks and blooming chrysanthemums around them.

He squeezed her shoulder tightly, seeming relieved. He stopped on the bridge, gazing into the rushing falls below.

"Do you believe Jesus is God's son?" He held her closely, as if afraid she'd run off.

"Yes." Vanessa squirmed beneath his scrutiny.

Yet he wasn't even looking at her. He stared into the water, holding her tight.

"Don't worry, Chad. Julia and I had this talk a long time ago. I know Christ died for our sins, but the way my family was, I didn't think God really cared about *me*. Although lately I've seen how others are praying for me. God's been speaking to my heart, and I'm listening."

Chad looked into her eyes with hope and uncertainty.

Turning away, she confessed, "I've accepted God's forgiveness, and received Jesus into my heart."

He released a pent-up breath and pulled her into a hug.

"Vanessa, you don't know how happy I am to hear that."

Wrapped in his embrace, her heart sang. God loved her, Chad loved her, and her father loved her. Did she deserve them? She pulled back, turning to look over the bridge at the gurgling waters of Crystal Creek and the beautiful falls.

God created a gorgeous world for her enjoyment. He died to save her. He gave her a loving mother and a dedicated brother who got her through some tough years. Now she had her real father, and this wonderful man beside her.

"I know I don't go to church as much as I should." She shrugged as guilt swept over her. "I just wasn't raised that way and it's hard to change. Sunday's my only day off. I like to sleep in and catch up at home." Laundry might not be as important as church, but the sermon wasn't going to provide clean clothes for work on Monday morning.

"Although I struggled with God, I never thought much about church until I met you," she admitted.

He turned her, cupping her shoulders with his warm hands. He looked into her eyes with utmost sincerity.

"No guilt." He shook his head. "I never meant to make you feel guilty. I just couldn't bear to think of you struggling with all of this alone. Church helps me focus on God, and I know God wants to help you."

"Hmm." She frowned. "But He wasn't much help until lately."

"Maybe it took longer than you wanted, but He did come through. Your mama is home and she's a new woman."

Vanessa couldn't help but smile at his optimism. "You think so, huh?" Not waiting for an answer, she grinned at him. "Are you gonna have a little talk with her too?"

"Do you want me to?" he asked earnestly.

She smiled. "No, Mama's a Christian. She just hasn't been able to live her life for Christ – you know – with Clyde around."

She hated speaking ill of the dead, but the truth was the truth.

"Do you think that'll be different now?"

Thoughtful, she didn't answer for a minute. She hadn't wanted to discuss this with Chad, but he was so easy to talk to.

"Mama and I both need to be more dedicated to Christ." She hung her head. "I feel bad that I've been ignoring God for so long. I was angry with Him because my life was so rotten."

"We go through bad times to build our character."

"Yeah, but I don't have to like it." She rolled her eyes.

"No one does. But it's easier with God at your side. I heard a pastor say that God's more interested in our character than our comfort."

She nodded. "Well, I need God to be my comfort. And I want to live for Christ from now on. After all, He gave His life for me."

Chad's face beamed. "That's what I wanted to hear."

The following Saturday night, Chad knocked on Vanessa's door with a potted violet in his hand. He had debated on red roses for the occasion, but violets held more meaning for her. Besides, since when was he traditional?

But this date was special, just like Vanessa. Enough with the cheap dates – he was serious this time.

He smoothed his sport coat over his best button-down shirt and black dress pants. He even skipped the ball cap and traded his work boots for leather shoes.

Would she ever answer the door?

Hurried footfalls scurried toward the opposite side of the door and the dead bolt scraped. With a whoosh, the door opened to a vision of beauty.

Vanessa's beaming face glowed. Her eyes sparkled a deep, clear blue, and her long blonde hair flowed in loose curls the way he liked it. Her dress in a soft shade of purple cast a flattering radiance on her fair complexion. Not to mention the way it swathed her slender body.

He kissed her cheek, not wanting to smear her lip gloss. She pulled him to her for a quick hug. Taller than usual in strappy heels, she gracefully stepped aside.

"Come in." She stretched a lovely arm to motion him inside.

He held the flowers out to her.

"Flowers? For me?" She reverently took the blooms and set them on a table. "No one but you has ever given me flowers." She raised an eyebrow. "Except Lee's puffy dandelions when we were kids. Then he'd blow the white seeds all over my hair."

He smiled, unable to take his eyes off her.

She fidgeted as he gazed at her, color rising in her cheeks.

"You're absolutely stunning."

"Thank you." She nervously smoothed her dress. "I splurged and went shopping. I've never been this dressed up before."

"We'll have to give you a reason to dress up more often." He waggled his eyebrows and her blush deepened. He couldn't resist another kiss on her cheek.

She clung to him. As much as he was tempted to throw her onto that cushy old sofa and ravish her, he had other plans first. And he didn't want to mess up her hair – at least not yet.

"We have reservations at seven." He checked the clock on the wall. "Should we get going?"

"Sure." She wrapped a stylish ivory coat over her shoulders and grabbed a tiny purse before they headed into the crisp November evening.

Patrons filled Devon's, the expensive upscale restaurant in town. The maitre'd led them to a quiet booth in back with a window overlooking the creek. Twinkle lights glittered on the bare autumn trees, and spotlights showcased the gurgling creek below.

Vanessa nervously opened her menu. She wondered what Chad had planned. He'd never brought her to such a fancy place before, never with such mystery or wearing a sport coat.

She ordered the petite prime rib. When the waiter asked how she wanted her meat cooked, she had no idea what he meant.

"Well done, Medium, Rare?" he inquired.

"Medium," she replied, clueless. It sounded like a good answer. When Chad ordered his jumbo rib eye 'well done,' she worried that might have been better. If it wasn't well done, was the meat properly cooked? Yet certainly they wouldn't serve uncooked meat at this fancy place.

She noticed they agreed on food – beef for dinner. She knew Chad loved chocolate for dessert and so did she.

His conversation took her mind off her worries. She enjoyed

his company, the beautiful décor, and the amazing creek side view outside her window.

The waiter brought their salads. She stared down at the table.

At the tea room, they brought silverware with each course. At Devon's, she had two forks, two spoons and a knife beside her plate. She decided to wait for Chad and watch what he did with them all.

"All this silverware," he muttered conspiratorially. "I'm glad they put the ones you need first on the outside. Otherwise, I'd never be able to figure out what to do with it all."

He had such a way of helping without ever making her feel inadequate. Confidently eating her salad, she couldn't believe her good fortune.

Everything in her life was so new: her relationships, her family, her wonderful career with the prospect of actually owning her own business, and most precious of all – the charming and handsome man staring at her.

The waiter took their salad plates and brought the entrees.

Breathing in the delicious aroma of beef, she was in awe and her dinner partner seemed to be eating it up right along with his steak.

"How's your mom doing?" he asked.

"Really well." Vanessa brightened. "Since she was cleared, she's made a complete turnaround."

"That's wonderful. Amazing how stress affects the human mind and body."

"She wants to come back to the tea room – now that Myrtle's had a change of heart."

"That's great! Myrtle will get a slap on the wrist – but apparently she learned a lesson." He paused. "Has Baldy been around?"

"Only every day." Vanessa grinned from ear to ear. "I caught them kissing again yesterday. I kept on walking. Later they acted all embarrassed but I pretended not to notice."

He laughed heartily. "Who'd have thought?"

"Yeah. Almost like I might have normal parents. I'm wondering if they might get married." She stared down at her plate. "How weird is that?"

Chad took a sip of water.

"I have more good news too." She perked up. "Lee sold

Clyde's traps and his old car to scrape up money for the taxes. Then he got a permit for the campground."

"He did?" Chad looked like he'd jump for joy.

"Yeah. Thank goodness those greedy developers can't ruin the land."

"So you're not mad that I butted in?"

"No, I'm grateful." Vanessa bowed her head sheepishly. "You were trying to help, and I'm glad you did."

He took her hand. "I don't mind at all."

"I can't believe how you stuck your neck out for me." She seemed incredulous. "Didn't you feel threatened, thinking whoever beat up Clyde would come after you?" She held her breath.

"I don't let people like that intimidate me. Todd's a big blow-hard. He pushed the old guy to the edge. Huh – literally." He shook his head at his own pun. "With that on his conscience, I suppose it's punishment enough."

"Wow. I'm relieved we didn't lose our property to a man like that."

"'Our property?' So do you have a stake in the campground?"

"Yep. Lee gets a salary since he's doing all the work. We split the profit three ways with Mama. He'll buy us out when he can, and that's fine with me. I'd love to buy the tea room and give Aunt Julia a nest egg."

She felt tremendous hope, along with a peace and joy she'd never experienced before.

"May I interest you in dessert?" The waiter courteously interrupted.

"No thank you," Chad answered before she could reply.

Disappointment washed over her. The dessert case out front made her mouth water.

"Have a good evening, then. And please join us again soon." The man left a leather wallet on their table.

"We have other plans for dessert." Chad waggled his eyebrows at her.

Delighted, she giggled.

He checked the time on his cell phone and slipped it back into his pocket. "Are you ready?"

"Sure," she said eagerly, watching him closely as her nerves jumped.

He paid the check and left a generous tip. Walking to the door, she felt anticipation – and apprehension.

Something was definitely up.

Heading to Chad's house, Vanessa had the feeling this was a turning point in their relationship. After all she'd been through, his doting attention felt wonderful.

Yet her feelings for Chad frightened her. She couldn't even hope that he might want to be with her for more than right now. Forever didn't happen to girls like her. Their kind of forever was the tormented kind like her mother had known.

Real love was something you wished for, but couldn't really have. Like her real father had loved her mother, but couldn't be with her. Yet they were together now.

Was her life turning around?

Chad parked the truck and led her onto his porch. Bright yellow chrysanthemums flanked the front door. Eyes full of mystery, he kissed her lightly on the cheek. Then he threw open the unlocked door.

Vanessa stepped into the foyer overlooking his great room.

"Oh my."

Soft music played and a robust fire burned on the hearth. A blissful cinnamon aroma wafted from glowing candles on the mantel. On the coffee table, champagne chilled near two crystal glasses. Fresh strawberries and swirls of sauce garnished two glass plates laden with creamy chocolate silk pie.

"Look what you've done." Awestruck, she gaped at the romantic scene before her.

"I had a little help from the neighbors while we were out." He grinned with a nod toward the farmhouse next door.

His parents were in on this?

A tingle of hope shivered through Vanessa. He came up behind her. Wrapping his arms around her, he pulled her back against his chest. Engulfed in his warmth, she knew what heaven must feel like. For the longest time, he held her that way.

Reveling in his comfort, she didn't care if he never let her go. But her shoes were killing her. She slipped them off.

"That's my girl. Take 'em off. My home is your home."

If only. She turned in his arms.

"You don't mean it," she teased.

Chad's gaze grew intense. "Oh yes I do."

Wide-eyed, she stared into his face.

He didn't flinch. His hands ran up her sides with a luxurious caress. They nuzzled beneath her hair to cradle her neck. Then his touch slid slowly away as he dropped to one knee.

Her breath caught. This was like something from an old movie, when they knelt to propose. Things like this didn't happen in the twenty-first century, and they certainly didn't happen to Vanessa Gallagher.

Chad reached into his pocket and pulled out a tiny black velvet box. He snapped the box open.

A brilliant diamond solitaire glittered on a narrow platinum band. With her jaw hanging, she stared at the ring.

"Vanessa, will you marry me?"

She'd never seen Chad James so earnest. Joy flooded her senses like she'd never experienced.

Chad James, the handsomest, kindest, most adorable man on the planet wanted to marry her. Forever!

"Yes, Chad. Oh yes."

Her heart floated so high in the clouds she couldn't contain it. Lost in the moment, she felt his lips lock on hers. Warmth, love, and passion swept through her body and her brain.

Chad loved her.

God loved her and truly blessed her – with eternal life, with Chad, and with unique gifts and talents.

For the briefest second, she wondered if love and independence could co-exist.

But who needed independence? She had love.

Chapter 24 – Independence or Love?

In the morning, Vanessa called Darla and Baldy to invite them to the James farmhouse for Sunday dinner right after church. Both agreed to come to the service, thrilling Vanessa's heart. Her brother was unlikely to be so cooperative.

"I hope Brandy will come too," Vanessa added after Lee accepted her dinner invitation.

"She'd like that," Lee said. "What time is right after church?"

"You're welcome to join us at The Olde Methodist and find out," she teased. "Or meet us at the farmhouse around noon."

"I'll see what Brandy wants to do." He sounded perplexed.

Brandy usually attended church alone. Vanessa suspected she'd invited him before and he was wearing down.

She dressed with excitement, wearing gloves to hide the enormous rock on her finger until they announced their engagement at dinner.

To her surprised delight, the entire family showed up in church. Baldy and Darla wore their best clothes. Lee wore his characteristic overalls, but he shaved and he showed up. Brandy beamed beside him, holding his hand and singing exuberantly.

What a classy girl like Brandy was doing with a redneck like Lee was anybody's guess. Sort of like Chad and herself, she supposed. Opposites definitely attracted.

She got through the entire service wearing gloves, removing only the right one to take communion. At the farmhouse, she removed them to avoid questions. She hid her hand in the folds of her dress.

Fortunately, Chad wasn't one to beat around the bush. As soon as everyone settled around the table, he stood up, pulling Vanessa up beside him.

"We have an announcement." Chad pulled her hand into the open, waving the diamond for all to see. "She said yes."

In moments, everyone was hugging, laughing, and examining her ring. The James family heartily welcomed her to the family.

"Congratulations, honey." Darla hugged her and Vanessa felt an indescribable depth of love.

"Congratulations." Shy Baldy laid a hand on her shoulder.

Vanessa enveloped him in a hug and he responded with warm vigor. She felt so grounded, so secure. Being part of a family was the best feeling in the world – nearly as good as being a child of God, and being in love.

Tears of joy streamed down her face.

"Do we have your blessing?" Chad asked Baldy.

"You sure do. I'd be proud for my daughter to marry you, Chad." Baldy thumped him on the back.

"Will you walk me down the aisle?" Vanessa asked.

"Would I have to dress up and go out in public?" the old hermit asked nervously.

"Church was really pushing it, wasn't it?" Chad wrapped an arm around him. "Come on old man, I'll show you how it's done."

"Will you do this for me?" Vanessa pleaded. "Please...Dad?"

Baldy's face brightened as he nodded. Darla grinned beside him. Chad now had an arm around them both. Like a real family.

Vanessa's heart warmed as her eyes overflowed.

Finally everyone settled around the table. She picked up a napkin to dry her face, but Chad kissed the tears away. Smoothing a tendril of hair from her forehead, he whispered, "I love you." He smiled when her lips quivered with emotion.

Chad's father said grace, a personal prayer of gratitude that had fresh tears welling in her eyes.

No sooner had he said 'Amen,' than tiny Amelia shoved a basket of rolls into her face.

Chad snickered. Winking at Amelia, he shared the basket. Bowls passed until their plates mounded with food.

The James women could cook! With homemade rolls and fresh salad, they served hearty beef Wellington – Chad's favorite dish – with mashed potatoes, thick beef gravy, and glazed carrots.

When Vanessa thought she would burst, they pulled out a

mountainous chocolate torte.

"I don't think I can eat another bite," Vanessa bemoaned.

"I'm eating for two," Laura said from across the table.

"Me too!" Rachel chimed in, rubbing her swollen belly.

Their husbands, Brett and Elliot, exchanged worried glances. Rachel's daughters, Jessica and Amelia, giggled. Laura's baby Kate kicked in her high chair, happily smooshing mashed potatoes all over her face.

"Will we have chocolate cake at the wedding?" Amelia asked.

"I don't know," Vanessa said. "We haven't planned it yet."

"We're having chocolate cake, don't you worry," Chad assured his niece.

"Are you getting married at The Olde Methodist like Mommy and Elliot?" Jessica asked.

Chad grinned – a mischievous, devilish grin. "It's a family tradition to get married where your courtship started. Your mommy and Elliot met at the church. Aunt Laura and Uncle Brett met in the gazebo, and that's why they got married there."

Puzzlement clouded Vanessa's mind. With sudden clarity came dread. "I am not getting married on the side of the road! Nor in that truck of yours!"

Subdued chuckles surrounded them, but Jess and Amelia flat out guffawed. Baby Kate erupted in squealing laughter.

"We'll have to discuss this further," Chad said with a wink at Lee. "We haven't decided yet."

"I thought you weren't traditional," she hissed in his ear.

He kissed her neck, whispering not to worry. Yet she stewed the remainder of the afternoon.

After meaningful goodbyes, Chad walked her to his truck.

"Let's go for a drive," he suggested.

"Sure." She loved riding through the countryside and she was anxious to discuss this wedding location issue in private.

Barely seated in the truck, she rounded on him. "What's this business about getting married where we met?"

"Just a family tradition. I rather like the idea. Quite romantic, don't you think?"

"That depends on where you met. The side of the road is not romantic."

"Well it was that day." He wiggled his eyebrows with another mischievous grin.

She wanted to pound him.

"Actually, the first time we met was at the bait shop. Remember?"

"How could I forget? I was humiliated!"

Chad snickered, heading out Lake Road toward the bait shop.

"We are not getting married there, Chad James. If you won't agree to a respectable location, the wedding is off."

"Oh really? Getting a little feisty there are we?" He howled with laughter.

"It's not funny!"

"Lucky for you, I'm not a traditional kind of guy."

"Since when?" Relieved, she realized he was yanking her chain. Yet she'd never met anyone as traditional as Chad.

"When my entire family named their horses after *herbs*, of all things – how lame is that? – I named mine Midnight. And when the cats and dogs were named after jewels – Topaz, Emerald, and the like – I named mine Bluto and Popeye. Everyone followed my grandparents' footsteps in being florists. I took up carpentry and don't have a single flower in my yard. And I – "

"So you're a rebel are you?"

"You could say I'm a rebel of sorts," he said proudly.

"But you still ride horses, just like the rest of your family. Your dogs' names have a theme, so you followed that too."

He scrunched his face.

"You're an independent businessman, just like your father and grandfather before you. And you have houseplants and a thriving vegetable garden!"

"Hold the phone, just a doggone minute here. I took up with you, even after your father gave us nothing but grief. You can't say there's not something rebellious in that."

"Okay, that's a bit rebellious."

He smiled smugly.

"Just like the rest of your family."

"They are not!"

"Ha! Rachel was married to Jake Santos before Elliot came along. Laura married the son of that infamous Wayne Mitchell. I admit Wayne's a changed man, but still. Your father married your mother. No offense, but you told me yourself she was a poor girl from the wrong side of the creek – just like me. Stories of her childhood are a lot like mine. She told me even your grandpa was some kind of rogue – running off to America and your grandma never saw her family again."

"When was that little chat?" He stared in disbelief.

She didn't answer; she was on a roll.

"For all your pious 'I'm different' nonsense, you're just like the rest of your family. You are the most traditional man I've ever met. If I'd stand for it, you'd have me barefoot and pregnant, serving you like some king on a throne."

The grin returned. "What's wrong with that?"

She groaned. "What am I getting myself into?"

He pulled off the road by the lake where they'd spent so many happy hours talking and getting to know each other. He jumped out and opened her door.

She crossed her arms, trying to ignore him, but he pulled her down into his arms and buried his face in her hair.

"I'll tell you what you're getting into." He whispered in her ear so passionately she nearly melted with the heat of wanting him. His hands ran up her back as he kissed the top of her ear. His tongue trailed to her earlobe until his lips engulfed it.

With a gasp, she was lost.

"Picture this," he whispered. "July at the lake. I'll build a pretty arbor or pergola or whatever you want. Family and friends all around. Water rippling, cattails swaying, birds singing, and wildflowers blooming. Oh, and of course, paths lined with violets."

"You remember the violets," she breathed.

"Did you think that potted violet was a coincidence?"

"I was afraid to ask. But there are no violets at the lake," she said. "And no paths."

"Lee's building paths. I'll plant the violets," he said. "With help from the *real* gardeners in my family."

"You'd plant violets for me?" She thought she'd faint from the depth of his sweetness. "That sounds beautiful, Chad.

And very romantic."

Vanessa's bridal shower was a dream come true. Rachel invited everyone they knew to her home on Rose Hill Drive for afternoon tea. After eating endless yummy savories and sweets and drinking pots full of tea, they played a couple fun games and then Vanessa opened a mountain of gifts.

As the guests said goodbye, Vanessa admired Rachel's home.

"I can't believe this house is brand new. It has all the architectural details and old world charm of a century home."

"That was the plan." Rachel smiled proudly as she piled cookies on a platter.

"Rachel has awesome taste," Brandy chimed in as she carried a stack of gifts toward the door.

Rachel smiled. "You could make Chad's house more Victorian with just a few touches here and there."

"He'd never go for that," Vanessa said.

"You never know." Rachel lifted a brow. "Chad would do just about anything to please you."

"Don't be telling her that." Chad stood in the doorway with a wrapped present.

Vanessa ran to him, smooching him full on the lips.

"She's right you know," he whispered against her lips. "I'd do anything to please you."

Her heart could not contain any more joy.

"One more present." He pulled her onto the sofa and laid the heavy box on her lap.

The white on white paisley gift wrap was decorated with lavender ribbon and a spray of silk violets. Eyeing Chad, she carefully slid her finger beneath the tape. As the paper fell away, she recognized the violet-patterned tea set on the box.

With a gasp, she looked up into his eyes.

"When did you do this?"

Grinning, he shrugged. "I have my ways."

Vanessa hugged him with all her might.

"I'll build you a shelf to display it. Or we could get a china cabinet if you like. My house is your house, and you can decorate however you please." He beamed at her.

"Living in your house, just like it is, will please me beyond words."

He smiled into her eyes with admiration and love.

His colonial was simple, traditional, and oh, so *Chad*. The Victorian tea room was enough for her.

She had no more desire to change him than she wanted him to change her. Love and independence could co-exist, and they would prove it.

Epilogue

Darla Gallagher & Wilbur Calvin
And
John & Emily James
Cordially Invite You
To the Wedding Ceremony Of Their Children
Vanessa Mae Gallagher
And
Chadwick John James
Held at the Violet Arbor
At Crystal Lake
On Saturday, July 24
At Three in the Afternoon
Reception to Follow
In the Crystal Lake Pavilion

Vanessa checked the mirror as Sarita fussed with her veil in the newly built lodge at Crystal Lake Campground. Lee and Chad had built the beautiful outdoor pavilion complete with a commercial kitchen, spacious restrooms and the spectacular lodge just in time for the wedding.

"What do you think Chad's surprise will be?" Rachel asked.

Vanessa felt the color drain from her face. "Surprise?"

"You know Chad." Rachel raised an eyebrow. "He built this fancy lodge and planted violets along the path and designed the prettiest arbor I've ever seen. The man has limits you know. He's got to do something rebellious."

"Getting married at a campground isn't rebellious enough?" Vanessa had a scary vision. "He better not show up in overalls."

Rachel laughed. "Or hang a shotgun over the arbor."

"Or switch the menu to BBQ and cornbread," Laura chimed in.

"I planned this wedding to the last detail," Vanessa fretted. "It might be a campground, but the lake is beautiful."

"I better take a look around." Sarita slipped out the door of the lodge.

Vanessa peeked out. Chad stood close by, but his back was to her. At least he wore a tux. He stood talking with handsome Max Carter as Sarita walked by. Max watched her and some kind of passionate look transpired between those two. Sarita sidled past but Max never took his eyes off her. Vanessa shamelessly eavesdropped on the men.

"Who's that beauty?" Max leaned toward Chad.

"Sarita Santos," Chad said. "Man, you're in trouble."

"What do you mean?" Max asked.

"She's a beauty, but you ain't seen nothing yet."

Max gawked at her stunning form, grinning like a fool. Chad began to turn, so Vanessa shut the door before he spotted her.

"I can't believe we're flower girls *again*!" Jessica thrust her hands onto her hips in a sarcastic gesture.

"Three weddings in three summers." Rachel fluffed Amelia's hair. "Don't you think it's about time Uncle Chad got married and gave you more cousins?" She winked at Vanessa.

"Uncle Chad's too slow. He wants boys but you and Aunt Laura beat him to it." Jessica giggled as the door shoved open.

"What's this about boys?" Laura ambled in with two blue bundles of joy in her arms.

"Lemme see Cameron!" Amelia tugged her tiny cousin's foot.

Laura's baby giggled and she leaned toward Rachel with Elliot III. "Here, take Number Three."

"You've got to stop calling him that. It's gonna stick." Rachel gladly took her son off Laura's hands.

"Chad started it," Vanessa admitted.

Rachel shook her head. "That brother of mine. Do you know what you're getting into?"

"I have a rough idea," Vanessa said.

"Rough being the operative word." Sarita snuck back in, smoothing her violet maid-of-honor dress.

"So what'd you find?" Vanessa asked eagerly.

"Nothing unusual." Sarita shrugged. "Everyone's in a tux who's supposed to be, the caterer's setting up as planned, and there's not a shotgun in sight."

The wedding march began to play.

"That's our cue!" Vanessa grabbed her bouquet as Rachel handed the girls baskets of violet petals and opened the door. Waiting outside, Baldy looked nervous, but handsome in his tux.

"Thank you for doing this." Vanessa gave him her arm with a grateful smile. They lined up behind Jess, Amelia, and Sarita.

"My pleasure." Beaming, Baldy Calvin, *her real father*, would walk her down the aisle.

The music heightened. Vanessa's gaze shot to Chad. Breathtakingly handsome in his black tuxedo, he wore a devastating grin that told her something was indeed up.

She scanned the grounds. Blooming violets bordered the stone path and a white paper ribbon led the way from the door to the pretty arbor. Purple clematis climbed the arbor flanked with enormous pots of violets. No guns of any kind.

Tiny white lights twinkled in the rafters of the pavilion and billowing tulle bows decorated each supporting beam. The tables were set with neat white tablecloths, potted violets, and floating candles. The catering van was from the firm she'd hired and she smelled the roast beef.

Their guests were seated in padded white chairs on the lawn. Her mother sat in the front row beside Aunt Julia with John and Emily James on the opposite side.

Chad smirked like a kid with fingernails poised on a chalkboard. Beside him, Brett looked ready to burst out laughing.

Jess and Amelia reached the arbor and the white ribbon was covered with violet petals. Beautiful – and she'd missed it. Sarita was halfway down the aisle already.

Vanessa gathered her wits and adjusted her bouquet of violets in front of her. With a fortifying smile at her father, she straightened her spine and grinned for all she was worth.

The music intensified. One foot in front of the other. Here comes the bride. Don't slip in these heels.

What was Chad up to?

As she approached, he winked at her.

She gave him a look, hoping it said, "Don't you dare do whatever you've got up your sleeve." She feared the telepathic message wasn't received.

Her father kissed her cheek and let go of her arm to take his place beside her mother. The gold medallion at her neck shone almost as much as her glowing face.

Chad met Vanessa at the arbor and took her hand. They faced the minister.

"Today we celebrate a special union." The pastor opened his Bible. The reading on love from I Corinthians 13 almost made her tear up. Everything was perfect and beautiful. She glanced at her handsome groom. His eye caught hers with a roguish sparkle.

The pastor prepared to recite their vows. Would Chad dare doctor his vows? He squeezed her hand and drew her to face him. When she turned, that's when she saw it.

A procession of trucks, decked out with ribbons and bows, parked behind the building where she'd dressed. Chad's blue beast led the way, followed by Brett's black four-by-four, and Elliot's silver extended pickup. Max had offered his Porsche for their drive around town and to the gazebo for pictures. Yet there it sat in the parking lot with the mini-vans and SUVs.

Her eyes widened, and then she glared at Chad. His dark eyebrow tilted up with a smirk and his deep blue eyes glinted violet.

How could she be mad at him? She'd just hike her dress and climb into his truck. Rachel's girls would love it. She swallowed a chuckle, looking at the ground to compose herself.

Chad wore black work boots with his tux.

Vanessa tried to stop the giggles, but they spurted out.

The infernal man would never stop making her laugh. He was his own man, rebel that he was. And she was her own woman.

Independence and love – she and Chad had both.

Violets for Vanessa Reader's Guide

1. Did you catch the prophetic double meaning of the song "Who's Your Daddy?" playing on Chad's radio at the beginning of the story?

2. Vanessa and Chad met as children. Although five years apart, they were aware of each other over the years growing up in small town Crystal Falls. Discuss how their feelings toward one another changed once they were reacquainted as adults.

3. Vanessa grew up in a run-down cabin attached to a bait shop. Her father is a trapper and her mother cleans horse stalls. Discuss the significance of Vanessa's career at The Porcelain Teapot and her gravitation toward civility and beauty.

4. How does the rural small town setting of Crystal Falls help or hurt the circumstances of Vanessa's family? How does it affect Chad's family?

5. Domestic abuse is confronted in the story. Have you ever witnessed this type of abuse? Do you believe domestic violence has increased in modern society or occurred just as often in the past but was more hidden?

6. Do you understand Darla's point of view when she refused to leave her home despite Clyde's abuse?

7. *Violets for Vanessa* deals with sexual abuse as well. Do you believe the open sexuality of modern society has affected this type of abuse?

8. To protect Vanessa, and herself, Darla hid the truth about Vanessa's real father. Did Darla do the right thing by keeping this secret?

9. When Clyde is found dead, can you relate to Vanessa's empathy and confused feelings?

10. Before the story revealed it, what scenario did you suspect resulted in Clyde falling off that cliff? Were you as shocked as Vanessa by the truth?

11. Was Chad being selfish when he wanted to spend time alone with Vanessa while her mother was ill? How do you feel about Vanessa's reaction to him?

12. Vanessa's father was a hermit who shunned society. Discuss how her independent spirit results from both genetics and her upbringing.

13. Both Vanessa and Chad rebel in some ways. How do their very different family backgrounds contribute to their needs for independence?

14. Can you relate to Vanessa's fear of losing her independence? Does Chad's behavior warrant that reaction?

15. Were you surprised by the irony that Julia is Vanessa's aunt? Do you think Julia suspected this when she hired Vanessa?

16. If Julia had offered The Porcelain Teapot to Vanessa as a gift or inheritance, do you think independent Vanessa would have been as willing to accept ownership?

17. At what point did Chad win Vanessa's heart?

18. Can you relate to Chad's concern about Vanessa's faith? Do you find it interesting that in pursuing their relationship, he was more apprehensive about her feelings toward God than her tormented family history?

19. Vanessa is reluctant to trust God because she feels He wasn't there for her when she needed Him most. Chad argues the ways God protected her despite her suffering and severe trials. Discuss your thoughts.

20. Throughout the story, Vanessa feels she cannot have both love and independence. Yet in the end, she finds both. Or does she?

Next in The Crystal Falls Series…

SUNFLOWERS FOR SARITA,
BOOK IV in The Crystal Falls Series

Chapter 1 – Broken Sunflowers

Hot August sun streamed through the display window of Willow Pond Interiors, but Sarita Santos stood frozen, chills running through her as the voice of the small town Ohio police chief reverberated from her cell phone.

"Ramone got parole. He was released this morning."

Icy fear prickled her scalp, surging through her with a sudden trickle of sweat down her back, all the way to the tips of her frigid toes.

"His attorney appealed to get him out early. I don't know how or why, but he won." Chief Hunter heaved a sigh. "We'll do all we can to protect you, Sarita. Stay away from Riverside and his old haunts."

Shivering, she dabbed perspiration from her brow. Her stomach pitched with the rush of heat and cold, nausea churning as if she'd just contracted the flu.

Ramone Valdez had murdered her best friend. When Sarita refused to abort his child, he tried to kill her too. Then she testified against him, and he swore revenge. After he went to prison, she'd moved to nearby Crystal Falls, cut all connections to her sordid past, and started a new life. But Riverside was only twenty-five miles away.

He'd track her down.

"Don't go near anyone connected to him," the chief warned.

Sarita sucked in a jagged breath. "What if he finds my mother? She watches Gracia." Scenes of horror flashed through her mind: Ramone busting through the door, yanking Gracia from her mother's arms, torturing her screaming child.

"Don't panic. Where does your mom live?"

"Here in Crystal Falls. In the apartment above the music shop." Bile burned her throat.

"Stay here in town. Your phone's unlisted, right? And your

mother's?"

"Yes." Her voice cracked. "We only use cell phones."

"Good. Lie low for a while. Watch for anything suspicious and let us know. I'll ask the department in Riverside to keep an eye out for him. We'll do the same here."

"Thank you."

"I'll be checking in with you. Keep your daughter close and be safe."

Trembling, Sarita fumbled the phone into the pocket of her dress. Only then did she feel the bristles across the palm of her other hand. The woody stem of a sunflower crushed in her fist. Its fresh green scent filled her nostrils and oily sap covered her hand.

She dropped the broken flower as if it were razor wire.

Would Ramone hunt her down? Had prison deterred his promise of revenge, or hardened his heart even more?

She swallowed the acid taste and wiped her hand on a dust cloth. With a desperate prayer on her lips, she dialed her mother's number.

"Hello, mama?" she stammered.

"Sarita, what's wrong?"

"Mama, where's Gracia?"

"She's napping." An edge of irritation tainted her mother's voice as the opening music of her favorite soap opera played in the background.

"Will you check on her, please?"

"Why? What's wrong?"

"Quickly, Mama, please. Then lock all the windows and doors – especially the balcony over the back alley."

"But – "

"Ramone's been released from prison."

"No – " Maria Santos gasped and the phone clamored as she dropped it. Rushed footsteps scuffled away and a door creaked shut. The click of a deadbolt, more rushed footsteps and heavy breathing coursed through the phone line. Muted sounds assured Sarita she was locking the windows.

"She's safe." Her mother sounded more rattled than confident.

"Thank you, Mama. Please stay home and keep your eyes open. Don't let Gracia outside. The police will be watching the area."

"Okay." Maria heaved a breath. "Whew. It's hot in here

already. Is it really necessary to lock the windows on the second floor?"

"I'm sorry, Mama. We can't take any chances. I wish you had air conditioning."

"Yeah. It's usually not this hot up here."

Northern Ohio summers rarely required more than an open window and a fan to circulate the breeze. A native Puerto Rican, her mother spent her youth in tropical heat without air conditioning. But she was older now, overweight, and acclimated to the cooler climate.

"We'll have to figure this out. Please just be careful and I'll be there as soon as I can."

"Okay, honey. Try not to worry."

"I will. Thanks, Mama. Please pray."

Ramone would need more than a day to find her. After four years in the slammer, his first order of business would be booze and sex. He would likely return to Riverside and hole up with one of his drunken floosies.

When she and Ramone were together, he'd cheated plenty while Sarita had worked her tail off to support them. Furious when she got pregnant, he could no longer rely on his star stripper to bring in the cash. He insisted on an abortion. When she refused, he orchestrated an 'accident' by cutting the brake lines on her car.

Injured and close to miscarriage, she'd gotten out of the hospital in time to testify against him. He was in prison by the time Gracia was born. He might not know she that survived.

And surely he'd never suspect Sarita had gone to interior design school and landed a job in swanky Willow Pond.

She couldn't stop shaking. Even in small town Crystal Falls, her precious daughter could be in danger.

Her stomach roiled. She needed food but the last thing she wanted to do was eat. Sipping her chocolate espresso to settle her stomach, she resolved to keep busy. No customers wandered about for the moment.

As turmoil churned her mind, she struggled with an arrangement of sunflowers in the front window of the store. The warm sun, once welcome, now felt garish as she massaged her forehead to fend off a migraine. Taking deep breaths, she scanned the quaint main street of Willow Pond, checking pillared corners and brick alleys for any sign of Ramone.

A well-dressed man passed the window and caught her eye. After initial surprise, he grinned. Men gawked at her looks without a care for the person inside. Much less what she was going through this minute.

As he opened the door, Sarita groaned inwardly. Drained and terrified, she just wanted to be left alone. She needed to focus on a way to protect her daughter and hide from Ramone without leaving her job and everything she'd worked for.

The handsome man smiled as he approached her. "You look as sunny as those flowers."

"Thank you." She felt like a wreck after that phone call. She climbed from the display window, careful not to hike up her slim yellow dress. Ah – he must have meant her yellow dress and dark hair matched the sunflowers.

Wobbly on spiked heels, she righted herself on the slick tile floor.

He stuck out a hand and she braced herself for the onslaught of emotion his touch could bring. Handsome men still held power over her.

His firm handshake steadied her. Like a gentleman, he helped her regain her balance without letting on he was doing so. Too upset for his touch to cause the anticipated effect, she felt an odd comfort instead. She pulled back with cool grace and mentally shored up the talented interior designer she'd trained to be.

"Welcome to Willow Pond Interiors. I'm Sarita."

"Nice to meet you, Sarita. I'm Max Carter. I believe we've met before. I'm a friend of Chad and Vanessa James. Weren't you in their wedding?"

His sandy hair and trim frame looked familiar. She met his gaze. With a jolt of surprise, she remembered him. He'd caught her eye at the wedding two summers ago, and Vanessa hinted hard that he was interested. But after all Sarita had been through, she'd sworn off men.

She had her hands full raising a three year old and building a career. Now she had Ramone to worry about.

Besides, as memory served, Max Carter, millionaire tycoon, lived a few notches above anyone who'd be interested in an ex-stripper with a toddler in tow.

"I'm surprised you remember." Her raw emotions precluded flattery.

"How could I forget?" Heat radiated from him in waves of spicy cologne and overheated male, threatening to melt her resolve like the chocolate stashed in her purse. *Lord, give me strength.*

"It was a beautiful wedding." She tried not to stammer, determined to be professional and get to business. "It's nice to see you again. So how can I help you today?"

His expression registered disappointment, but he let the conversation shift.

"Vanessa recommended you to redecorate my great room. I have a large stone fireplace and cathedral ceilings. I'd like to make the big room feel more intimate." He cleared his throat as if fortifying his businesslike manner. "Cozy, that is." Avoiding eye contact, he glanced around the store.

"All right." She ignored the double meaning of his words. "We need to find your style. Let me show you around." Still shaken, she led him toward a grouping of sofas and chairs on tottering heels. She put on her professional face and fought an inclination to touch his arm for support. "Point out anything that strikes you, without concern whether it fits the room. I need to get a feel for your taste."

That was *all* she needed a feel for. His kindhearted gaze made her want to lean into him for a hug. How she needed one right now. But her weakness for affectionate comfort had betrayed her time and time again. Irresistible men had gotten her into this mess.

With this one, she'd have to be ultra careful to subdue her natural tendency toward physical contact. Any association with a client not only undermined professionalism, it could prove detrimental to her priority of protecting her daughter.

At least his presence distracted her from that looming threat. Pushing Ramone from her mind, she strived to focus.

They wandered through the store, perusing various styles and woods and colors. Max stopped to rest his hand on the back of a bold-shaped couch in a banana color much like her dress.

"I like this." He studied the sofa, and then looked toward a chair upholstered in a mango print. "That's interesting." He eyed bamboo tables and lamps. "I like the whole grouping."

"Do you like a tropical style?" Having grown up in Puerto Rico, Sarita gravitated toward Caribbean colors and forms.

"It reminds me of the beach, of carefree vacations." His smile reflected fond memories.

"What if we mix it up a bit?" She tossed lime and turquoise throw pillows onto the couch and chair. "Too much?"

Without batting an eye, his face broke into a childlike grin. "It's wild, but I like it." He scrubbed the sandy stubble on his chin. "I don't know how it'd go with my stone fireplace, though." He pulled snapshots from the pocket of his creamy linen shirt.

Excited to decorate in the style she adored, Sarita took the photos. Careful not to graze his fingers, she noted his tanned arms and lack of a wedding band. She glanced at the photos.

"How do you feel about plants?" she asked.

"Love them. Gardening is my hobby."

"Perfect!" She brightened. "Garden rooms and bringing the outdoors inside is my specialty. We could create a tropical oasis in your living room."

"Sounds great." With hesitant enthusiasm, he added, "But what about the rustic fireplace?"

"I'm sure we could make it work."

He smiled over a pause. "Yes, I'm sure we could."

His alluring tone implied much more than decorating.

Barely able to breathe, she handed back the pictures with shaking hands. She needed air, needed space from this man and his tantalizing scent. She'd settle for a chair with a large table between them.

"Let's sit down and formulate a plan." The words came from some autopilot in her brain.

Max glanced at his watch. "Can we discuss it over lunch? There's a wonderful little bistro on Main Street and I'd be honored to buy you lunch."

If only she could lie and say she'd already eaten. Given the frightening call from Chief Hunter, she had no appetite whatsoever. As her mind darted for an excuse, the elderly store owner ambled to her rescue.

"Mrs. Kentosh," Sarita said gratefully. "This is Max Carter. He's redecorating his great room."

Reaching arthritic fingers toward Max, Mrs. Kentosh shook his hand with more gusto than a woman her age had a right to.

"Sarita, dear," she said. "Why don't you show Max our gallery." With a wink, she nodded toward the private conference room.

Relief swept over Sarita as she continued toward the room.

Her elderly boss seemed to read her mind.

"Actually," Max addressed Mrs. Kentosh, "I wondered if I might take Ms. Santos to lunch while we discuss her ideas. I'd be happy to see the gallery later."

"How sweet of you!" the older woman gushed. "After that disturbing phone call, dear Sarita could certainly use a nice lunch out with a handsome young man."

How did she know about the phone call? Practically deaf, she had to be telepathic.

Sarita stared at Mrs. Kentosh. Read this: I don't want to go.

Mrs. Kentosh clasped Sarita's hand in hers. "Go have a nice lunch. And take your time, honey."

Max grinned from ear to ear.

She had no way out now.

Have you read

LILACS FOR LAURA,
Book I in The Crystal Falls Series?

Chapter 1 – Broken Lilacs

An eerie shadow crossed the window of Rosebuds Flower Shop. Laura James looked up from her arrangement of lilacs with a tingle of alarm.

Only May sunshine peeked in the window, filtering colorful light through the stained glass border of pink roses and green leaves. Yet a sense of impending doom lingered.

How silly. Nothing remotely dangerous ever happened in Crystal Falls. That security was exactly why she loved her small Ohio hometown. Too bad her family heritage wasn't so secure.

Worries over finances were making her jumpy.

Breathing in the heady fragrance, she lifted a crystal vase overflowing with lilacs. Her grandfather had planted lilac bushes years ago on family land. Heaven forbid if her parents lost the farm.

She carried the vase toward a round wooden table in the center of the shop.

A shadow returned.

The door burst open, banging the wall.

Laura jolted as the antique bell jangled wildly.

In slow motion, the vase fell through the air. Shards of crystal exploded across the wooden floor.

Her eyes widened at water splashing her sandaled feet among broken lilacs and remnants of her grandmother's vase.

The antique door shut with a tinkling thud.

Her gaze jerked up to see her sister's husband.

As he sashayed toward her, lust settled in his dark eyes. Even more than the last time.

Self-conscious of her generous curves, she smoothed water droplets from her skirt. Heat crept up her neck, but she glared at

Jake Santos and casually tossed her long blond hair over her shoulder.

Too handsome for his own good, Jake shot her a look that made her stomach churn. She stiffened, refusing to let him see her tremble.

"Grandma brought that vase from England," she growled. "I can never replace it." Rising panic made her breathing erratic.

"That's too bad." A strand of ebony hair fell to his forehead, Elvis Presley style. His gaze crept over her as one corner of his mouth lifted in a wicked grin.

"Jumpy today, sis?" With a bawdy laugh, he waltzed toward her like he owned the place.

At the faint smell of whiskey, Laura backed away, teetering on heels that didn't remedy her height disadvantage. Fighting hysteria, she stumbled to the closet and snatched a broom.

Willing her arms not to shake, she ran it over the edge of one sandal, where a sliver of glass threatened her lavender-polished toes. She swept glass into a dustpan, and banged it on the rim of the trash can in the closet. Maybe a show of anger would mask her panic.

The wooden floor creaked with Jake's nearing footsteps. The reek of alcohol intensified.

"All alone?" His husky voice hung in the air.

Her mind raced. Her father was home recovering from knee surgery. Her mother wouldn't be back from deliveries for at least an hour. She was on her own.

With a deep breath and a silent prayer, she propped the broom in a corner.

"Can I help you?" She set her jaw, crossing her arms over her chest.

"Oh yeah, you can help me." He raised an eyebrow.

His stare made her realize, too late, that crossing her arms created more cleavage where she had too much already. She dropped her arms, digging fingernails into her palms.

Jake slowly surveyed her body. All too aware of her clingy top and fitted skirt, she wished she were wearing the shapeless apron that made her feel fat.

"Do you need some flowers or are you just here to ogle the merchandise?" She narrowed her eyes, trying to look fierce.

"Both." He cocked his head with amusement and moved closer.

Grabbing the broom, she backed up until her elbow banged a wall. Gulping air, she was cornered in the closet.

The vacuum cleaner jutted into her back. Just like the leather armrest pressed into her spine on that starless night eight months ago. Her heart pounded.

Not again. The scene flashed through her mind – a wooden steering wheel, shiny chrome gauges, and tan leather seats. Not tan. Biscuit, her then-boyfriend had indignantly corrected her. Blond hair fell across his blue eyes. His wet, greedy mouth had smelled of sickly sweet peppermint.

She hated peppermint.

Liquor was worse.

Jake's silhouette filled the closet doorway. Grinning like *The Grinch Who Stole Christmas*, he reached for her.

"No!" Swinging the broom frantically, she whacked at his legs.

"Ow!" He stumbled backward, rubbing his shins.

She ran for the counter and skidded behind it.

"What's wrong with you, woman?"

"Get out," she hissed, brandishing the broom like a weapon. Hair stood up on the back of her neck.

Jake laughed. "But I need flowers, and you need business."

"I said get out!"

"What am I supposed to tell Rachel? That you kicked me out and wouldn't sell me any flowers? How do I explain that?"

Horror rose like bile in her throat. Her sister could never know about this. Desperate not to let Jake further diminish Rachel's fragile self-esteem, Laura glared at him.

"What do you want?" she snarled.

"Gimme the usual." He raised his eyebrow again. Leaning an elbow on the counter, he adjusted his collar to display his bronze chest. He was gorgeous and she hated him. Disgusted with her own intrigue, she looked away.

Keeping the broom handy, she half-turned to the cooler behind her. She slid open the glass door. Cool, moist air wafted over her flaming skin as she felt his eyes burn through the fabric of her dress. The invigorating floral scent clashed with Jake's alcoholic stench.

She chose eleven red roses. The twelfth one pricked her. She resisted a flinch and swiped away a drop of blood with her thumb. She laid the blooms in a long, thin box with a red bow.

"That'll be $20.00 – family rate," she stated smartly.

"Put it on account. You know the drill."

"Yeah, I know it all right. What did Rachel find this time – lipstick, a bra, maybe another pair of panties in your car?" She pushed the box across the counter. "And you think red roses make everything okay."

Hurt glinted in his eyes. "No matter what I do, it's not good enough. Doesn't mean I don't love her."

"Yeah, right."

He frowned. "Your sister doesn't understand me."

"She's not the only one."

"Come on, Laura," he pleaded. "You know I love Rachel. But I love you, too." He came around the counter.

"Get out!" She screeched, reaching for the broom.

The bell jingled and the door creaked open.

Jake stepped back. Pressed against the cold glass doors of the cooler, Laura trembled. Her gaze darted between him and the wide-eyed lady at the door.

"Later, little sister," he said under his breath. He tucked the box under his arm and smiled at the woman. Weaving between plants and flowers, he regained his swagger along the way.

"Mornin', Mrs. Hunter," he greeted the police chief's wife with an extra dose of charm. His words reverberated off the embossed tin ceiling as he waltzed out the door.

Laura shivered. He loved her too? Surely he wouldn't have done anything more than steal a kiss, even if Mrs. Hunter hadn't walked in.

Would he?

ROSES FOR RACHEL,
Book II in The Crystal Falls Series?

Here's an excerpt...

Chapter 1 – Crumb Cake

Gripping the steering wheel, Rachel Santos shivered despite the warm June weather. A chill ran up her spine as a bad feeling washed over her.

Chugging up the rural Ohio road, her rusty yellow Toyota headed for a familiar white rattletrap coming toward her. Sunlight glinted across its windshield, hiding Mr. Gallagher's shaggy white head and scraggly beard.

Yet that face plagued her mind. Ten months ago, he'd threatened revenge – slow and sweet. His daughter had died in a car accident – Rachel's husband had been the other driver. She felt horrible for his loss, but she'd had nothing to do with it. Although her husband was now dead, Mr. Gallagher's boat-sized car drove past her house frequently – slowly enough for the toothless driver to deliver an evil glare.

Watching him draw ever closer, she heard a gasp from the back seat. Screams jarred her.

"Mommy, look out!" her girls shouted.

To her right, an old pickup barreled out of a driveway. She screeched as faded green paint filled her windshield. The driver's cueball head gaped in terror. Tromping the brake, she braced herself.

Shrieking filled the air. Tires squealed, metal crunched, and glass shattered. The engine roared and clunked to a stop. Screams turned to frightened sobs.

Thank God her girls were alive.

Frozen in shock, she forced her eyes open. Steam poured from her Toyota's mangled yellow hood, obscuring her view. Her chewed gum lay on her lap. Bits of glass, broken china, and piles of crumbs littered the passenger seat and floor. So much for the tea cakes she'd baked for her sister's party.

Crumb cake, she thought with sick humor.

"Mommy!" Jessica cried, shaking her shoulder.

She had to move, had to make sure her daughters were all right. She pried her fingers from the steering wheel. In slow motion, she pivoted to stare into their scared little faces.

"Jessica, Amelia, are you hurt?" Fear tied a knot in her gut as she scanned their tiny, trembling bodies for blood or wounds. Relief flooded her soul when she saw none.

She leapt into the back and gathered them in her arms. Fat tears rolled down five-year-old Jessica's cheeks. Blond hair stuck to her wet face. Four-year-old Amelia's eyes overflowed. She pulled from the booster seat and clung to her mother.

"Thank God you're all right." Squeezing them tightly, Rachel rocked on her knees. "My precious girls." She kissed their cheeks and foreheads. "I love you so much."

She heard Mr. Gallagher's old rattletrap approach. Angry with the bitter old man, she scowled out the window.

Mr. Gallagher's wrinkled face pushed to the windshield for a better look at the accident. With a vengeful, toothless smile, he drove two tires through the ditch to get past without even stopping to see if they were all right.

Shuddering at the extent of his hatred, she held her daughters protectively. Turning, she faced the windshield and gasped with fresh horror.

"Baldy..." Beyond the subsiding steam of the pickup truck, Old Bald Calvin slumped over the pickup's steering wheel.

Panicked, Rachel yanked her door handle. Hinges groaned as she forced her way out of the car. Burnt rubber and leaking antifreeze stung her nostrils.

She ushered her girls from the wrecked car, but struggled with leaving them in the front yard alone.

"I have to check on Mr. Calvin. Stay in the grass. Don't go near the road. I'll be right back." She kissed their cheeks.

They nodded dumbly, huddled together.

Twisted yellow and green metal crushed the driver's side of the truck. She ran to the passenger door and jerked it open.

Tremendous dread threatened to paralyze her. She forced herself to reach in, to gingerly touch his arm.

He stirred. She released a pent-up breath.

"Mr. Calvin, thank God you're alive."

He moaned, lifting his head from the steering wheel. Blood ran down his pale forehead toward bewildered, glassy eyes.

"Be still now," she soothed. With renewed purpose, she snapped into action. She climbed inside and helped him lean back. His groggy compliance overwhelmed her with guilty fear.

God, please let him be all right. She'd been distracted and could have killed this poor old man – and her daughters too.

"Rachel!" An urgent, familiar voice yelled. "Are you okay?"

In a daze, she turned to see her mother running from the cottage next door to Mr. Calvin's.

"Grandma!" The girls ran toward their grandmother.

"We're okay, but..." Rachel couldn't finish.

"Thank God." Emily James rushed to her granddaughters with breathless hugs, and then pulled back to look them over. She watched Rachel with caring concern.

"But Mr. Calvin's not," Rachel choked out.

"Laura called 911," her mother said.

"Rachel!" Her sister Laura came running from the cottage, a dishtowel still in her hand. "You okay? Jess? Amelia?" She threw her arms around Rachel.

A painful groan came from the truck.

Rachel turned to pat Mr. Calvin's bony shoulder.

"Here." Laura handed her the towel.

With a pang, Rachel recognized the blue linen that had belonged to Grandma Kate.

She dabbed Mr. Calvin's head as a wailing ambulance screeched to a halt beside them. Paramedics rushed out and shooed Rachel and Laura into the yard – just like when they'd taken Grandma Kate away last summer.

Her world had turned upside down since then.

Mr. Calvin groaned loudly as paramedics checked his vitals and carefully pulled him from the truck. Her stomach churned while they eased him onto a stretcher. As she stood in silence, the ambulance doors slammed shut.

With a howl of sirens, they whisked off to the hospital.

"What if he dies?" She searched her sister's face.

"It's not your fault," Laura said firmly.

"I never saw him coming..."

"I did." Compassion filled Laura's deep blue eyes. "I saw it all from the kitchen window. He pulled out without stopping."

"But I was distracted. Did you see Mr. Gallagher? He drove right by and didn't even stop to see if we were all right."

"He's lower than worm spit," Laura seethed. She spontaneously hugged Rachel again, even tighter this time.

Rachel knew Laura loved her. She yearned to restore their relationship, yet couldn't get past feelings of betrayal.

After the accident that had killed Mr. Gallagher's daughter, Rachel's husband was missing. Since his convertible crashed into the creek, everyone assumed Jake had drowned. He'd hidden in the woods behind Laura's house, afraid of being arrested for vehicular homicide. He'd turned to Laura for help, and she'd kept his secret.

Although she was protecting Rachel, the deception still hurt. Not to mention the fact that her husband had turned to her sister in his time of need.

Rachel watched the spinning red lights of the ambulance fade into the distance. She could forgive her sister.

But could she ever forgive herself?

Thank you for purchasing this third book in
The Crystal Falls Series.

**The Crystal Falls Series
by Dianne Miley:**

Lilacs for Laura, Book I
Roses for Rachel, Book II
Violets for Vanessa, Book III
Sunflowers for Sarita, Book IV

Coming Next:

Time to Enjoy Your Blessings, Second Edition

Zoe

The Charleston Series:

Jasmine for Jessica
Magnolias for Amelia
Gardenias for Gracia
Camellias for Kate

About the Author

When she's not writing or reading, Dianne Haynes Miley enjoys walking on the beach, swimming, flower gardening, entertaining, hosting tea parties, cooking, decorating, and traveling. She spends as much time as possible with her husband, son and daughter.

Dianne and her husband both grew up in northeastern Ohio where they raised their family. Once their grown children went off to study engine building and photography, the couple moved to Charleston, South Carolina. Upon graduation, both children joined their parents on the sunny South Carolina coast. Dianne was thrilled with God's answer to her prayers!

In addition to writing, Dianne works at a local pregnancy center where she encourages young women in unplanned pregnancies. She founded a non-profit with hopes of building a maternity home in the Charleston area.

To learn more about Dianne and her writing, visit www.diannemiley.com where you can find her books, sign up for her quarterly newsletter, or connect with her on Facebook, Twitter, Linked In or Good Reads.

" 'For I know the plans I have for you,' declares the Lord,
'plans to prosper you and not to harm you,
plans to give you hope and a future.
Then you will call on me and come and pray to me,
and I will listen to you.
You will seek me and find me when you seek me with all your heart.' "
Jeremiah 29:11-13 NIV